THE
STARLIGHT
CONSPIRACY

Praise for **The Dreamwalker's Child**:

'Ingenious premise, relentless pace and a sprinkling of thought-provoking philosophy – I loved it.' Herbie Brennan

'This elegant, intelligent book has a good sprinkling of wisdom – about what you miss, for instance, if you don't look carefully at your environment . . . It is Sam's friendship with Skipper that makes this not just an ordinary action adventure but a tale to remember.' *Sunday Times*

'Steve Voake's debut, *The Dreamwalker's Child*, is an ingenious and fast-paced thriller . . . his book buzzes and hums with ideas.' *The Times*

'It's a brisk, adventure-filled quest, complete with a gung-ho girl companion named Skipper and hordes of grisly adversaries.' *Observer*

THE
STARLIGHT
CONSPIRACY

Steve Voake

faber and faber

First published in 2007
by Faber and Faber Limited
3 Queen Square London WC1N 3AU

Typeset by Faber and Faber Limited
Printed in England by Mackays of Chatham plc,
Chatham, Kent

A CIP record for this book
is available from the British Library

ISBN 978—0—571—22998—7

2 4 6 8 10 9 7 5 3 1

for Ed Jaspers & Julia Wells

Whoso loves
Believes the impossible.

Elizabeth Barrett Browning, *Aurora Leigh*

PROLOGUE

6 July 1947. White Sands, New Mexico, USA. 3.15 a.m.

SPECIAL AGENT SAMPSON of the FBI pulled into the parking lot of the Ranch Horn Motel, cut the motor and coasted silently to a halt. Three more unmarked cars slid past him, lights and motors off, the hiss of their tyres masked by the chirping of cicadas in the trees.

'Are we sure he's in there?' whispered Special Agent McCarthy as the other cars emptied and a dozen or so agents approached across the vacant lot.

Sampson nodded towards a sky-blue Ford parked beneath the glare of security lights and unsheathed his revolver. 'No question. That's his vehicle. He checked in less than an hour ago.' Sampson pointed back up the dirt track to where several squad cars had set up a roadblock. Armed officers crouched in the dust, aiming their guns across the hoods.

'We've got the whole place locked down tight. He ain't going nowhere.'

Sampson nodded to a uniformed officer who lifted a loud-hailer to his mouth. As it crackled into life his amplified voice echoed loudly around the parking lot:

'Joseph Mitchell, this is the FBI. We are armed. We have your motel room surrounded. Come out with your hands up. I repeat, come out with your hands up or we will shoot.'

Sampson heard the *chk-chk* of automatic weapons being loaded.

The cicadas fell silent.

'Look,' said McCarthy. 'There.'

The curtains twitched and Sampson saw the silhouette of a face appear briefly at the window before the curtains fell back again. He signalled to the officer with the loud-hailer.

'All right,' he said. 'Once more.'

'Joseph Mitchell.' The voice was more insistent now. 'We are armed police and we have your room surrounded. Come out with your hands up or we will shoot.'

In his head, Sampson counted 1, 2, 3, 4, 5, 6, and knew Mitchell wasn't coming out.

'OK,' he said. 'Put one in.'

Two agents ran to the window, crouching either side. The first smashed the glass with his wooden baton. The second pulled the pin on a tear-gas canister and lobbed it through the hole. There was a muffled explosion and white smoke billowed through the gap in the curtains.

Any second now, thought Sampson.

But there was nothing.

And when, two minutes later, no one had emerged, he nodded to McCarthy and they ran towards the door, McCarthy pointing his shotgun at the lock and blowing it apart in a ribbon of flame. As McCarthy stepped back, Sampson kicked the door off its hinges and ran forward, smoke and tear gas clawing at the back of his throat.

'Armed police!' he shouted, sweeping his standard-issue revolver around the darkened room. 'Stand still or I'll shoot!'

But as the smoke cleared, it quickly became apparent that this would not be necessary.

The room was empty.

Mitchell had vanished into thin air.

I

BERRY

'NO,' SAID BERRY, pushing a lock of dark, straggly hair out of her eyes and glaring at the woman opposite. 'I've told you. I don't want to.'

'Well, love, there are lots of things in life that we don't want to do, but sometimes we just have to do them.'

As she spoke, Angie from Social Services clutched her file to her knees and stared around at the inside of the old, broken-down bus as if to make a point.

'It'll be for the best in the end. You'll see.'

'How can you say that?' snapped Berry, her eyes bright with anger. 'You don't know me. You don't know me at all.'

'Well, I know some things,' replied Angie. 'I know that you don't go to school. And I know that you're living alone in this old van.'

'It's a bus, not a van,' said Berry. 'And anyway, I'm

not alone. The other travellers look out for me.'

'They might look *out* for you,' said Angie. 'But they don't look *after* you. Anyway, you know as well as I do that there's an eviction notice on this site. They'll all be moving on in a couple of weeks. Has anyone said they'll take you with them?'

Berry didn't reply. She knew that times were hard and no one wanted an extra mouth to feed.

From now on, she was on her own.

'Look at you,' Angie continued. 'You're all skin and bone.' Her voice softened a little as she added, 'I just want to help you, that's all.'

'I don't need your help,' said Berry. 'I don't need anyone's help.' She pushed up the fraying sleeves of her green woollen cardigan and hugged her arms tightly to her chest. 'I can look after myself.'

'Look,' said Angie gently, trying another tack. 'I know you're upset. Who wouldn't be? I'd be angry if my mother had died and left me to cope on my own. I know you must be hurting. But that's why I'm here. We've finally got a local family who can take you until we find something more permanent. And the Head of Hillgrove School says you can start there next week.'

She gave Berry an encouraging look, as if this was supposed to be the best news ever.

'That'll give you a whole month to make friends before the end of term. Then you'll be able to start afresh in September, along with everyone else.'

Berry stared out of the window and imagined herself drowning in a sea of uniforms.

'You're not listening,' she said quietly. 'I'm not going.'

'Well, I'm sorry, sweetheart,' Angie replied, her voice sympathetic but firm. 'I'm afraid that staying here is not an option. You're too young. In fact, I'm amazed it took us this long to find out about you.' She stood up, smoothing the creases from her skirt. 'Look, why don't you take the weekend to think things over? Maybe have a chat with the others, sort some of your stuff out. Meanwhile I'll get things organized my end and come back and see you on Monday. Then we'll talk some more. OK?'

She smiled, a reassuring smile.

'I know this is difficult for you, Berry. But it'll be for the best in the end. You'll see.'

Berry didn't look up until she heard the door click shut. Then she put her face in her hands and sobbed, not just for the mother she had lost, but for the life she had always known.

The life that was slipping away from her with every passing second.

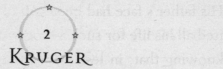

2

KRUGER

HIS VOICE TREMBLING, William Kruger pressed the phone against his ear and stared at the red and black Swastika flag pinned to the wall of his apartment. Outside, cicadas chirped in the hot New Mexico night.

'Are you absolutely sure it's him?' he asked. Although he was nearly fifty, Kruger was experiencing the kind of excitement he hadn't felt since his father first told him about Joseph Mitchell all those years ago. Now it seemed too good to be true.

Could they really have found him?

He listened for a few moments, nodded into the phone and then smiled. 'You have done well, my friend. Keep watch until I get there. I'll be with you as soon as I can.'

Replacing the phone, Kruger reached for the silver picture frame which took pride of place on his desk. In it was a black and white photograph taken in 1944, a few months before everything had changed. It showed his father standing proudly with his fellow scientists outside a secret research facility in Germany. He was shaking hands with Adolf Hitler.

His father's face had been full of pride, as if he had waited all his life for such a moment. He'd had no way of knowing that, in less than a year, Germany would lose the war and he would be captured by the Americans. Captured and flown halfway round the world to New Mexico, where he would be made to work for them instead.

So by the time William Kruger was born in 1957, his father's spirit had already been broken, trying to feed his family on a few measly dollars a week. Right up until his death, he would sit on the end of the young William's bed and tell him, over and over, how the Americans had taken him away from the Fatherland and destroyed everything that he loved.

But he would also tell William his favourite story of all: about a strange, mysterious object that he had found many years ago, and a man called Mitchell who had taken it from him.

'I am dying,' his father told him one night, close to the end. 'But when I am gone I want you to do something for me, William. I want you to find it. Find Mitchell and take back what was mine. For this will be my final gift to you. If you succeed, it will be within your power to become the greatest leader that Germany has ever known.'

In the playground, the American children would chant, 'Daddy was a Nazi, Daddy was a Nazi!' And as William lay sobbing in the dust, they would kick him and shout: 'Tell us, pig! Who's the master race now?'

But after his father died, something had hardened inside the young William. He had learned to stay on the fringes, melting into the background and silently holding on to his father's dream of bringing back what had been lost. *If only I can find it*, he had thought, *my whole life will be better*.

And now, after all these years, it seemed his dream was coming true.

He would catch a plane to England before dawn.

But first, there was something else that needed attending to.

Kruger left the car a couple of blocks from his destination and walked the rest of the way. It was one thirty in the morning and no one saw him walk up the suburban driveway and slip beneath the silver Buick that was parked there. Less than thirty minutes later, the job was done and he was driving along the main freeway towards Albuquerque airport.

At about the same time as the stewardess was checking Kruger's boarding pass and wishing him a pleasant flight, Andy Sampson of the FBI was closing his front door and watching the sun rise above San Pedro mountain, thinking how it was setting up to be another beautiful summer's day. Throwing his brief-case on the passenger seat of the car, he started the engine, engaged reverse gear and turned round to make sure he didn't scrape the wall on his way out.

This, as it turned out, was to be the least of his problems.

As the back wheels moved off the flat part of the drive and the car tilted backwards down the slope, there was the tiniest of clicks and then a massive explosion ripped through the interior with such force that a ball of flame punched its way through the roof, sending shards of jagged metal spinning high into the air. By the time the young woman across the road had opened her front door and started to scream, smoking fragments of debris were already pattering down into the streets and gardens all around her, falling from the sky like hot, black rain.

3
THE BIRTHDAY PRESENT

THROUGH HER TEARS, Berry could still see the childish painting of the house, pinned to the wall of the bus. She thought back to the afternoon art lesson when her mother had said:

'Close your eyes, Berry. Close your eyes and imagine that you could build your dream house. What would it look like?'

And in her mind, Berry had seen a field of golden corn rippling in the summer breeze. Beyond the cornfield, looking out across the ocean, was a blue weatherboard house with a cherry tree in the garden. She had dreamed of it many times and painting the picture had felt comfortable and familiar, like painting an old friend.

Looking at it now she could still remember how long she had spent mixing the paint, trying to achieve the exact sky-blue colour of the house from her dreams and the ocean beyond it.

On the wall next to the painting were some photographs. There was one of her mother, dark hair blowing in the wind, standing next to the motorbike on which they had taken so many trips: to a small stone church where the air was heavy with dust and silence; to a quiet art gallery where the colours of dead summers lit up the room or, once, to an ancient woodland in winter, watching the sunlight flame through the branches and sparkle in frozen ditches like something rare and mysterious.

Berry's mother had never made her go to school. She had believed that Berry should learn about the world through experience and spent hours teaching her how to read and write, to dig the earth and to sow seeds in succession so that there was food all the year round.

'These are the things that matter,' she said.

But occasionally, when they walked to the baker's or the wholefood shop in town, Berry would hear the sounds of children playing. She would catch sight of them, shouting and laughing beyond the railings, and her heart would beat a little faster. Sometimes, in the lengthening shadows of the evening, she would feel the gentle ache of her heart and imagine it lying trapped in the darkness behind her ribcage, like a bruised animal.

'Are you all right, my love?' her mother would ask. And Berry would smile and nod, and busy herself with the evening's supper.

Sometimes, on days when the weather was warm and the sky was blue, they would ride down to the coast and swim until the sun dissolved into the sea, picnicking on the sand as the moon rose pale and strange above the clifftops.

These were Berry's favourite times, moments that burned themselves deep into her memory so that, years later, she could still feel their warmth, even on the darkest of days.

Now she stared out of the bus window at the field of maize where she had first learned to ride the motorbike. It had been winter then, the corn reduced to a sprinkle of white stubble across the frost-hardened ground and Berry had shrieked with delight as they bounced and skidded over the ruts, sending startled rabbits racing for the tangle of brambles.

'Now it's your turn,' her mother had said as they skidded through a gateway into a narrow country lane. So Berry had stood on tiptoe and learned to keep the heavy bike balanced above its centre of gravity as she kick-started the motor and let the clutch out slowly with her left hand, twisting the throttle with her right to keep the powerful motor ticking over. The first few times she had stalled the engine, either by letting the clutch out too fast or by not keeping the revs up with the throttle. But quickly she had learned to let the clutch out smoothly and gradually, twisting the throttle just enough for the gears to engage and spin the back wheel until it gripped the tarmac and sent her wobbling away up the lane.

After ten minutes she was no longer falling off.

After an hour, her braking was so smooth that she was confident enough to put her foot down on muddy corners, letting the back wheel slide out just enough for her to take them at speed.

'Bravo, Berry!' her mother had cried, clapping her hands together in the cold, brittle air. 'What did I tell you, my darling? You can do anything!'

Berry gazed up at the photo she liked best of all: the one of her mother, smiling at the camera with the Golden Gate bridge and the lights of San Francisco behind her. She was eighteen years old then, at the end of a trip that had taken her on a Greyhound bus right the way across America. There was hardly a day went past when she wouldn't tell Berry some story about it.

'One day,' her mother had said, 'when you're older and I've saved some money, we'll go. OK? Just you and me.'

Berry stared at the last photograph she had ever taken, the one of her mother in the hospital bed. Her hair had fallen out and she had said, *No, Berry, don't take me looking like this*. But Berry had reminded her of her own words:

'It's what's inside that counts, Mum, remember? Now hold still!'

And she had held still, and smiled.

As Berry looked at the photograph now, she remembered that her mother had thought she was getting better.

She had thought she was coming home.

A knock at the door interrupted Berry's thoughts and, to her surprise, Maria walked in. Since her mother's death, the other travellers had tended to keep their distance. They had been kind enough during her mother's illness, inviting Berry in for meals and giving her money for bus fares, but since her mother had died it had been different somehow. Berry and her mother had always been quite self-sufficient in the camp, friendly with the others, but never close. Now that the travellers had to move on, it seemed no one wanted to take responsibility for her.

'Hello,' Maria said, shutting the door behind her. 'I saw you had a visitor. Is everything OK?'

'No,' said Berry. 'Not really. That was my social worker, apparently.'

'I know,' said Maria.

Berry heard the awkwardness in Maria's voice, saw the way she was looking at the floor and guessed that she had been the one who contacted her.

'You *know*?'

'She said . . . she said you were too young to be living here on your own. She said you should be going to school.'

Berry nodded. 'And what did you say?'

Maria shrugged and looked embarrassed.

'What could I say? I mean, she's got a point, hasn't she? In a way?'

Berry stared at her, more in sadness than in anger.

'Why is it,' she asked softly, 'that everyone thinks they have the right to tell me how I should live my life?'

'But they'll look after you,' Maria said. She shook her head. 'Look at you. You're so *young*.'

'Please don't,' said Berry. 'I've already heard it from the social worker.'

'She's right, though, isn't she? She is right. You need to be with people who can look after you. Not stuck on your own all day.'

'Look,' said Berry. 'I know you're just trying to be kind. But I think I need to be alone for a while.'

'All right,' said Maria, moving back towards the door again. 'I understand. But give it some thought, OK? Everyone here only wants what's best for you, that's all.'

'Sure,' said Berry. 'Of course they do.'

When she was alone again, Berry's eyes fell upon the tickets to Glastonbury Music Festival, pinned next to the photographs on the wall. The two of them would have been going there tomorrow, just as they always did. Her mother had taken her every year since she was a tiny baby, pitching their tent in the middle of a thousand others and cooking supper on a rickety gas stove.

Berry remembered how she would sit beneath the stars listening to the bands warming up, drinking hot soup and reminding herself how lucky she was to have such freedom. She didn't have to be like everyone else, wearing school uniform or keeping up with the latest fashion. She wasn't confined by the walls of a schoolroom. And although there was a tiny part of her that wanted to be like all the others, to laugh, share secrets and feel the crisp whiteness of a new shirt next to her skin, she still believed that her mother was right. It was only by living outside of the world that you could truly be free.

Berry bit her lip, bunched up her fist and hit herself hard in the leg. 'Stop it, you baby!' she told herself. 'Stop crying. Stop it!'

But whichever way she looked at it, she couldn't see a way out.

Her days of freedom were over.

With tears rolling down her cheeks, Berry opened the old chest of drawers and began to pack.

As she was sorting through her clothes, she noticed something tucked away at the back of the drawer. It was a blue envelope with her name on the front, written in her mother's handwriting.

'Oh!' said Berry, taken aback. She had completely forgotten.

It was her birthday.

She was fourteen years old today.

Her hands shaking, Berry opened the envelope and took out the card. On the front of it, her mother had painted a little blue house on a clifftop with a cherry tree in the garden. Beyond it was the ocean, with little white splashes of spray flecking the waves. It was just like the dream house in Berry's picture.

Inside the card were two plane tickets to San Francisco. It seemed her mother had planned that they would go straight after the festival.

The card read:

To Berry

HAPPY 14th BIRTHDAY!

Let's make our dreams come true!

Love always

Mum x

With a sob, Berry snatched up the little rucksack she used for shopping, threw the card and some loose change inside and ran blindly out across the yard. She didn't know where she was going and right now she didn't care. She just kept on running, through the gate and away down the lane, desperate to be somewhere – anywhere – far away from the hopelessness she felt inside.

In a few minutes she had reached the town, traffic buzzing all around her. She smelled dry dust and petrol fumes mixed up with the thick aroma of chip fat floating from the fish shop doorway. Ladies with tartan shopping trolleys hobbled past babies in prams who gurgled and pointed at the sky. Two boys sat on a bench outside the Town Hall, smoking and spitting, watching the cars and staring at the pavement. Berry didn't stop. She ran past them all, faster, faster, down through the High Street, people side-stepping out of her way as the shops and cars and faces whirled past in a blur of colour and sound.

Then, stepping off the kerb, she turned around just in time to see the large green bus that was about to hit her.

4
An Accident Avoided

There was a squeal of brakes and Berry felt herself pulled backwards at great speed. A second later she thumped down on to the pavement, the kick of unyielding stone hard against her shoulder. She heard the crump of metal as a car skidded off the road and crashed into a lamp-post.

Somewhere, someone screamed.

A man grabbed her hand, saying, 'Come on, get up, you're fine. Let's go.' Stumbling to her feet in a daze, she allowed herself to be led through a puzzle of streets, wondering:

Is this what it feels like to die?

The sky slid overhead, blue and slippery as ice. Clouds hung ragged above the trees, snagged in their branches like wool on a fence.

Berry turned and saw that her companion was a

white-haired old man. He was wheezing with the effort of walking so fast. He looked frightened, she thought.

'Are you all right?' she asked.

'We have to get away,' he replied and Berry detected the slightest hint of an American accent. 'They are close now. I can feel it.'

'Who?' she asked. 'Who is close?'

But the man did not reply.

Confused, Berry touched the side of her face and realized that she was bleeding.

'What happened?' she asked as they walked down a street of terraced houses. 'Did the bus hit me?'

'No,' said the old man, coughing into the curled flesh of his fist. 'Luckily I saw you in time.'

Berry frowned.

What on earth did he mean?

They came to a quiet, tree-lined street of terraced, redbrick houses. A ginger tomcat watched from a windowsill as they passed and Berry could see through the glass to the long, narrow gardens beyond.

Halfway down the street, the man stopped and pushed at a small iron gate which creaked as it opened. Flakes of rust fluttered and fell on to weeds that grew up through cracks in the paving stones.

Following him up some steps to a blue front door, Berry realized how thin and frail he was. Although the day was warm, she could see that he wore an old grey cardigan beneath his brown tweed jacket and his hands shook as he fumbled with the key. Was he cold, she wondered, or was he frightened?

Perhaps she would just make sure that he was all right and then go home.

Wherever home was.

'Please,' said the old man, gesturing towards a couple of brown velour armchairs. 'Sit down for a moment and I'll make us some tea.'

As he shuffled off into the adjoining kitchen, Berry glanced around the small living room and saw that it was virtually empty. There were none of the things one might normally expect to find; no pictures on the wall, no photographs of friends or family on the mantelpiece, no gold-plated carriage clocks or china mugs celebrating the Queen's Silver Jubilee.

Just a brown, battered suitcase by the front door, a portable television on an upturned box and a telephone on a small wooden table.

She wandered across to the kitchen and leaned on the door frame. The old man was laying a little wooden tray with a blue and white sugar bowl, a plate of digestive biscuits and a silver spoon on each cup and saucer. Berry saw the care he took with everything and it made her sad for him.

'Have you lived here long?' she asked. She looked at

the kitchen cupboard above his head and saw that it was empty except for a can of baked beans and a jar of Marmite. The old man followed her gaze and guessed what she was thinking.

'I don't stay anywhere long,' he said.

He ran a piece of kitchen paper under the tap and offered it to her. 'Here,' he said. 'That should stop the bleeding.'

When they were back in the lounge again, the old man leaned forward and offered Berry his hand which, she noticed, was no longer trembling.

'Forgive me,' he said. 'In all the excitement I have forgotten my manners. My name is Joseph.' He pointed at the cut on the side of her head. 'I hope that's not too painful.'

Berry shook his hand and smiled.

'It's fine,' she said. 'I'm Berry, by the way.'

Joseph nodded.

'Tell me something, Berry,' he said. 'Why were you in such a hurry?'

'When?' asked Berry.

'Just before I pulled you away from the bus. You looked as though you were running away from something.'

Berry looked at Joseph's thin, bony fingers holding the handle of the teacup and she raised her eyebrows in astonishment.

'It was you that saved me?'

'Yes,' replied Joseph matter-of-factly. 'The bus hit me instead, which was unfortunate. They watch all the time for such things, you know.'

Berry stared at Joseph, perched on the edge of his chair like a small, delicate bird and knew that the idea of him being hit by a bus was completely ridiculous. And yet . . . for some reason, his words sounded like the truth. To her surprise, she realized that she trusted him.

'Now it's your turn', he said, 'to answer my question.'

And as she watched him sipping tea from his little china cup, all the emotions of the last few weeks suddenly came frothing up to the surface and, before she could stop herself, she was telling him everything.

'My mother died a couple of months ago,' she said. 'We lived in a travellers' camp and now everyone's being moved on. Social Services say I have to go to school and live somewhere else. But today is my birthday and I found out that my mum had bought me a ticket to go to America.'

She stared hard at the brown, leaf-patterned curtains in an effort to stop herself from crying.

'So I suppose I was running because today I saw how my life could have been. I'm running away from a life that I'm not sure I want any more.'

Berry wiped away her tears with the back of her hand and looked at Joseph.

'Don't cry,' he said. 'I think I may be able to help you.'

He stared at Berry intently, as though he was seeing her for the first time.

'Help me?' she asked. 'How?'

'First things first,' said Joseph, leaning forward and placing his teacup back in its saucer. Berry noticed that his whole demeanour had suddenly changed. He seemed more animated, more alive. 'Tell me about this ticket. Where will it take you?'

Berry shrugged. 'San Francisco. But it doesn't matter, does it? I'm not going now.'

'Oh, my dear girl,' said Joseph. 'On the contrary. You *have* to go.'

'What?' asked Berry, shocked by this reaction and deciding that maybe she had been wrong to trust him so readily. He was beginning to sound a tiny bit mad.

'Thank you very much for the tea, Joseph,' she said, standing up, 'but I think perhaps I should be going now.'

Joseph nodded, almost as though he had been expecting this.

'Of course, of course,' he said, using the arms of the chair to push himself unsteadily to his feet. 'How silly of me. We have only just met, after all. These things cannot be rushed.'

He accompanied Berry to the door and, although she was still puzzled by what he had said, she looked into his eyes and saw that she had been mistaken; there was not the slightest trace of madness in them.

'I don't know what to do, Joseph,' she said quietly. 'I don't know what to do about anything any more.'

Joseph rested a hand gently on her shoulder. 'Well, my dear,' he said, 'you're certainly not alone in that.' He shook his head and opened the door. 'You know, most people are so busy rushing around that they forget to listen to what life is trying to tell them. But not you, Berry. You're different. I can feel it.'

Berry stood at the top of the steps and watched the shadow of a cloud slide silently across the pavements and gardens. As the sun came out again and warmed her face, she felt as though she was standing on the edge of something; something beyond her understanding.

'What do you mean?' she asked, hearing herself talk in a whisper.

'I mean,' said Joseph, 'that life is giving you a chance. If you want to take it, then come back and see me tomorrow.'

He closed the door and, all at once, Berry was alone, standing at the top of the steps and staring out into the bright, sunlit world, listening to the birdsong and wondering what on earth was to become of her.

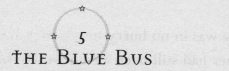

5
THE BLUE BUS

IN REALITY, the 'travellers' camp', as the locals referred to it (usually when giving directions to passing motorists), was little more than a small collection of dilapidated vehicles and caravans. It was situated at the end of a narrow country lane and had once been the site of a small haulier's yard serving the nearby quarry. But the quarry had long since been abandoned and the lorries had moved on.

Now the lane was overgrown and rarely used.

The yard itself was bordered by fields of maize. In summer the crop grew tall and thick, surrounding the camp with a sea of green which effectively absorbed the noise of distant traffic, leaving only the rustle of wind in the leaves.

Aside from the bus in which Berry lived, there was a rusty wartime ambulance with faded red crosses painted on the sides, four caravans in varying states of disrepair and a yellow 1970s Ford Capri which always stayed exactly where it was, owing to the fact that its axles were up on bricks and the motor was in oily bits behind the wood store.

Berry was in no hurry to get back there today. If her mother had still been alive it would have been different; she would have raced home breathlessly to tell her about her strange encounter with the old man. But since Berry's mother had died there was no one left who would be the slightest bit interested in her story. No one whose eyes would light up at the sound of her footsteps or smile at the rattle of the door handle.

Just a handful of travellers who in their minds had already moved on, leaving her behind to fend for herself.

Walking up the grass-banked lane, its hedgerows choked with bindweed and brambles, she caught sight of the bus beyond the five-bar gate and remembered how her mother had arrived home excitedly one summer morning, clutching pots of blue paint and a couple of paintbrushes.

'Today,' she had exclaimed, 'we are going to create your dream house!'

They had worked for hours, spending the whole day covering the pale green bus with a colour as blue as the sky. On the side, next to the wheel arch, they had painted a cherry tree with pink blossom splashed across its branches. As the sun coloured deep orange against the evening sky, her mother had surrounded the bus with sheaves of yellow corn, stuffing them into flowerpots. 'There now,' she said at last. 'What do you think?'

And Berry had stood with her paintbrush dripping pink flowers into the dust and whispered, 'It's beautiful, Mum. It's beautiful.'

Resting her chin on top of the gate, Berry stared at the blue bus that had been her home for so long and knew that everything had changed. She listened to the drone of bees among the clover and suddenly the sound seemed desperately sad. The world was unconcerned with her and would always remain so. Things would carry on just the way they always had and, one day, sooner or later, she too would be gone. But the world would keep on turning and the bees would keep on buzzing; the seasons would come and go and nothing really mattered in the end.

Inside the bus, Berry undressed and pulled the blankets over her head, shutting out a world that had no need of her; a world that she no longer wanted.

The next morning, however, she felt lighter, as though the sensation she'd experienced on the steps of

Joseph's house had grown and blossomed inside of her as she slept. She couldn't explain it exactly, but as she pulled on her clothes and put the kettle on the stove to boil, she realized that something had changed. Instead of feeling as though it was the end of everything, she suddenly felt quite the opposite.

As though something was about to begin.

6
JOSEPH'S STORY

'YOU CAME,' SAID JOSEPH, opening the door and ushering her into the narrow hallway. Berry sensed the
relief in his voice and immediately began to wonder
whether she had done the right thing in coming back.
But it was something he had said yesterday that had
brought her here.

'Life is giving you a chance,' he had said.

That was all she needed, wasn't it?

A chance.

'I'm sorry about yesterday,' he said as he fetched a
tray with two glasses of lemonade from the kitchen.
'I'm afraid I didn't explain myself very well.' Berry put
down her rucksack containing the bread and milk she
had picked up from the paper shop and took one of the
glasses from the tray.

'Don't worry,' she said. 'It was a strange day

altogether.'

Joseph nodded. 'To be honest, I didn't think you'd come back.'

Berry shrugged. 'Nor did I,' she said. 'But here I am.'

She settled into an armchair and watched Joseph sip his lemonade, sensing that he was desperate to tell her something. She could feel it in the space between them, an invisible bundle he seemed hesitant to unwrap.

'You told me yesterday that life was giving me a chance,' she said. 'What did you mean by that?'

Joseph put down his glass of lemonade, took out a handkerchief and dabbed at his mouth. 'I meant exactly what I said,' he replied, replacing the handkerchief in his top pocket. 'But before we come on to that, I think perhaps I need to tell you about something that happened to me a long time ago. Would that be all right with you?'

Berry saw how cautious he was being and it made her want to make things easier for him.

'Of course,' she said. 'I like stories.'

Joseph seemed to relax a little at this. He passed a hand over his eyes and when he spoke again his voice was much quieter, as though he was afraid that someone else might hear.

'Many years ago,' he began, 'back in the 1940s, I

was a scientist in the United States, working as part of a Flight Research Team in the south of New Mexico. One night, we got called to an area in the desert where an aircraft had apparently come down. When we arrived, there was a two-mile cordon around the crash site and the place was swarming with government officials. They weren't letting anyone through. But my pass got me in there, and most of my life since has been spent living with the consequences of what followed.'

'Why?' whispered Berry, suddenly intrigued. 'What happened?'

'I was partnered with another man, a German scientist captured at the end of the Second World War. Although he never said, you could tell he hated us for what we had done to his country. Anyway, the wreckage wasn't from any plane we recognized, so we took it back to the lab for analysis. That night, while we were pulling it apart, we found something that I knew I should tell my superiors about right away. But while I was heading for the phone, this guy pulled a knife and tried to kill me.'

'Why would he do that?' asked Berry incredulously.

'Because', said Joseph, 'he wanted it for himself. Anyway, I knew how to look after myself in those days and I hit him a good one. But then I panicked and drove to a motel. I was afraid, you see. Afraid of what we had found. I decided then that I didn't want to hand it over right away.'

'Why not?'

'I was worried that it might fall into the wrong hands. I just needed time to figure out my next move. But the other guy must have realized the trouble he was in and tried to save his own skin by calling Security. Probably told them I'd attacked him and stolen it. Next thing I knew, the Feds were surrounding my motel room, waving their guns about. But by then I knew I didn't want anyone else to have it. So I took it and escaped.'

'I thought you said you were surrounded?'

'I did,' said Joseph.

Puzzled, Berry waited for an explanation, but when it was not forthcoming she asked the question she had been dying to ask.

'What was it? This thing you took?'

'Believe me,' said Joseph, 'it's better for you not to know. Knowing would only make it more difficult for you to succeed.'

'Succeed?' asked Berry, utterly confused. 'Succeed in what?'

'In returning it,' said Joseph. 'I want you to take it back to New Mexico for me.'

'*What?*' Berry stared at him in amazement. 'Why me?'

'Because they'd never suspect you. That's the beauty

of it, don't you see? You have no connection with me and, from what you say, no one will ever miss you. I felt it when I passed you in the street. It must have sensed you weren't like all the others. It must have *known*.'

Berry shook her head in bewilderment. 'I don't know what you're talking about,' she said. 'It doesn't make any sense.'

'Look,' Joseph went on. 'Don't you see? This is your chance, Berry. You said yourself that you were running away from your life. If you do this one thing for me, I'll give you money, set you up, everything. You'd never have to speak to a social worker again. Think of that!'

'But why can't you do it?' Berry asked, the reminder of her current situation keeping her interested.

Joseph shook his head.

'I should have done it a long time ago. But I always resisted, always wanted to keep it for just one more day. And now it seems I've left it too late. The doctors tell me I am suffering from deep-vein thrombosis. A long transatlantic flight would almost certainly kill me. But I have to get it back. I *have* to.'

'But why?' asked Berry.

'Look, I won't lie to you,' said Joseph. 'There are some dangerous, vicious people out there who want this thing, and they're closing in. I can't run from them any more. It's only a matter of time before they catch up with me.'

Berry didn't know who *they* were or if they even existed, but when she saw the desperation in Joseph's eyes she realized that he was genuinely scared, that he really believed all this madness that was spinning around in his head.

'Listen,' he went on, fixing her with a grave stare. 'I genuinely believe that this could be a way out for you. But in the end, it doesn't matter *why* you do it. You can do it for the money, you can do it because I saved your life, or you can do it because you don't like the way your life is turning out. I don't care. But you *have* to do it, Berry. You must believe me when I tell you that the safety of the world depends upon you returning this item. So *please*. We don't have much time. Just say that you'll do it.'

'Look,' said Berry, feeling uncomfortable now and wishing that she had never come back. 'I don't want to be rude or anything, but I'm afraid that this isn't what I expected at all. It's all too . . . weird.'

She stood up again and gave Joseph an apologetic smile.

'I'm sorry I can't help you with your problem, Joseph. But listen – thank you for looking after me so well. I really appreciate it. Is there anything else I can do for you before I go?'

'Yes,' said Joseph, suddenly calm again, as if her refusal had been something he had been expecting all along. Holding out his cup he asked, 'Could you possibly make me another cup of tea?'

Ten minutes later, Berry slipped quickly away through the back garden, puzzled by the sudden change in Joseph's behaviour. When she had returned from the kitchen, he had become agitated, seemingly desperate for her to leave.

'I'll call you later,' he said, pushing her rucksack into her hands and ushering her out of the back door. 'In case you change your mind. But in the meantime, don't tell anyone and don't open it. Now quickly – go.'

What was that supposed to mean? *Don't open it.*

Open what?

The safety of the world depends upon you returning this item.

The poor man was obviously deluded. How did he think he could call her later? She didn't even possess a phone. And anyway, why on earth would she want to go halfway around the world to deliver something she hadn't even seen? It was ridiculous and – she had to admit – disappointing too. What she had hoped might be an answer to her problems had merely turned out to be a lot of rambling nonsense.

As she walked down the path behind the rows of terraced houses, a jogger in a blue tracksuit suddenly appeared from around the corner and knocked her sprawling to the ground.

'I am so sorry,' he said, helping her to her feet. 'Are you all right?'

'I'm fine,' said Berry and it was then that she noticed the hypodermic syringe sticking into the strap of her rucksack.

'Are you sure?' he asked, pulling out the syringe and handing the rucksack back to her.

'Yes,' said Berry, suddenly feeling uneasy. 'I'm quite sure.' Then she turned and ran as fast as she could up the lane, not stopping until she reached the door of the bus and fell gasping on to the worn, threadbare carpet inside.

7
THE VISITORS

STANDING IN THE COOL shade of a beech tree, William Kruger lit a cigarette and looked across the street at the line of Victorian terraced houses. Although he was still tired from the long flight, excitement kept his senses keen. He focused his attention on number 27, its faded brown curtains drawn against the sunlight. Paint flaked from the window frames, drifting like dandruff on to the blowzy shoulders of last season's hydrangeas. Could it be that this drab, grey-stoned building really contained the treasure he had been seeking for so long? It was hard to believe that such an ordinary place could house such riches. But his people had been thorough and it seemed that, after years of frustration, they had finally located the old man. He had been followed, identified, and now here he was, sitting alone behind the curtains of number 27.

Apparently there had been a girl too; possibly just a relative but Grezne had tagged her as a precaution. They could catch up with her later if necessary. As for Mitchell, well . . . this was one Kruger wanted all to himself. This wasn't just about retrieving the item; it was a settling of his father's accounts.

The lock was a simple three-lever mortise and it took him less than a minute to deal with it. Standing silently in the kitchen, he heard the sound of the old man talking quietly upstairs. Was someone else here too?

Taking off his shoes, Kruger began to climb the stairs, slowly, carefully, one at a time.

'Who is it? Who's there?'

The voice was weary, its strength worn down by the passage of time until now it could only rustle softly, like paper.

But there was fear in it too.

Kruger's father had warned him that success would depend on how fast and furiously he struck. Pulling a silenced pistol from the concealed holster under his jacket, he leapt up the last few stairs and ran into the bedroom, the gun held out in front of him. As he entered the room, he heard the old man say, 'Take it to Eddy Chaves!' and saw that he was speaking into a telephone.

'Calling the police?' he asked.

'Please,' said Joseph Mitchell. 'I don't have it.'

But Kruger wasn't falling for that one. He pulled the trigger several times in quick succession and the silenced pistol jumped and squeaked in his hand. Mitchell folded slowly to the floor, still clutching the telephone. 'Eunice . . .' he gasped into the receiver. 'Vaughn . . . Anthony . . . Centre.'

Kneeling beside him, Kruger wrenched up Mitchell's sleeve and realized, with a cold fury, that the old man had been telling the truth.

He didn't have it.

The item was gone.

Despite the increasing strangeness of the day – or perhaps because of it – Berry's thoughts had moved from disappointment to a mixture of annoyance and excitement. She discovered, to her surprise, that while she had been making the tea Joseph had secretly placed a mobile phone, two bulky envelopes and a small blue package in her rucksack.

Sitting cross-legged on her mattress, she tore open the first envelope and pulled out a bundle of crisp, hundred-dollar bills. Raising an eyebrow, she whistled softly and began to count.

One, two, three . . . she counted a hundred in all.

Ten thousand dollars.

Stunned, Berry shuffled the notes back into a neat pile before carefully tearing open the second envelope. This one contained more cash, only this time it was in fifty-pound notes – one thousand pounds' worth in total.

I'll give you money, set you up . . .

What was Joseph playing at?

Outside, Berry heard the sound of a car pulling up in the lane. She frowned, knowing that the other travellers had gone to check out new sites and wouldn't be back until evening. Hurriedly scooping up the money and the package, she thrust them into her rucksack, crawled across the floor and squinted through the window.

A four-wheel drive with blacked-out windows. The doors opening, three men getting out. One dark-haired – fit and hard-muscled – smartly dressed in an expensive lounge suit. One older – early fifties – wearing neatly pressed khaki slacks and designer sun-glasses. One wearing a blue tracksuit.

The jogger!

As Berry watched them talking together, something told her they weren't from Social Services.

I won't lie to you. There are some dangerous, vicious peo-ple out there . . .

Crawling back across to the storage unit beside her bed she upended the drawers on to the floor, scooped up a bundle of clean socks, pants and T-shirts and thrust them hurriedly into the bottom of her ruck-sack, followed by the plane tickets, her passport and the phone, which she skimmed from the top of the chest. Her heart pounding, she ripped the Glastonbury tickets and the photograph of her mother from the wall before wrenching open the wardrobe and pulling a small two-man tent from beneath a pile of clothes. Tying it quickly beneath her pack, she ran back to the window again.

The man in the tracksuit unlatched the gate, pointed towards the van and suddenly she knew with a terrible certainty that Joseph had been telling the truth.

They are closing in.

These were the people he was so frightened of.

And now they were after her.

8

†HROVGH †HE CORNFIELD

BERRY'S MIND FLEW into overdrive, accelerating through her options in a desperate race for self-preservation. Throwing a frightened glance at the door of the bus, she realized there was no way of leaving by that route without being seen. Frantically, she looked around for possible hiding places. Under the mattress? In the wardrobe beneath the coats?

Not a chance.

They would find her in a second.

Picking up her rucksack, she ran the length of the bus, pushed the driver's window open and hurled her rucksack on to the dry ground. Grabbing the motorbike keys from the hook above the sunshade, she stuck her feet through the window and jumped down into the dust. At the same moment, there was a loud banging on the door and a voice shouted,

'Open up! It's the police! Open the door!'

Dropping low, Berry ran behind the back of the bus towards the wood store. Crouching next to the wood-pile, she heard the sound of breaking glass and saw that the man in the suit was using a hammer to smash out the bus window. Reaching through, he twisted the lock and the door swung open. One by one, the men climbed the steps and disappeared into the bus.

Terrified, Berry fumbled in her pocket for her mother's keys.

This was it. It was now or never.

She ran to the back of the woodpile and pulled back an old tarpaulin to reveal a black, mud-spattered motorbike.

'She can't have got far!' said a voice. 'The signal's still strong.'

Her fingers shaking, Berry unclipped the helmet from the side of the bike and buckled the straps tight-ly under her chin.

Swinging her right leg over the seat, she thrust the key into the steering lock and twisted it. To her relief, a green light illuminated on the instrument panel but as she brought her right foot down hard on the kick-start lever, the motor grumbled, spluttered and died.

'Hey!' shouted a voice. 'Over here!'

Fighting the urge to scream, Berry remembered the motor hadn't been used in a while and pulled the choke handle. Then, jumping into the air, she brought her whole weight down on to the kick-start and twisted the throttle.

The engine spluttered and coughed.

Then it roared into life.

Waiting until the men were nearly upon her, Berry pulled in the clutch, revved the engine and released the lever. The back tyre spun in the dirt as the hot rubber found its grip, then there was a howl from the exhausts, Berry's head snapped backwards and the bike accelerated through the men like a bullet from a gun, scattering them in all directions.

Recovering quickly, Berry jammed on the brake lever and thrust her foot down hard so that the back wheel slewed around in a cloud of dust. To her horror, she saw that the jogger was already sprinting across the yard to close the gate and block her escape. Seeing the man in the suit reach into his jacket, Berry blipped the throttle and let the clutch out fast. There was a surge of power and the bike's front wheel clawed at the air before slamming down into the dirt again, catapulting her at high speed towards the thick hedge that ran along the back of the yard.

At that moment an image flashed through Berry's mind of a winter's day when the hedgerow was bare . . . her mother squeezing through a gap, pushing the bike through . . . somewhere just to the left of that patch of weeds . . .

Berry put her head down, twisted the throttle back as far as it would go and the bike took off into the hedgerow like a scalded cat. There was a heavy thump as the front wheel struck a tree root and then the bike twitched, skidded and reared up on its back wheel. Hanging on desperately to the handlebars as brambles whipped across her chest, Berry experienced a brief sensation of flying as the bike left the ground, its front wheel spinning through empty space before thudding down to earth once again. Suddenly she was surrounded by tall green stalks that towered above her, their brown feathery tops stirring in the breeze.

'There!' shouted a voice. 'In the maize field!'

Berry heard three sharp cracks and the whine of bullets as the ground exploded around her, flinging fragments of earth into the air.

Stamping her foot down through the gears, she released the clutch and with a roar the bike leapt forward into the maize. The plants had grown so high that she was unable to see where she was going; tall stalks of corn shredded and buckled in front of her, clattering against her helmet as the bike gathered speed and tore a path through the centre of the field. Berry knew she was driving blind and that crashing at this speed could be the end of everything. But she had no choice; the men were dangerous, they had guns and they were after her.

Bumping and jolting across the field's uneven surface, Berry remembered that the gateway to the road had been somewhere over in the right-hand corner. With a light touch on the brakes, she leaned the bike over on a diagonal course, hoping it would bring her out in the right place. Changing down a gear, she watched the speedometer drop to twenty miles an hour. Quicker than running pace, but not much.

She slowed to 15 mph.

The edge of the field had to be here somewhere.

Any second now . . .

Suddenly, in a clatter of stalks, the bike emerged from the maize and Berry found herself heading straight for a hedge. As she slammed the brakes on, the back wheel slid sideways and the front wheel dug into a rut, flipping her off into a patch of stinging nettles. The bike somersaulted through the dust and came to rest beside the gateway where the motor spluttered and died.

'Aaaaaaagh!' she yelled, thrusting her stinging hands beneath her armpits. '*Damn* it!'

'This way!' shouted a hidden voice in the maize. 'I think she's crashed!'

Forgetting her injuries, Berry jumped to her feet and pushed open the gate. Wrenching the bike off the ground, she straddled it, jumped on the kick-start and heard the engine splutter and fade.

'Oh please,' cried Berry as she heard the rustling in the cornfield. '*Please!*'

She jumped on the starter again, and again it stuttered to a halt. They could be only seconds away now. Weeping with fear and frustration, she leapt on the kick-start once more and this time the motor exploded into life just as the man in the tracksuit emerged from the corn clutching a semi-automatic pistol.

For a brief second, Berry and the man stared at one another.

Then, as he raised his gun, she released the clutch and spun the bike around, trailing clouds of dust as she powered through the gateway and up the lane.

As the sound of the bike grew fainter, the man swore and put his gun back in its holster.

'How'd she do that?' he said. 'How the hell did she do it?'

The other two men reached the edge of the field and began brushing dirt and pollen from their trousers.

The blond, middle-aged man in expensive glasses seemed calm as he watched the dust settle, but the thin set of his lips betrayed his true feelings.

'You tagged her, right?' he asked quietly. 'Promise me you tagged her.'

'Sure thing, Mr Kruger,' said the man in the tracksuit nervously. 'I definitely tagged her rucksack. That's how we found her in the first place.'

'All right then,' said Kruger. 'From now on, no more mistakes.'

9
BLUE LIGHTS AND BRIDLEWAYS

As soon as she reached the junction with the main road, Berry turned left and then immediately right towards the bridleway. She knew that if she stayed off the main road, it would be harder for them to track her down.

She decided she had to try to warn Joseph, let him know that these people were on to her. She would return the money with the package and make it clear that she wanted nothing more to do with it. Then perhaps she would go to Glastonbury Festival after all. The gates would already be opening and it would take her less than an hour from here on the bike. At least she could lose herself in the crowds and chill out for a while until she decided what to do next.

Reaching a gateway partially hidden by brambles, Berry guided the bike through and turned off the ignition. The silence that followed was broken only by the soft cooing of a wood pigeon and the occasional hum of a bumblebee. Leaning the bike against the hedge, she kneaded her bruised shoulder with her fingers. Her hands were covered in little white bumps from the nettle patch and although the stings had faded into a kind of dull heat, they were beginning to itch. She picked a dock leaf, spat on it and rubbed it into the stings, which cooled them a little.

Her hands shook and she felt sick with fear. She had never been so threatened, so frightened. But, strangely, she also felt more alive than at any time since her mother had died. Everything in the world seemed closer now – the birdsong, the wild roses in the hedgerow; even the sky seemed bluer and brighter than she remembered. The thought that her life could be taken from her at any second gave it a terrifying sweetness, poised between past and future in the heat of a summer afternoon.

Twenty minutes later, Berry parked the bike a couple of streets from Joseph's house and made her way on foot to the narrow access path which ran behind the rear gardens. She decided she would check that no one was around and then sneak in the back way. But as she turned the corner, she saw that the back garden was cordoned off with long strips of plastic tape printed with the words: 'Police line. Do not cross.' Two men in white boilersuits and blue rubber gloves were stepping into the house while a uniformed police officer stood guard outside the back door.

'Oh no,' Berry whispered, steadying herself against the fence. For a moment she thought she might be sick. She bent over and put her hands on her knees, breathing deeply until the waves of nausea passed. Then she walked around to the front of the house where two police cars were parked outside, their blue lights flashing. She could hear the hiss of static from the radios and a voice crackling across the airwaves, asking for 'an update on the situation'.

She stood by the low front wall and stared across the unkempt lawn as another boilersuited man emerged from the front door, snapping the elasticated wristband of his blue rubber gloves. Several neighbours had emerged from their houses and were standing around in little groups, whispering and pointing.

'Can I help you?' asked a voice behind her.

Berry turned to see a young police officer staring at her. She glanced down and saw what he saw: jeans covered in mud and grass stains, the elbow of her cardigan ripped and her hands cut and grazed from the fall.

The policeman's arms were folded and Berry sensed a professional curiosity.

'I said, "Can I help you?"' he repeated.

'Oh s—sorry,' she stuttered, still in shock. 'Umm, no, not really, I just, sort of, wondered what was going on.'

'I see,' replied the police officer. Berry stared past him at the other officers knocking at front doors and realized that her fears for Joseph were probably well founded.

'Has someone died?' she asked, trying to sound unconcerned. But her voice trembled and the police officer narrowed his eyes.

'Did you know the person who lived here?' he asked.

The person who *lived* here, thought Berry. *Past tense.*

'No,' she said. 'I was just curious, that's all.'

The young police officer eyed her suspiciously.

'Shouldn't you be in school?'

'Yes,' said Berry. 'That's where I'm headed.'

'Uh-huh,' said the policeman, sounding sceptical. 'And which school would that be, exactly?'

'Hillgrove High,' said Berry.

'Hillgrove High,' repeated the policeman. 'Name?'

For a moment, Berry wanted just to tell him, wanted him to put her in the back of his police car with the blue light flashing and drive her somewhere safe, somewhere far away from all the dangerous, crazy people. But then she remembered that somewhere safe meant school and strangers, living and dying just like everyone else. Her mother had taught her not to fall for that one. Staying on the outside was the only way to be free.

'My name's Janice,' she said. 'Janice Johnson.'

The young policeman stared at her, less than convinced, and Berry felt herself beginning to weaken. *If he asks me again*, she thought, *I'll tell him the truth.*

But he didn't ask her again. Instead, he looked at his watch.

'Well, Janice Johnson from Hillgrove High. Seeing as how it is now ten minutes to two, I would politely advise you to get a move on.'

'OK,' said Berry, making to walk back up the road again. 'I'll do that.'

'But', the policeman added, holding up a hand to detain her, 'perhaps I might make a small suggestion?'

Berry squinted back at him in the afternoon sunshine and waited.

'The next time you get stopped by a police officer, they may not be quite as busy as I am. In which case, your story will need to be a bit more convincing.' He winked and Berry saw from his smile that he was nicer than he had first appeared. 'Go to school on Monday, Janice. You never know, you might actually learn something.'

'Thanks for the advice,' said Berry. 'I'll try and remember it.'

Once around the corner, she ran as fast as she could

and by the time she reached the bike she was exhausted. Unbuckling the helmet from the handlebars, she
glanced around to see if anyone was watching, but the
streets were empty. Putting her hands over her eyes,
she let the tears fall silently as her body tried in vain to
wash all her grief and fear away.

After a while she wiped her face with the sleeve of
her cardigan, buckled up her helmet and rode away up
the street, past the houses with their lawns and drives
and neatly trimmed privet hedges, past the park where
a young mother stared silently into her second-hand
pram, past the chip shop, the newsagent's and the
empty hairdresser's until at last she turned on to the
High Street, where soon she was swallowed up in the
smoke and the noise.

10
4/20

IN ALL THE TIME he had worked at the New Mexico office of the FBI, Special Agent Bill Horton had never seen it redecorated. The paint in the corridors was still the same dull brown he had noticed when he arrived twelve years ago and each year a bit more flaked off, revealing a dull beige plaster beneath. He didn't know what the Feds spent their annual budget on, but it wasn't paint and it certainly wasn't his salary.

Dropping a couple of quarters into the slot of the vending machine, Horton pressed the button and waited for his morning delivery of black coffee. He was just about to take his first sip when the door of Jack Layton's office swung open and he saw his boss standing in the doorway.

'Come in, Bill,' he said. 'We need to talk.'

Horton sat opposite the window, watching the streets of Albuquerque coming alive through slatted blinds. Layton closed the door and sat behind his desk.

'I'm sorry about Andy, Bill. I know you two were close.'

Horton nodded. Andy Sampson had been his line manager for over a decade and although, at fifty-six, Sampson had only been a few years his senior, Horton had always looked up to him. He still found it hard to believe that he had been blown away by a bomb outside his own front door. Harder still that he would never, ever see him again.

'I guess you've heard what the CIA are saying?' Layton asked.

'No,' replied Horton. 'What are they saying?'

'They're saying the bomb was probably planted by Colombian drug barons, trying to protect their interests.'

Horton snorted with derision.

'You don't believe that?' he said.

Layton shrugged.

'It's possible. You and Andy were following up a drugs lead when all this happened, weren't you?'

Horton shook his head dismissively. 'Small-time dealers, that's all. We'd already decided they were hardly worth the paperwork. Closest those guys ever got to Colombia was drinking a cup of coffee.'

'OK, Bill. Let's just say — for the sake of argument — that the CIA got it wrong. That it wasn't the Colombians. Who the hell else is going to want to plant ten pounds of high explosive beneath Andy's car?'

When Horton didn't answer, Layton raised his eyebrows, encouraging an answer. 'Come on, Bill. Help me out here. I want to know what you think.'

'No, you don't, Jack,' said Horton. 'Really. You don't.'

'Try me,' said Layton.

'All right,' said Horton. 'I don't buy any of that CIA drugs stuff. Not for a second. You want my opinion? I think it's got something to do with the Mitchell case. And I think the CIA think so too. They just don't want to admit it.'

Horton saw his boss's expression change and knew this was something he really didn't want to hear. He knew that Sampson had become something of an embarrassment to both the FBI and the CIA in recent years, trying to get the investigation into Mitchell's disappearance reopened. But no one had wanted to know and, looking at Layton's face, Horton could tell that he didn't want to know either.

'Listen, Bill,' said Layton, leaning forward and putting his elbows on the desk. 'We all know Andy was obsessed with finding Joseph Mitchell. But things have moved on. Sure, when Mitchell first disappeared, he was on the FBI's 'Most Wanted' list. But that was sixty years ago. It's ancient history, Bill. In today's world, it's irrelevant.'

'Andy didn't think so.'

'No, he didn't. But then maybe that's because it was

his dad who let Mitchell get away in the first place.'

'That's not fair, Jack. Have you read the "Project Paperclip" report?'

'Oh no,' said Layton. 'Please. Don't start on me with the whole UFO thing.'

'What UFO thing?'

'You know what UFO thing. That whole conspiracy theory back in the forties and fifties. About flying saucers crashing near Roswell and the government covering it up. About people seeing flying saucers landing in the desert and all that top-secret stuff at the White Sands Missile Base. That *is* what you're talking about, isn't it?'

'Well, that's part of it,' Horton admitted. 'But it's not the part that was worrying Andy and it's not the part that's worrying me.'

'OK,' said Layton. 'All right. So if we're not talking about little green men here, what exactly are we talking about?'

'We're talking about US forces', said Horton, 'capturing a bunch of German scientists at the end of the Second World War and bringing them across to New Mexico to work at the White Sands Missile Base. Each of them had a paperclip on the front of their file.'

'So nothing to do with flying saucers from outer space, then?'

'Well, I guess it was the same time as all the rumours started. But that's all they were. Rumours.

Nothing was ever proved.'

'OK. So remind me. Why did they bring the Germans over?'

'Because their research on new flight technologies was way ahead of anything the US government had done. Once the war was over, the US wanted the German scientists to work for them.'

Layton rubbed his eyes and squeezed the bridge of his nose between finger and thumb. Horton figured that if Layton didn't have a headache before, he had one now.

'I'm sorry, Bill. You're losing me. What does all this have to do with the disappearance of Mitchell?'

'Mitchell was an American research scientist working alongside the German team at the time. There was some sort of crash and he was involved in figuring out what had happened. According to the report, he suddenly disappeared, taking some piece of top-secret technology with him. So secret, in fact, that, to this day, no one will say what it was. But it was obviously pretty important back then. They spent a lot of time and money trying to track him down.'

'Yes, but that's exactly the point, isn't it?' said Layton. 'Back *then* it was important. Not now, Bill. Not any more.'

'Well, that's kind of what I thought,' said Horton. 'But then Andy showed me this.' He pulled out a piece of paper and pushed it across the desk.

'What is it?' asked Layton.

'It's an email,' said Horton. 'Sent to Andy Sampson a few months back. He showed it to me at the time.'

Layton looked at it. It read:

We're both getting warmer, Andy. But will you be able to stand the heat . . . ? 4/20

Layton frowned.

'4/20. Isn't that slang for cannabis or something?'

'That's what we thought at first. It came from a downtown internet café, so it was local and seemed to make sense as we were working on the drugs thing. But you know how Andy was with the Mitchell case. Something about it set his alarm bells ringing. Do you have an internet connection on that computer?'

'I have, but I don't . . .'

'Just type "4/20" into the search engine.'

'What? Look, Bill, I really don't see –'

'Please, Jack. I just want to show you something.'

Layton sighed and glanced at his watch.

'All right, Bill. But let's not be too long about this, OK? I've got a meeting with the Mayor in an hour.'

Horton watched Layton tap the keyboard, look at the screen and then back at Horton.

'What am I supposed to be looking at here?' He stared at the screen. 'I've got drug culture, a passage from the Bible, a New Zealand nightclub . . .'

'How about the word "hate"?' asked Horton. 'Anything starting with that?'

Layton peered at the screen again and nodded. 'Yep. OK. Here we go.' He clicked his mouse, raised his eyebrows and began reading:

'Hate Number Symbols. 4/20 is a number symbol commonly used by neo-Nazi groups to denote their allegiance to Adolf Hitler.'

Layton shrugged. 'So?'

'So the twentieth of April was Hitler's birthday. The way I figure it, Andy must have made contact with some kind of terrorist group that still has connections with those Nazi scientists from sixty years ago. And I think that, because he asked too many questions, they got rid of him. My guess is, these people are close to finding whatever piece of technology it was that Mitchell stole all those years ago. And maybe, if they get it, they'll use it to attack America in some way.'

Layton, whose eyes had been growing wider all the time that Horton had been speaking to him, now held up both his hands.

'OK, Bill, you know what? I haven't got time for this any more. I understand that you're upset, but just listen to yourself for a minute. The stuff about Mitchell and weird technology was bad enough, but a Nazi plot against the US government? You're moving into fairyland territory here.'

He sighed and looked Horton straight in the eye.

'I'm speaking as a friend now, Bill,' he said. 'What you're saying has absolutely no basis in fact. If you carry on with these crazy theories then you're going to waste a lot of valuable FBI time and, what's more, you're going to make yourself a laughing stock. You're a good agent, Bill, with a good reputation. Don't throw it away over this.'

'But what if I'm right?' asked Horton. 'What then?'

Layton sighed. 'You're not going to let this one go, are you?' he asked wearily.

'I just want the truth,' said Horton. 'Not the CIA's version of it.'

The phone rang.

Layton held up a finger and picked it up.

'Layton.'

Horton watched as Layton nodded at the phone and began to wonder whether he really was reading too much into all this. Maybe the 4/20 thing was just a coincidence. Maybe it *was* a drugs reference.

Maybe he needed a holiday.

'Are you sure?' Layton was saying. He sounded worried. 'When did they find out?'

Horton watched him scratch at the polish on his desk and wondered what the guy on the other end was telling him.

'OK,' Layton said. 'Let me get back to you.'

He replaced the phone and stared thoughtfully at his desk as though he had asked it a difficult question and was waiting for an answer.

'That was police forensics,' he said at last. 'They've found traces of ammonium nitrate and the remains of a Primadet delay system at the bomb scene. They're saying – unofficially of course – that it's not the kind of device the Colombians would generally use.'

Horton nodded. He was no expert, but he recognized the type of bomb. It was the same home-grown kind that extremist groups had previously used against US government targets. A fertilizer bomb.

'You know, Jack,' he said, 'Andy always knew that people weren't interested in the Mitchell case. He knew that everyone thought he was obsessed with it. But he was convinced that whatever it was that went missing back in 1947 was still a huge threat to national security. The night before he died, you know what he said? "Look out for the unusual. That's where you'll find it."'

Layton stared at Horton for a long time.

'All right, Bill,' he said finally. 'I still think your theory is crazy. Hell, I think you're even crazier. But if you feel like wasting your time making a few enquiries, well then I guess I'm going to be too busy talking to the Mayor to even know about it.'

Horton got up and smiled.

'You're the boss, Jack,' he said.

II
THE PACKAGE

BERRY APPROACHED THE Shepton Mallet roundabout
at fifty miles an hour. With a quick dab on the brakes
she indicated right and transferred her weight across
the bike so that it leaned neatly into the turn and swept
smoothly across the junction on to the road sign-
posted 'Pilton'. A green and white camper van loomed
up in front of her and with a quick twist of the throttle she scorched past it like a rocket, hugging the white
lines down the centre of the road before flicking the
bike back on to the left-hand side again. Less than a
minute later she entered the village of Pilton, slowing
down to join a line of traffic backed up behind a slow-
moving tractor. She trundled along in first gear for a
while, watching a colourful assortment of people
laden with rucksacks and bedrolls, making their way
along the narrow pavements towards the festival.

As she pulled level with the village stores, she noticed a thin, wiry boy of about sixteen emerge from the doorway, carrying a carton of milk in one hand and a packet of liquorice allsorts in the other. He wore bright purple trousers and a striped, multi-coloured jumper of red, yellow, green and blue. On his feet were a pair of bright green boots.

'Hello,' he said as he spotted Berry looking at him through her open visor. She pretended to look at something else, but it was too late. He did a neat pirouette on the pavement and walked across the road towards her. 'You look like a woman of taste,' he said, pointing one toe forward like a dancer. 'Tell me – do you think these boots are too much?'

Berry looked at his long eyelashes, heavy with mascara beneath glittering blue eye-shadow and saw that his smile was as wide as the moon. She looked down at his shiny green boots and found herself smiling too.

'On you?' she said. 'Never.'

'That,' replied the boy as his smile grew wider, 'is the right answer. And for that, you win a prize.'

Keeping his eyes fixed on Berry, he dug his hand into the packet of liquorice allsorts and, with a flourish, pulled out a pink one.

'Of such sweet moments are our lives made up,' he said, holding the sweet delicately to Berry's lips. She opened her mouth and he pushed the sweet in before tapping her lips lightly with his finger. 'May yours be made up of many more.'

Berry looked into his dark brown eyes, and for a moment, the world seemed to stand still. Then a horn blared loudly and a man in a pin-striped shirt leaned out of his window.

'Get out of the way, you crazy rag doll!' he shouted.

'Rag doll?' repeated the boy and Berry saw that he was not angry, but amused. 'That's a new one.' He held up a finger to Berry as if to excuse himself and then spun around to face the man.

'I'm sorry,' he said. 'Did you want one too?'

With that, the boy leaned down, popped a liquorice allsort into the astonished man's mouth and rolled neatly across his bonnet before disappearing up a side road with a friendly wave. As the man swore loudly and spat the sweet out, Berry smiled, feeling as though she had shared some kind of secret. Reaching the brow of the hill, she could see queues of cars lining up at the festival entrance and, in the distance, thousands of coloured tents stretching over the fields as far as the eye could see. Flags fluttered in the breeze and she could hear the rhythmic thud of a bass drum above a crackle of guitar chords. Tapping the gears into neutral, she freewheeled down the hill past the line of traffic and headed towards the main entrance, the taste of sweet, pink coconut still dancing across her tongue.

'ID?' said the man on the gate as she handed him her ticket. Berry fished out her passport and flashed it in front of him, hoping he wouldn't make the connection between her age and the fact that she was riding a large motorbike. But if he did, it obviously wasn't his job to worry about it.

'Follow the red route,' he said, 'and park in the secure compound. They'll give you a pass so you can get your bike when you need it.'

'Thanks very much,' said Berry as he fastened a coloured bracelet to her wrist.

'No problem,' he told her. 'Welcome to Glastonbury.'

It was just after eight thirty when she finished putting up her tent, surrounded by countless others. The sun was still hot, but the clouds had coloured a candy-floss pink and Berry tasted the scent of oil and spices floating up from the food stalls beyond the Pyramid Stage. In the shade of her tent, she checked the contents of her rucksack: clothes, plane tickets, passport, money, and the strange package that Joseph had given her, still thickly wrapped in shiny blue paper. Berry picked it up, amazed by its lightness. It felt like holding air and feathers.

The safety of the world depends upon you returning this item.

It was ridiculous, of course. How could something

so important weigh so little? And yet . . . Berry was scared. Now she had the package and Joseph was dead. She was sure that the men had killed him. So had Joseph been telling the truth – did this small package actually contain the incredible thing he had spoken of? Was it really what they were after?

Carefully, Berry turned it over in her hands, trying to gain some sense of what lay hidden inside. But the box underneath the paper was too rigid, giving no clue as to its contents.

'You really didn't want me to know, did you, Joseph?' she whispered.

She held the box up to her ear and shook it gently from side to side, listening for a tell-tale rattle or clink. But instead, she was amazed to hear the tiniest of sounds, so distant and strange that whenever she tried to think of it later, it was almost impossible to remember. The closest she could get was to imagine a waterfall of stars tumbling through space, each one splashing silver notes into the darkness. The music wove a pattern of such beauty and sadness into Berry's mind that after a few seconds she could bear it no longer and dropped the package to the ground.

Immediately, the sound stopped.

Berry stared at it for a long time, her insides fluttering as though she were standing on the edge of a very high cliff.

'What are you?' she whispered. 'What *are* you?'

But the sound was gone and all she could hear was the laughter and shouting of a thousand people outside. Somewhere in the distance, a band began to play. And because she suddenly felt a dreadful longing to know what was in the package, and because she knew that she mustn't, she quickly snatched it up and flung it to the bottom of her rucksack, pushing her spare clothes and everything else on top of it. Then, zipping up the tent, she threw the rucksack over her shoulder and made her way towards the crowds that were gathering beneath the darkening sky.

12

THE ONE THAT SAVES ME

IN AN EFFORT TO TAKE her mind off the package and all the problems that went with it, Berry spent the next couple of days wandering around the site in a daze, trying to listen to a few bands and soak up some of the atmosphere. Her recent experiences had left her exhausted, however, and she would often return to her tent during the day, the sounds of music and laughter becoming a jumble of noise as she drifted fuzzily in and out of sleep. She heard people in the next tent talking about a change in the weather, but each day the sun continued to shine down upon the colour and clamour so that, even when she was awake, Berry felt as though she was stumbling through some hot, confusing dream.

Now, early on Sunday evening, she emerged from her tent to the sound of guitars, then stretched her arms above her head and looked around. Two huge screens on either side of the main stage showed a man in a striped suit, smoking and singing above a thundering bass while a slide guitarist bottle-necked a tune over the chopping chords of a Fender. As the crowd danced, stewards in yellow vests sprayed water to keep them cool and high above them a tiny red kite sailed lazily through a darkening sky.

Ambling down the hillside, Berry made her way past the stage towards the stalls and cafés in search of something to eat. Following a path through a row of tents, she found herself surrounded by giant wooden sculptures of mushrooms, each carved in such intricate detail that she could pretend she had shrunk down to the size of a beetle. A man wearing swimming trunks and a green woolly hat was sprawled untidily across the smallest one, snoring quietly beneath the setting sun. Berry swung around one of the stalks and watched a woman in pink and yellow trousers wobble past on a unicycle. Then, quite unexpectedly, she came across a stall selling little bird puppets on strings. Her mother had bought her one the very first time she came to Glastonbury and now, as she watched them dance, she remembered how she had lost sight of her mother in the crowds soon afterwards. She could have been only about four or five, but she still remembered the ache of her loss and the joy when, a few minutes later, her mother had found her again. Now the ache was back and Berry knew that, from now on, it was here to stay. This time, she would not be found.

Stumbling past a multi-coloured sign inviting her to 'Make Your Own Dreamcatcher', her eyes filled with tears as she wandered into a field of tall, cream-coloured tepees where smoke from open fires drifted through the holes in the tops, spreading out and hanging in a light blue haze above the field. At the entrance to one of the tepees, an old man was stirring soup over an open fire.

'Here,' he said, holding out a wooden spoon as she approached. 'Would you like some?'

Berry pointed at herself in surprise. 'Me?' she asked.

The man nodded.

'Of course. My soup is for sharing.'

'Thank you,' said Berry. She knelt down and as she wiped away the tears with the back of her hand, the man asked, 'Are you all right?'

Berry smiled, even though she had started to cry again. 'I will be,' she said. 'Just give me a minute.'

Silently, the man waited for Berry to dry her eyes and then handed her the spoon. Realizing how hungry she was, Berry dipped it into the thick brown soup and a rich aroma of carrots, aubergines and sweet potatoes filled her nostrils.

'Oh,' she exclaimed, sipping from the edge of the spoon. 'This is so delicious! How much do I owe you?'

She fumbled in her bag for some money, but the man put his hand on her arm.

'Please,' he said. 'This soup was made from the fruits of the earth and the earth belongs to all of us.'

Berry took another sip and then handed him a two-pound coin. 'Well then,' she said, 'this will help you to plant some more.'

'You have a good heart,' said the old man as Berry got up to go, 'and in time it will heal itself. But remember: go lightly upon the earth and always try to listen when your heart speaks to you.'

'I will,' said Berry, surprised at how deeply his words touched her. 'Thank you.'

Following a thread of people up a slight incline, she scrambled over a wooden stile and saw that someone had painted the words 'This Way to Lost Vagueness' on a large cardboard sign in the shape of a finger. She walked along an old railway track for a few minutes until she heard the sound of an organ over some twanging guitars.

'Yeehaw!' someone shouted. 'Welcome to the Chapel of Ho—lee – Matrimony!'

Berry wandered beneath a mysterious purple sign announcing that she was 'Now Entering the Field of Lost Vagueness' and suddenly found herself in a field where strange, outlandish figures flitted in and out of the shadows like characters from a dream.

Two men dressed in flowing black coats towered several metres above her, their huge legs striding across the grass as they peered down at her through silver masks, poking at her jacket with their long, scissor-like hands.

'Snip, snip, snip,' they cried in unison. 'Snippety, snip snip!'

Realizing that she must have walked into some kind of street theatre, Berry laughed nervously and backed away behind a giant rhinoceros that had been constructed from straw. A man with a blue face and pointy ears — who up until that moment had been lying on the grass — rose up into a sitting position, put a silver funnel to his mouth and shouted, 'Beware of the stick men! Beware of the stick men!' Then he placed the funnel on his head and said, 'I am ready to receive your messages, Sky People.'

Berry giggled and ran beneath the rhinoceros, weaving through a group of children with painted animal faces who were watching a sad-faced juggler. She came to a red and white striped tent where a man in a white tuxedo beckoned her through the doorway.

'Welcome to the poetry tent,' he told her. 'May our verse . . . be your nurse.'

As Berry ducked inside the doorway, a hush fell across the crowd and she looked across to see a lone figure walking towards the middle of a small stage. He was lit by a single spotlight and Berry saw that he clutched a piece of paper to his chest. A crowd of a hundred or more were gathered around the stage, and as the figure approached the microphone, she saw that it was the liquorice-allsorts boy.

'Hi, everyone,' he said in a voice that was soft but confident. 'I saw the sign saying that there were poetry readings, so I thought I'd write you a poem. Hope that's OK.'

The crowd remained silent, waiting.

The boy unfolded his pad, cleared his throat and began to read:

> listen
> I am here to tell you
> I am all you'll ever need
> I'm the doctor who will heal you
> I'm the plaster when you bleed
> I'm the net for your mosquitoes
> I'm the rabbit in your hutch
> I'm the pack of new Doritos
> When the hunger gets too much
> I'm the poetry you're reading
> The umbrella when it rains
> I'm the oxygen you're needing
> For the blood inside your veins
> I'm the colours in your palette
> I'm the sunshine in your day

I'm the heavy wooden mallet
That will smash your fears away
So when you're feeling like you're falling
And you're lost without a trace
That's the time when I'll come calling
Any time and any place

The boy looked up into the glare of the spotlight and as Berry watched him blink and swallow, she felt as though she had fallen into a dream that was not her own.

He looked down at his piece of paper and began to read once more.

I'm the net for your mosquitoes
I'm the pack of new Doritos
I'm the poetry you're reading
I'm the only one you're needing
If you ask me I will die for you
I'll walk into the sky for you

The boy stopped, lowered his notebook and looked straight at Berry.

You're the love that no one gave me
Won't you be the one that saves me?
Won't you be the one that saves me tonight?

Then his head fell forward and the spotlight faded to black.

13
Standing on the Outside

There was silence for a fraction of a second, and then the stage lights came up again and as everyone clapped politely, the boy just shrugged, said, 'Thanks — thanks very much', and disappeared into the crowd.

The man in the white tuxedo walked up to the microphone and, reading from a piece of paper, said, 'That was Ell, ladies and gentlemen, with a poem he tells me he wrote about an hour ago. Next up, from this afternoon's poetry workshop, we have Bronwen with her poem entitled "When the moon grows cold".'

A rather nervous-looking woman wearing a purple corduroy dress shuffled out of the shadows and approached the microphone cautiously, her fingers trembling as she held up the sheet of paper like a barrier against the crowd.

'When the moon grows *cold*,' she began, at which

point Berry spotted Ell walking out through the exit. She tried to follow him through the crowds, but it was getting dark and harder to see. Outside, people had lit small wood fires and the field was dotted with the flickering light from paper lanterns that hung from the branches of trees. Berry wandered past bright cafés and food stalls, scanning every face, but there was no sign of him. She didn't know why it suddenly felt so important to see Ell again – didn't even know what she would do if she found him – but as she watched a moth flutter against a bright shining lantern she knew that something drew her towards him.

After a while, her feet began to ache and she approached the counter of a stall selling hot drinks and sandwiches.

'Hello, love,' said the lady with the hooped earrings and the yellow cotton apron. 'What can I get you?'

Berry looked up at the menu board and realized how tired she was.

'I'll have a cheese and tomato sandwich, please,' she said. 'And a hot chocolate.'

'Coming up, darling. Do you want chips with that?'

Berry smiled. 'Go on then.'

She watched the woman tuck a loaf of wholemeal bread under her arm, butter the end of it and cut a thick slice which fell neatly on to a waiting plate. She placed a wedge of cheese on it and then skilfully sliced a tomato so that it fanned out neatly across the top of the open sandwich.

'Now *that*,' said a voice behind her, 'is real poetry. Art you can eat.'

Berry felt her skin tingle and knew without turning round that it was Ell.

'Are you after something?' asked the woman as she pressed another slice of bread on top of the sandwich and drew a sharp knife through the middle.

'Not at all,' said Ell. 'Just admiring your work.' He paused before adding, 'Mind you, if you've got any chips going spare, I wouldn't say no.'

He winked at Berry as the woman stuck a small plastic sword into the sandwich and handed it to her.

'You're a cheeky one,' she said. Then she shovelled out two portions of chips and placed them on the counter. 'There,' she added. 'Enjoy.'

'Don't suppose you've got any ketchup?' asked Ell.

'I'll eat them for you if you like,' replied the woman, tossing a handful of sachets on to the counter.

'Don't worry,' replied Ell, ripping open one of the sachets and squirting it over his chips, 'I can take it from here.' He picked up a handful between finger and thumb, tilted his head back and dropped them neatly into his mouth.

'Manna from Heaven,' he said.

As Berry paid the woman, she smiled, shook her

head and went off to serve someone else.

'Better than Doritos?' asked Berry quietly.

'Sorry?' said Ell.

'The chips,' said Berry. 'Are they better than the Doritos you were talking about?'

Ell grinned as the penny dropped.

'You heard my poem?'

'Uh-huh.' Berry pointed a chip at him and added, 'You read it like you meant it.' She dabbed the chip in some ketchup and popped it into her mouth. 'Do you write a lot then?'

'Nope. Just wandered in by mistake. Thought it was the beer tent.'

'Well, it was a nice poem,' said Berry, not believing him. 'You should write some more.'

Ell smiled and put his head on one side.

'Don't I know you from somewhere?'

Berry ate another chip and reached for her hot chocolate.

'You gave me a liquorice allsort. A pink one, as I recall.'

Ell frowned, then remembered.

'The girl on the bike!' He looked at her quizzically. 'How was it for you?'

Berry shrugged. 'It was, you know . . . *liquorishy*.'

She offered him her Styrofoam cup and Ell took it without comment, as though they were already friends.

'So who was the poem about?' asked Berry.

'It was just a poem,' said Ell.

'I don't believe you,' said Berry.

'All right then,' said Ell. 'It was about someone, but I don't know who.'

Berry turned, expecting to find him smiling, teasing her, and was surprised to find that he was staring away into the darkness. 'I guess', he said at last, 'that I just haven't met them yet.'

Berry looked at her chips and wanted to say something then, something that would close the gap between them. But she couldn't think of anything to say and in the end it was Ell who spoke.

'So,' he said, draining the rest of the cup. 'Staying anywhere nice?'

'Oh, you know. Tent. Field. The usual arrangement.'

'Ah yes,' said Ell, and Berry sensed his mood lighten again. 'The Glastonbury experience. Tat, tents and toilets. Is this your first time?'

'No,' said Berry. 'I used to come with my mum but . . . things changed.'

'Things?'

'Well, everything actually.'

Berry had intended to keep the conversation on an ordinary, everyday level. She had wanted to pretend that everything was OK. But her voice trembled and Ell noticed.

'Come on,' he said.

He took her by the hand and led her gently away from the bright lights of the stall.

'Where are we going?' asked Berry, clutching the remains of her sandwich as she trotted along beside him.

'The stone circle,' said Ell as they walked back along the moonlit track. 'Have you been there before?'

'I think so,' said Berry. 'It's on a slope at the top of the festival, isn't it?'

'That's right,' said Ell. 'Beyond the Green Fields, out on the edge of things. That's always the best place to be – standing on the outside. It helps you get rid of the glasses.'

'Glasses?' asked Berry, puzzled.

'You know. The ones they make you wear at school so that you'll see things the same way everyone else does. The ones you end up wearing for the rest of your life.'

'I wouldn't know,' said Berry. 'I never went to school.'

'Well, now.' Ell sounded impressed. 'You're even more interesting than you look.'

'You don't know the half of it,' said Berry.

'I'd like to, though,' said Ell. 'Really I would. I'd like to know who you are.'

'The trouble with that is', said Berry, stumbling over a fallen branch in the darkness, 'I'm not even sure if *I* know.'

Ell held on to her elbow and steadied her.

'Well then,' he said. 'Let's see if we can find out.'

They made their way into the stone circle where groups of people huddled around bright, crackling fires, some dancing and singing, some laughing, some simply staring into the flames and the surrounding darkness.

'Here will do,' said Ell.

They sat together at the feet of a giant wooden phoenix and Berry looked up to see that it held a thick pole in one of its clawed fists. On the top of the pole, high above them, a flaming beacon burned fiercely, scattering glowing embers of red and orange into the night sky. There was a distant roar of appreciation from the crowd as someone began to play a guitar solo and Berry imagined the guitarist's fingers dancing across the strings, notes flying into the air like bright shining bullets. A tiny hot-air balloon made of white tissue paper rose slowly into the air above the fields and as Berry watched it float higher and higher, spinning and turning, it seemed to her a quite magical thing, distinct from the earth, like a wish or a dream. As it caught alight, flamed fiercely for a moment and then vanished, she looked out at the small fires flickering across the valley and felt strangely comforted by them, as if they might somehow protect her from the darkness that troubled her in the world outside.

She put her hands behind her head and lay back on the grass, looking up at a patch of stars just visible between the clouds.

'You see those seven stars?' she asked, pointing up at the sky. 'Those are called the "Plough".'

'No, they're not,' said Ell.

'Yes, they are!'

'No, they're not,' said Ell. 'That's what they *used* to be called. But I renamed them.'

Berry smiled.

'When?'

'About five minutes ago.'

'Oh, I *see*. Go on, then. What are they called now?'

'Doritos,' said Ell. 'See? Seven stars, seven letters. D–O–R–I–T–O–S, Doritos.'

'Very clever,' said Berry. 'Although not very poetic.'

She pointed at another constellation.

'What about that one then? The one on the left.'

'Monster Munch,' replied Ell. 'Barbecue Beef flavour.'

'Oh, of course,' said Berry. 'And there was me thinking it was Orion's Belt.'

'Hard to come by these days, Monster Munch. Retailers just don't seem to stock them.'

A cool breeze whispered through the grass and Berry felt a sudden jolt of fear as she realized that for the last hour or so she had almost forgotten about her problems. Now they came back and hit her in the stomach like a sledgehammer.

I mustn't tell him, she thought. *I mustn't tell anyone.*

Ell rolled on to his side and, as he faced her, Berry saw that some of his mascara was smudged. She reached over and brushed it away with her fingertip.

'Tell me about yourself,' she said.

'Hey,' he said. 'I thought we were going to find out who *you* are.'

Berry smiled and fluttered her eyelashes.

'Ladies first,' she said.

14
KISSES AND KILLERS

'LIKE DICK WHITTINGTON,' said Ell, 'I have run away from home to seek my fame and fortune. You can be my Puss in Boots if you like.'

'Thanks but no thanks,' said Berry. 'Biker in Boots, maybe.'

'Even better,' said Ell.

'Have you really run away from home?' Berry asked.

'Yup,' said Ell.

'Why?'

'Because my father was a total pig. Although actually, now I come to think of it, I didn't *run* away from home. I kind of sauntered. In a very stylish, yet under-stated way.'

'Can't you ever be serious?' asked Berry.

'Serious?' Ell frowned. 'Why on earth would I want to be serious?'

'Because,' said Berry, 'not everything in life is funny.'

'That all depends', said Ell, 'on which way you look at it.'

'Come on,' said Berry. 'Tell me. What was so awful about your dad?'

'Well, for one thing he used to hit me whenever he felt like it. Which was most of the time. But the worst part was, he made me feel like I should have been anyone else but me.'

'Is that why you wear the make-up and stuff? To annoy him?'

Ell raised an eyebrow and smiled.

'No, I wear it 'cos it makes me look *foxy*.'

He propped himself up on one elbow and looked at Berry. 'How am I doing? Serious enough for you yet?'

'Not bad,' said Berry. As she watched him chew the hard skin at the side of his thumbnail, she wondered what strange tides had washed him up next to her and how long it would be before they carried him away again.

'Did he really hit you?' she asked.

Ell nodded. 'He really did.' He pointed up at the dark, anvil-shaped clouds that were building in the sky.

'There's going to be a storm tonight. A big one, I reckon.'

'Why did he hit you?' Berry persisted, not wanting to change the subject.

Ell shrugged. 'I guess his life was just one big disappointment. When I was little, he left the army and
used his savings to start up his own window-cleaning
business. He thought he was going to be a millionaire.
But it didn't quite work out like that.'

'What happened?'

'Well, for a start, the only window cleaners he
could get were the sort who'd do a couple of weeks
and then decide they'd be better off working for themselves. So he'd train 'em up and then they'd run off
with his customers. They crashed his van three times
and nicked it twice. In the end, there were only two
window cleaners who didn't rip him off. Him and me.'

Berry smiled.

'You were a window cleaner?'

'Best-dressed ladder monkey in Hackney.'

'Shouldn't you have been at school?'

Ell laughed. 'That's good, coming from you. Anyway, school doesn't pay. Mind you, neither does cleaning windows. We'd be out there in all weathers,
working our socks off just so that he could lose a bit
more of his money. Then we'd come home and the
rows would start. I'd lie in bed listening to my mother
telling him what a waste of space he was. How if he
didn't start making money soon, she'd leave him. And,
God bless her, she was true to her word. She left us
both, in fact, to go and live with the owner of a betting

shop. And you want to know the really funny part?'

'What?'

'She met the guy while she was putting her weekly child allowance on the gee-gees in the hope of winning herself a better life. Which, I guess, is exactly what she did.'

'That's terrible,' said Berry. 'I'm so sorry.'

'I think it's quite funny actually,' said Ell. 'You've got to laugh, haven't you?'

'Do you?' asked Berry.

'Yes,' said Ell. 'Absolutely you do.'

And for some reason which she couldn't explain, that was the moment that Berry knew she had to tell him.

'Well, in that case,' she said. 'Here's something for you. Do you want to hear something really funny?'

Ell looked intrigued.

'Always and always. Funny ha-ha or funny peculiar?'

'Funny peculiar. Funny terrifying, actually.'

'Go on then. I'm all ears.'

'Well, I'm kind of on the run. I'm being chased by some men who are out to kill me.'

Ell looked at her mock sternly and waggled his finger.

'Are you messing with me now?'

'No,' said Berry. 'I'm not.'

'You are though,' said Ell, smiling. 'I can tell.'

'Look, Ell. I'm being deadly serious. There are

some people out there who want to kill me.'

Berry saw that Ell was having a hard time believing her.

'Why would anyone want to do that?' he asked. 'You're an absolute poppet.'

'Because they want something I've got,' said Berry.

'And what might that be?' asked Ell, looking her up and down. 'Dress sense?'

'Look,' said Berry, 'if you're going to be mean, then I'm stopping this conversation right now.'

'I'm sorry, I'm sorry,' Ell apologized. 'It's just, you've got to admit, it does sound a little . . . weird.'

'I know it does,' said Berry. 'I know, I know . . .'

She sighed.

'Look Ell, I haven't told a soul about this, but you told me what happened to you so I'm going to tell you what happened to me. Then it's up to you whether you believe me or not. OK?'

'OK,' said Ell. 'Go for it.'

'A few days ago, an old man saved my life,' she said. 'And when he found out that I had a ticket to America, he asked me to deliver a package to New Mexico for him.'

'Hang on,' said Ell. 'You've got a ticket to America? How come?'

'Long story,' said Berry, 'but basically a birthday present. Anyway, I said I wasn't going to do it. But then he said he'd call me and when I got home I found he'd put this package in my rucksack.'

'What was in it?'

'I don't know — he didn't say, apart from telling me it was really important. Anyway, I thought he was a nice old man but probably a bit mad. So I decided I would take it back to him and that would be that. But then these men came with guns and I got really scared and when I went back to see him there were police all over the place and I found out he was dead. I realized then that he wasn't mad and so I came here to get away from those people and work out what I'm going to do next.'

'OK,' said Ell evenly. 'Wow. That is certainly some story.'

Berry saw Ell's expression and shook her head. 'You don't believe me, do you? You think I'm making all this up.'

'Look, it's not that,' said Ell. 'It's just . . .'

'I should probably go,' said Berry, standing up. 'I'm a bit tired.' She forced out a smile. 'It was nice meeting you, Ell.'

Ell took hold of her hand and pulled her down again.

'You're serious, aren't you?' he said. 'You really are in trouble.'

'Yes,' said Berry and she had to bite her lip to stop herself from bursting into tears.

'Hey now,' said Ell, holding out his arms to her. 'Hey. Come here, little friend.'

'Don't,' said Berry, waving her hand at him as if shooing away a fly. 'I'll only start crying again. I've done too much of that already.'

'Tell me something then,' said Ell. 'What do they look like?'

'Who?'

'These men – what do they look like?'

'Oh, I don't know. A blond guy, a guy in a tracksuit.'

'Has it got a white stripe across the shoulders?' asked Ell and Berry noticed that he had lowered his voice and was looking at her strangely.

'Yes,' said Berry. 'Why do –'

Suddenly, Ell put his arms around Berry's neck and kissed her, then pushed her down so that he was lying with his body draped on top of her.

'Ell, what are you do–' Berry began but her voice was muffled by his lips. A hot, indignant anger rose up inside her and she began thumping him on the back with her fists.

'Get off me!' she hissed. 'Get off me get off me get *off* me!'

'Ow!' cried Ell, grabbing her wrists. 'Will you cut it out?'

Berry nearly exploded with rage. 'Will I cut . . .? Will *you* cu–' she squeaked before Ell threw himself forward again, practically suffocating her beneath his weight. For what seemed like an age Berry struggled beneath him, but he was a good two years older and much stronger than he appeared. Then, just when she thought she would be completely smothered, he rolled off and clamped a hand across her mouth. As she squealed and slapped his arm, he whispered in her ear:

'All right, I'm going to take my hand away now. And when I do, you're not going to make any noise, because I'm going to show you something and you need to be really, really quiet, OK?'

He pulled his hand back, flipped her on to her front and whispered, 'Look. Over there.'

Berry followed his gaze and saw that two men were standing in the shadow of the hedgerow. One of them was shining a torch in people's faces and, when they protested, showing them some kind of ID. The other's face was lit by the green glow of something resembling a mobile phone. A long aerial extended from the end of it. He was wearing a tracksuit with a white stripe across the shoulders.

Berry felt a sick, churning terror in the pit of her stomach.

'It's them,' she said, scarcely able to believe what she was seeing. 'It's *them*!'

'Well, they look as though they could be police,' said Ell, watching the first man flash his torch in a woman's face and flip open his ID. 'Are you in trouble with them or something?'

'They're not police,' whispered Berry. 'They must have fake IDs or something, just so that they can get to me.'

'But how would they know you're here?' Ell whispered back.

'I don't know,' replied Berry, her voice shaking. 'But if they find me, I'm dead.'

'You really think they're going to kill you?'

'I don't think,' said Berry. 'I *know.*'

'Well they're getting closer,' said Ell. 'Shall we make a run for it?'

'*We?*'

'Might as well.'

'No, Ell,' said Berry. 'It's me they're after, not you.' She glanced at him and saw – to her surprise – that his eyes were shining with excitement.

'Seriously,' she said. 'I mean it. Don't get involved.'

'I'm already involved,' said Ell. 'Now where's your bike?'

'It's in the secure parking area. But –'

'Right. I'm going to go talk to these guys. And as soon as I'm talking to them, you run and get it, OK?'

'Ell, I'm telling you – they're dangerous. They'll –'

'As soon as I'm talking to them,' Ell repeated. Then he jumped to his feet and began walking straight towards the two men. When he was nearly upon them he started to stagger and sway, holding his arms out as if greeting long-lost friends.

'Hello, boys!' he slurred loudly in a very drunken-sounding voice. 'You are very, *very* naughty, wandering off like that. Yes, you, are! Very naughty in*deed*!'

People were turning to look, pleasantly surprised by this unexpected sideshow.

'Never mind, my darlings,' Ell continued, stumbling forward. 'I've found you now and that's all that matters!' He threw himself headlong at the man with the torch, wrapped his arms around his neck and brought him tumbling down into the mud. Berry heard him swear, heard Ell squeal, 'Oooh I've *missed* you!' and then she was up and running, down the hill and through the gate into the crowds that clapped and cheered as the music played and laser beams lit up the night sky.

She kept on running, past whole-food cafés and signs offering astrological readings, past stalls selling jacket potatoes and tents hung with crystal jewellery, all of them blurring at the edge of her vision as she twisted and turned through the crowds, heading for the sanctuary of the bike park. She had thought that she would be safe here at the festival, just one more face among thousands. But she was mistaken.

It had taken them less than three days to find her.

She knew what had happened to Joseph and knew that this time they wouldn't let her go.

If they found her now, they would kill her.

☆ 15 ☆
DEATH IN THE RAIN

A BOLT OF LIGHTNING flashed across the sky, followed almost immediately by a tremendous crack of thunder. For a few moments, thick, heavy droplets pattered across the grass and then with a roar the heavens opened, turning the paths into rivers of rain. By the time she reached the entrance to the bike park, Berry was completely drenched. A security guard sat in a wooden hut, reading by the light of a small gas lamp. Berry could tell by the way he looked at her that his magazine was far more interesting to him than a mud-soaked girl waving a piece of paper.

'Hi,' she said breathlessly. 'I need to collect my bike.'

'*Your* bike?' he asked scathingly. 'Since when have they let little girls ride around on bikes?'

'Oh, I'm sorry,' replied Berry, checking over her

shoulder to make sure she wasn't being followed. 'I didn't realize this was the comedy tent.' She slapped her collection ticket on the counter and glared at him. 'See? My bike.'

The man picked it up and studied it for a while.

'How old are you, anyway?'

'Old enough,' said Berry, aware that every second was precious now. 'Please, can I just go and get my bike?'

'Well, OK,' said the man. 'But don't forget your stabilizers.'

Berry slipped and squelched along the ranks of motorcycles, soaked by the rain that had already turned the compound into a quagmire. She saw her bike near the end of the row. A gust of wind had blown it off its side-stand and it had fallen against a large Harley Davidson.

Pulling it upright, she unclipped the helmet from beneath the seat and buckled it under her chin. Swinging her leg across the seat, she turned the key and jumped down hard on the kick-start. To her relief, the engine caught first time and began burbling throatily beneath her.

'Oh, *thank* you,' she whispered and pulled in the clutch. Then the engine stuttered, cut out and died again. Puzzled, she looked up at the instrument panel just in time to see a hand twisting the key into the off position.

'Don't move,' said a voice. 'Keep perfectly still or I will shoot you. Do you understand?'

Berry nodded and felt herself tremble all over.

She was going to die.

'Get off the bike. Now. Do it.'

Berry kicked out the side-stand and carefully dismounted, allowing her eyes to flick up briefly as she did so. She saw straight away that it was one of them. He was pointing a small, snub-nosed revolver directly at her head.

'What do you want?' she pleaded above the white noise of rain, hissing all around them. 'I don't know what you want!'

The man pushed her down on to her knees and raised the gun so that she was staring straight down its barrel.

'Don't think you can make a fool of me twice,' he spat. 'Now give it to me!'

'Please,' begged Berry. 'I swear I don't know what you're talking about!'

'OK,' said the man. 'No problem.'

He pressed the gun into her forehead and Berry screamed.

There was a metallic clang, followed by a loud grunt and the soft squelch of mud. Realizing that the pressure on her forehead was gone, she opened her eyes and saw Ell holding a large metal sign in his hands.

Below him, the man lay spread-eagled in the mud.

'Sorry I'm late,' said Ell. 'Got held up.'

Berry looked anxiously over his shoulder. 'Where are the others?'

'Up at the stone circle where I left 'em. They weren't happy.'

Berry noticed that one of Ell's eyes was closed up and his lip was split. 'Are you OK?' she asked.

'Sure. One thing my dad taught me was how to take a punch.'

Ell glanced down at the man stretched out in the mud and kicked the gun away from his open hand.

'You really weren't joking, were you?'

Berry shook her head. 'I think we'd better get going,' she said.

'We?' asked Ell.

Berry fired up the motor and revved the engine.

'If you want,' she said.

As Ell climbed up behind her, she let out the clutch and the back wheel spun before finding its grip and propelling them forward into the storm. She had to put her feet down several times to stop the bike from sliding sideways but, eventually, they reached the compound entrance. As they passed the small wooden hut, Berry glanced in and saw to her horror that the security guard was slumped back in his seat with his eyes wide open. Blood from a chest wound pooled in his lap.

'What the hell is going on here?' Ell shouted into the wind.

But Berry wasn't staying to find out. Seeing the gate unlocked, she twisted the throttle and accelerated forward, the front wheel snapping the gate back against its hinges as the bike powered through. Putting her right foot down, she kept the power on and slid the back end round until they had turned through ninety degrees, increasing the throttle speed so that they shot away up the exit road in a flurry of mud and smoke. Bumping and jolting across the rutted ground, Berry wiped the rain from her visor and saw that they were now approaching the main entrance. Beyond it was the main road, and apart from two cars waiting to enter, the exit seemed clear. But as they got closer, Berry noticed a man standing on the opposite verge, sheltering beneath a tree. He was holding a radio to his mouth and watching the exit carefully. Immediately, Berry twitched the handlebars to the right and they skidded off the road towards a line of trees where she brought the bike to a stop and killed the engine.

'What's happening?' asked Ell, jumping off the back. 'What's going on?'

'One of them's waiting over there,' Berry replied, still in shock from her glimpse of the dead body in the hut. 'Out there on the road. Look.'

Ell squinted through the rain at the distant figure beneath the trees.

'Are you sure?' he asked. 'Could just be a security guard.'

'Could be,' said Berry. 'But you saw what happened back there. We can't take any chances. We have to get out quickly, before he realizes what's happening.'

'But how?'

Berry looked at Ell and saw in his eyes how much the dead body had frightened him too. Although he was older than her, she suddenly felt protective towards him and this gave her fresh courage.

'You see the smaller entrance?' she asked, pointing along the tree line. 'That's where the pedestrians come through. Now look at him. You see where he's watching? I reckon he knows we're on a bike and is expecting us to come out of the main entrance. So I say we push the bike to the end of the tree line, start it up there and ride through the pedestrian bit. What do you reckon?'

'Looks a bit narrow,' said Ell doubtfully. A metal post divided the centre of the gap to allow two people through at a time – one on either side. It had been put there to prevent too many people going through at once. But Berry could see why Ell was worried – it allowed very little room for error.

'Just keep your knees in,' she said with a good deal more confidence than she felt. 'You'll be fine.'

In silence they pushed the bike through the shadows beneath the trees, taking care not to move too quickly in order to lessen their chances of being seen.

'OK,' said Berry anxiously as they brought the bike to a halt beneath the dripping leaves of a sycamore tree. 'How's it looking?'

'Not so good.'

'What? Why?'

Berry looked across the road and realized with a sinking feeling that the man had moved. He was still on the opposite verge, but now he was standing further over and Berry could tell from the way his head moved that he was watching both entrances.

'Damn it!' she said. 'What's he doing that for?'

'Maybe we should go back,' suggested Ell. 'Wait until the whole festival turns out. It might be easier to slip away unnoticed.'

'No,' said Berry. 'You saw how easily they found me. If we stay here, we've had it. At least, I have.'

She stared past the brightly lit entrance to the sweep of road that climbed steeply up to the right. Stretching away to the left was a long, curving bend. As she watched, a lorry appeared, the front of its cab lit up like a Christmas tree. It was a long sixteen-wheeler and as it lumbered up the road, Berry jumped back on the bike and slapped Ell on the shoulder. 'Come on,' she said. 'We're going.'

Ell looked at Berry, then at the lorry, then back at Berry again.

'Oh, God, no,' he said, climbing on behind her. 'No, no, no.'

As the front of the lorry approached the main entrance with its engine revving and gears grinding, Berry kicked the motor alive and slammed her visor shut. If the lorry driver hadn't chosen that moment to remove his foot from the accelerator and change gear, her timing might have been perfect. As it was, the noise of the lorry's engine faded just enough for the sound of the bike to be heard and Berry saw the man across the road turn and look at her. As their eyes met and he reached into his pocket, Berry released the clutch and the bike shot out of the trees like a greyhound from the traps.

'Hold on!' she shouted as they raced towards the tiny gap, the lorry coming closer, thundering up the road towards them. Flicking the gear lever up a notch, she watched the needle on the rev counter climb past the red line and then, as the footpeg clipped the metal post in a shower of sparks, Berry flipped the bike hard to the right and its front wheel thumped on to the road in a squeal of smoking rubber.

Suddenly she became aware of everything at once: the angry blast from the lorry's air-horn, the lights of the cars speeding down the hill, the scrape of her knee on tarmac and the smell of the hot exhaust as she leant the bike over as far as it would go. Then, as she pulled the bike up vertical again, Ell's head cracked against the back of her helmet and she twisted the throttle hard to send them hurtling along the white lines at 70 mph, missing the oncoming cars by a whisker. Berry changed up a gear and they shot past the lorry before weaving back into the left-hand lane and accelerating at high speed over the brow of the hill into the darkness beyond.

'You're crazy!' shrieked Ell into the wind as Berry changed up into sixth gear and the needle on the speedometer nudged ninety. 'We could have died!'

But when Berry glanced in her mirror she saw not only shock on Ell's face, but also the beginnings of a smile.

She wasn't surprised, of course.

There was nothing like the touch of death to bring the whole bright world screaming back into life again.

But as she looked up at the night sky and saw the storm clouds moving away to the east, she thought:

Twice in one day.

This was becoming a habit.

16
THE LAUNDERETTE

IT WAS AROUND NINE THIRTY in the morning when Berry finally pulled the bike out of the chaos that was London traffic and parked it down a back street south of the river. Having decided that she had nothing to lose, she had made up her mind to go to America. Ell had offered to accompany her to the airport as he wanted to see if he could get himself a cheap flight to France. His plan was to hitch south and get a job working in a beach bar or a restaurant somewhere. But, as Berry's flight wasn't until the next day, the first plan had been simply to get as far away as possible from their pursuers. Apart from a couple of stops to fill up on petrol and coffee, they had ridden all night through driving rain and it was only now that the sky was beginning to clear. A smudge of blue was visible through the clouds and steam drifted from rain-soaked pavements as the morning sun warmed them.

The combination of cold wind and vibration from the motor had numbed Berry's fingers, and as she staggered stiffly across to the wall she rubbed her hands together in an attempt to bring some feeling back.

She watched Ell dismount and walk uncomfortably towards her like some bow-legged cowboy. Seeing her amusement, he stopped and held his hands poised above imaginary holsters.

'This town ain't big enough for the both of us, missy,' he drawled. 'Where ah come from, we shoots first and asks questions later.'

A woman pushed her tartan shopping trolley through the space between them and looked at Ell distastefully, as though he were something that she had nearly stepped in.

'Ma'am,' said Ell politely, lifting his imaginary hat.

Berry wrapped her arms around herself and shivered as her damp clothes pressed against her skin.

'I'm wet,' she said. 'Wet and freezing.'

Ell pointed along the street to a small parade of grubby little shops.

'Look,' he said. 'Down there.'

'What about it?' asked Berry.

'Launderette,' replied Ell.

Berry followed him past over-stuffed rubbish bins

and faded shop fronts, listening to her socks squelch in her shoes and wondering how – short of climbing into a dryer and closing the door behind her – a launderette was going to help. But she was too tired to protest and, right now, too tired to even care.

'Here we go,' said Ell. 'Dry Clothes 'R' Us.'

They had stopped outside 'Jennifer's Laundromat' and Berry peered through the window at a middle-aged woman pulling wet clothes from a machine. They walked in and sat down facing the dryers.

'Hello,' said Ell in a friendly, how-are-you-today kind of voice which made Berry marvel at his ability to recover from the events of the last few hours. 'Are you the owner?'

Berry blushed as the woman stopped what she was doing and eyed them suspiciously.

'No,' she said, in a tone that was meant to discourage further conversation. 'I just work here.'

'Oh,' said Ell, sounding disappointed. 'So you're not Jennifer then?'

'No,' replied the woman, carrying an armful of clothes across to the dryer and slinging them in. 'I'm not Jennifer.'

Berry hoped this might be enough to shut Ell up, but guessed it wouldn't, and she was right.

'Now that', said Ell, 'is a shame. Meeting a launderette owner is one of the things on my "To Do" list.'

'Stop it, Ell,' whispered Berry, mortified. 'She'll think you're crazy.'

'Were you actually wanting something?' asked the woman.

'Actually, yes,' said Ell. 'If it's not too much trouble.'

'Well, I don't know yet, do I?'

The woman's expression suggested a certain resignation to the fact that her day was now taking a different course to the laundry-folding she had expected.

'I was just wondering, could we borrow a couple of towels?'

'Towels?' She couldn't have sounded more surprised if Ell had asked for machine-guns.

'Yes, towels. You know . . .'

Ell did a little mime of someone drying themselves.

'What do you want towels for?'

'Well, we got rather wet and need to dry our clothes. But the thing is, if we take all our clothes off, it could get a bit – oh, you know – embarrassing.'

As Berry blushed a deep crimson, the woman's horrified expression indicated that she was already picturing the scene.

'But I guess, if you haven't got any towels,' said Ell, removing his boots, 'then you haven't got any towels.'

He placed his boots on top of the dryer and stuffed his socks – odd ones, Berry noticed – neatly inside them. Then he began unbuttoning his trousers.

'Wait,' said the woman hurriedly. 'I can find you some towels.'

'You', said Ell, pointing at her with his index finger, 'are one of God's little angels.' He stopped unbuttoning his trousers and put his hands behind his head as though he was relaxing under tropical skies.

'See?' he said. 'Dry Clothes 'R' Us.'

They sat wrapped in a couple of pink towels, watching their clothes flop around in the drier. An old lady walked in with a bag of washing, took one look at them and walked straight out again.

'Brilliant,' Ell chuckled happily, watching her disappear off down the High Street again. 'She didn't even break step. Saw us, turned . . . gone.'

The launderette lady had scuttled off into the back room, leaving them alone in the empty shop.

'So tell me,' said Ell. 'What are we going to do about your little problem?'

'Well, let's see. I've got this package which Joseph wanted me to take to New Mexico.'

'Whereabouts in New Mexico?'

'I don't know. Somewhere in the south. He didn't say exactly.'

'He didn't *say*?'

'No. He just said it was incredibly important. Now

he's dead and these other people want to get their hands on it.'

Ell looked at her.

'Can't you just ditch it?'

'No,' said Berry firmly. 'I couldn't live with myself if I did.'

Ell shook his head. 'Look, at this rate you might not have to. I saw those guys, Berry. They weren't messing about back there. It could be drugs or anything. I really don't get why you have to do this.'

'He saved my life, Ell. I feel like I owe him.'

'Hang on, now. Let me get this straight. Just because some old guy saved your life, you've agreed to take something — you don't know what — halfway around the world to a place you don't exactly know where — whilst knowing that some other guys want it so bad they'll kill you in order to get it?'

'Yeah, I know,' said Berry quietly. 'It sounds crazy, doesn't it? But the thing is, it's not just that.'

She gazed into the dryer, watching her blue socks dance with the sleeves of Ell's jumper.

'What is it then?'

Berry pushed a lock of damp hair off her forehead and sighed.

'For thirteen years, it was just me and my mum, doing stuff together. She showed me how to grow things, taught me about the earth and the stars —

everything I needed to know about the world came from her.'

'You really never went to school?' asked Ell.

'No,' said Berry. 'Never. Social Services tried to make me, but Mum was too smart. She got all the books she could lay her hands on to prove I was getting a good education at home. They came a few times a year to check up on us, but apart from that, they left us alone. So I never had to sit in a classroom sweating over spelling tests or anything like that. I just talked to my mum and she told me stuff. She told me about life.'

Berry reached into her rucksack and pulled out the crumpled photo of her mother.

'That's her,' she said. 'When she was younger.'

Ell took the photo and nodded. 'She looks like you,' he said. He handed the picture back to Berry and she smiled sadly.

'I don't get it though,' said Ell. 'If life is so good, why run away from it? Why risk everything?'

'Because', said Berry, 'she died.'

17
THE RIGHT THING

'I'M SO SORRY,' said Ell, putting his hand on her arm. 'I didn't know.'

Berry shrugged. 'It's funny. She'd always wanted to take me to America. Turned out she'd been saving from her social money for years, planning the trip of a lifetime for us both. It was going to be my birthday treat, you see. She'd got the passports, organized visas, everything.'

'Is that why you want to do this?'

'Partly, I suppose. But it's more than that. She was my whole world, you see. And now she's gone, there's just this big hole which feels as though it'll never be filled. And it makes me think, well, what is there left to be afraid of? What can possibly be worse than that?'

'Perhaps you just need to keep believing there's some happiness out there,' said Ell, 'waiting to find you.'

'Perhaps,' said Berry. 'But my mum once said you don't find happiness by looking for it. You find it by doing the right thing. And I suppose that's what this feels like, Ell. It feels like doing the right thing.'

'Really?'

'Yes, really. And, anyway, what's the alternative? If I go back, they'll send me to school and I'll forget all about the things that really matter. So actually this isn't a risk, Ell; it's a chance. A chance to live right. The truth is, I've got nothing to lose.'

'Wow,' said Ell. 'And there was me thinking I was crazy.' But Berry could tell that he meant it kindly and when she looked at him she saw that he was deep in thought.

'When did you say the flight leaves?' he asked.

'Tomorrow morning,' said Berry. 'But I've never been on a plane before. I won't have a clue what I'm doing.'

'Don't worry,' said Ell. 'It's as easy as catching a bus, these days. And you're flying all the way to San Francisco?'

'Yep,' said Berry. 'Courtesy of British Airways.'

'They won't let you fly alone, you know that, don't you?'

'What? Why not?'

'Because', said Ell, 'you're too young. You've got to be sixteen.'

Berry stared at him in surprise. She hadn't even considered this.

'Are you sure?'

'Positive. A couple of years ago, just after my parents split up, my grandparents paid for me to fly over and visit them in Connecticut. I had to have a signed letter with me, saying that I had permission to travel by myself.'

'Perhaps they won't notice,' Berry suggested. 'If I stand up straight and look serious.'

'Well, you could try,' said Ell, 'but it's not going to help you much when they look at the date of birth in your passport.'

Berry wrapped her arms around her knees and huffed into her towel. Then she lifted her chin and looked at Ell.

'Come with me,' she said quietly.

Ell stared at her. 'Are you serious?'

Berry nodded.

'Why not? You're sixteen. You said you were planning to go off travelling anyway. If we were travelling together, I could say you were looking after me.'

'But I was talking about Europe,' said Ell. 'I couldn't afford a ticket to America.'

Berry reached down into her bag and pulled out the wad of notes that Joseph had given her.

'But *I* could,' she said.

Ell stared at the money.

'Blimey,' he said.

He sat for a while without saying anything. Berry watched as he stood up and opened the dryer.

'Well?' she asked. 'What do you think?'

Ell turned towards her with his arms full of dry clothes and said, 'We could have died today, Berry. You know that, don't you?'

'I know,' said Berry, suddenly wishing that she hadn't said anything. 'Look, I'm sorry, Ell. I should never have asked. I've caused you enough trouble as it is.'

'No,' said Ell. 'That's not what I'm saying. What I'm saying is, it changed the way I think about things.'

'What do you mean?' asked Berry.

'I mean that if I had died today, what would I have done with my life so far? Cleaned a few windows, watched some telly and argued with my dad. And it made me think, I've got to start living, I mean *really* living, before it all gets taken away. Sure, it's crazy and everything, no doubt about it. But it's like you said. Somehow, it just feels like the right thing.'

'So what are you saying?' asked Berry uncertainly.

Ell threw Berry her green cardigan and closed the door of the dryer with his foot.

'Put some clothes on, woman,' he said. 'We've got a plane to catch.'

'I saw a telephone box near where we parked the bike,' said Berry as they walked down the street. 'It's not far. We can phone the airport from there.'

'You really were educated at home, weren't you?' said Ell, pulling a mobile phone from his pocket. 'I'll get the number from Directory Enquiries.' He jabbed at the buttons for a few moments and then snapped it shut again. 'Damn. It's got no charge. Silly question, but I don't suppose you've got one?'

'Yes,' said Berry, remembering the phone that Joseph had given her. 'Actually I have. No idea how to use it, though.'

'Cave girl,' said Ell, holding out his hand. 'Come on. Give it here.'

Berry pulled the phone from her rucksack and as Ell turned it on she heard it play a little welcome tune, followed by a chime.

'Ooh,' said Ell. 'You've got a message.' He stopped walking and listened for a few moments. 'Now that is weird,' he said. 'That is *very* weird.' He handed the phone to Berry. 'Have a listen to that — see what you think.' Berry pressed the phone to her ear and immediately recognized Joseph's voice. He sounded scared and desperate.

'Berry?' he said. 'Berry, listen to me. They're coming. You must go to America straight away. Take the package to New Mexico.' There was the sound of a door opening and a sharp intake of breath from Joseph. 'Take it to Eddy Chaves!' he said. Then a man's voice in the background, faint but unmistakable, saying, 'Calling the police?'

Joseph's voice, pleading, 'Please, I don't have it', followed by three muffled thumps in quick succession.

Joseph gasping out four final words: 'Eunice Vaughn Anthony Centre.'

Then silence.

Berry stood, white-faced, knowing that she had just heard Joseph die.

'What does it mean?' asked Ell.

'It means it's too dangerous, Ell,' said Berry, close to tears. 'I don't want you to come with me any more. Go and have the life you would have had if you hadn't met me, OK? I mean it. Just go.'

'Sorry,' said Ell. 'Can't do it, missy.'

'Why?' asked Berry. 'Give me one good reason.'

Ell shrugged. 'Something you said earlier.' He hooked an arm in hers and began walking her in the direction of the bike. 'If you want to find happiness, then you've got to do the right thing.'

'So you really think this is the right thing?' asked Berry.

'No,' said Ell. 'But I think *we* are.'

18

A MINOR MIRACLE

WHAT WAS IT THAT Andy Sampson had said to him the
night before he died?

Look out for the unusual. That's where you'll find it.

Special Agent Bill Horton reached across his desk for
a thin, buff-coloured file that was marked 'PROJECT
PAPERCLIP: Ref: X3472' in faded pencil. Opening it
up, he saw the old black-and-white photographs of
Mitchell from the time when he had gone missing,
back in '47. An FBI team led by Andy Sampson's father
had traced his car to a motel and broken down the
door to find it exactly as he must have left it, the bed
unmade and his suit still hanging in the closet. A week
later he was straight in at number one on America's
'Most Wanted' list, charged with stealing Top-Secret
Government Property. But despite huge public interest, the cloak of government secrecy had swiftly

descended, hiding all further details from public view.

Once the story got out, the press had had a field day, and all the papers had been full of theories about crashed UFOs and alien invasions. Horton knew it was all nonsense, of course, but anyone who had tried to find out more had been met with a wall of silence. It seemed that whatever went missing that night was so important, so secret, that no one was allowed to talk about it.

Mitchell, however, had never been found. And now, nearly sixty years later, the case had become yesterday's news. Even the Bureau had downgraded it, leaving it to simmer on the back burner while they turned up the heat on new terrorist threats.

But Special Agent Andy Sampson had inherited his father's fear of what might happen if the item was not found. And Horton knew that Sampson hadn't been a man to scare easily.

He looked more closely at the photograph, a head and shoulders shot. Beneath it was written:

Joseph Mitchell (D.O.B. 17.01.1925).
Federal Air Investigation Unit.

He would have been in his early twenties when the picture was taken. What would that make him now? Eighty-two? Eighty-three?

An old man.

Horton suddenly thought of the milk cartons in his fridge. The ones with pictures of missing children on the outside, showing how they might look now. Would it be possible to do something similar with a person who had been missing for sixty years? His heart racing, Horton snatched the phone from its cradle and began tapping in the number of the Bureau's Intelligence Department.

'I hope so,' he said to the young receptionist who asked if she could be of any assistance. 'Could you put me through to the Image Enhancement Unit?'

The blinds were down and the streets were quiet except for the occasional lone taxi picking up late-night calls from the clubs. The only sound in the room came from the TV in the corner as the 24-hour news channel quietly recycled the day's stories on an endless loop, images of death and destruction flickering across the screen like a bad dream. Horton looked at his watch and saw that it was three thirty in the morning. He knew he should really be in bed. But the whole Mitchell thing was running around in his head and he couldn't sleep. He thought about his phone conversation with the guy from the Image Enhancement Unit and wondered if he would be able to come up with the goods. He had certainly seemed pretty keen on telling Horton all about the new 'age-progressive techniques' that had been developed to track down missing children. Apparently they took the original image and used a combination of a forensic artist and computers to make changes that would provide an accurate picture of how the person's face would have changed over time. This could then be fed into a recognition system which mapped the geometry of the face, comparing it with thousands of others on its database to find the nearest match.

All very clever.

But the guy had admitted that they had never done it for someone who had been missing for sixty years. 'Five is about the norm,' he had said. 'So this should be interesting. I'll do some work on it tonight and get back to you as soon as I have anything.'

Horton took a swig of beer and stuck his hand into a family-size pack of potato chips. Desperate to progress things, he had given the guy from the Image Enhancement Unit his home email address in case he managed to come up with anything before tomorrow. But so far nothing – and in just a few short hours it would be time to show up at the office again. The way he figured it, by the time he got undressed, got into bed and lay awake thinking some more about this stuff, it would be time to get up again.

So he would just stay here and watch TV for a while, try and take his mind off things. A quick doze, a shower and a shave and he'd be ready to roll all over again. Still, his head was aching and his throat was sore. Maybe he was coming down with something. He took another swig of beer and thought:

Welcome to the glamorous world of the FBI.

The TV newsreader had teeth whiter than polished pearls and he seemed pretty amused about something, although Horton couldn't quite make out what. Picking up the remote from the arm of the sofa, he sank back into the cushions and turned up the sound.

' . . . some news from across the water that is causing a good deal of head scratching in Britain. Some have called it a clever hoax, others a minor miracle, but what everyone agrees is that here is something for which there is no obvious explanation. Our reporter Julie Page has the full story . . .'

Horton took another swig of beer and leaned forward as the picture cut away to a young, breathy girl clutching a microphone. She seemed very excited, Horton thought. Maybe it was her first time abroad.

' . . . I'm standing in an ordinary street here in the country town of Slipton in Somerset. Behind me, you can see that the traffic is fairly busy – in fact, many of the local residents have been campaigning for a relief road over the past few years – but aside from that, there is nothing much to distinguish it from any number of small towns up and down the country. Not the sort of place you would expect to see anything out of the ordinary. But a few days ago, all that changed. When reports started coming in of a strange accident, the local police decided to examine footage from CCTV cameras in the High Street. What they saw left them astounded. Just take a look at this remarkable piece of film and you'll see why . . .'

The picture cut away to a grainy black-and-white film of the same street in the middle of the day.

'This was the scene in Slipton High Street on Thursday morning,' said the reporter's voice-over. 'Now keep your eye on the girl in the circle.'

A white circle duly appeared on screen to help the viewer identify the girl in question. Horton took his hand out of the potato chips and sat forward.

The girl seemed distracted and was walking erratically. Horton's training kicked in and he registered: early teens, dark shoulder-length hair, scruffy clothes.

Without looking, the girl stepped off the pavement, straight into the path of a double-decker bus. There was a blur of grey and a man leapt off the kerb behind her, pushing her violently backwards and sending her sprawling on to the pavement. A split second later the bus hit him full on, knocking him to the ground and thundering over the top of him. Smoke billowed from its tyres as it braked hard and squealed to a stop further down the road. The car behind bumped over the top of the man's body before skidding sideways and smashing into a lamp-post.

'Jeez,' said Horton. He watched as the girl struggled up into a sitting position and then the picture froze.

'A tragic accident it would seem,' said the reporter's voice-over. 'But just watch what happens next.'

Horton watched open-mouthed as the man in the road stood up and ran over to the girl. As he came nearer, the man glanced up at the camera and for a brief moment his face could be clearly seen. His expression was one of fear and panic which, in the circumstances, was only to be expected. What Horton had not been prepared for, however, was the man's age; the face staring into the camera lens was that of a white-haired old man. Turning away again, the man grabbed the girl by the hand and led her away along the crowded pavement until, moments later, they were lost from sight.

The picture cut to the driver standing next to his bus, looking pained and pointing to a large dent in the front of it.

'It all happened so quickly. One minute I was driving along minding my own business, the next minute this girl walks into the road and I'm slamming my brakes on. Then this guy just appears from nowhere and pushes her out of the way. But I couldn't stop in time and so I hit him. It was horrible – I was one hundred per cent sure he was dead. But when I went back to see if I could help, they told me he was gone and so was the girl. Just got up and walked off. And I was left with this great big dent in the front of my bus. I mean, just look at it – it doesn't make any sense. He should be dead, shouldn't he? The guy should be dead.'

The film cut back to the reporter, who was still looking very happy.

'And that's the story that's suddenly put the sleepy town of Slipton on the map. And the questions on everyone's lips are: Who were these people? And just how was this man able to walk away unharmed? But it seems that these questions may remain unanswered for some time to come. They've both disappeared and the simple truth is: no one knows. This is Julie Page reporting from Slipton, England, for CBS News. Back to you in the studio, John.'

Horton realized that he had been holding his breath and he let it out slowly before lifting the bottle to his lips once more.

'That is *crazy*,' he whispered. He pressed the standby button and the picture squeaked away to a little grey dot in the centre of the screen before disappearing completely. The apartment was silent now except for the low hum of the fridge and the sound of Horton's breathing, which soon slowed and became more regular as he drifted into sleep.

He awoke several hours later to the familiar bleep from his computer, informing him that he had mail.

Momentarily confused, he sat up and rubbed his eyes, took another sip of beer and then walked into the hallway, where his computer screen glowed from the small cubby hole beneath the stairs.

The new message subject read: 'Enhanced Image'.

Horton opened it and read:

We've had some fun working on this one, Bill. Based on the information received, I think what we've come up with is pretty accurate. Hope it's useful. John (FBI Image Enhancement Unit).

He clicked on the attachment and as the image flashed up on to the screen he stared at it for a long time, unable to quite believe what his eyes were telling him.

Could he be mistaken?

He looked again.

And the more he looked, the more certain he became. The image on the screen showed the face of an old man.

It was the same face he had seen on the television report.

Horton sat for several minutes, gazing at the screen,

trying to find a reason to doubt his own judgement.

But he knew that he was not mistaken.

The man involved in the strange accident was none other than Joseph Mitchell.

As he stared at his picture in the darkness, Horton remembered the words that Sampson had spoken to him the night before he died.

Look out for the unusual. That's where you'll find it.

19

Shopping

'OK,' said Ell, writing a number on the back of an envelope before snapping the phone shut and leaning back on the park bench. 'That's all sorted. We're booked on the same flight tomorrow morning. Apparently we catch a connecting flight in New York which will take us to San Francisco. I just have to go to the check-in desk with this confirmation number, fill in a 'Quick Collect' form and pay for my ticket. Plane leaves at six thirty.'

He handed Berry's ticket back to her and she placed it carefully inside her passport before returning them both to the bottom of her bag.

'I guess we'll be sitting apart though.'

'Not necessarily,' said Berry. 'My mum's seat will be free, remember. You can sit there, if you like.'

Ell squeezed her arm. 'If you're sure,' he said.

Berry looked at the time display on the phone and saw that it was 12.27. 'What are we going to do for the next eighteen hours?'

Ell shrugged. 'It's too early to go to the airport. Do you want to get something to eat?'

'In a minute,' said Berry, who was enjoying the warm sunshine that had burned through the morning clouds. 'Let's just sit here for a bit longer.'

They sat in silence, watching the lunchtime people wander into the park with their plastic sandwich packs, looking for empty benches.

'That could be us one day,' said Berry after a while. 'Clocking into our little jobs every day and waiting for the weekend.'

'If we live that long,' said Ell.

'Oh well,' said Berry. 'Who knows how long they're going to live anyway? I could have been hit by that bus and then none of this would ever have happened. You'd still be at Glastonbury, never knowing I even existed.'

'True,' said Ell. 'And now I'm stuck with you. Life's a bummer, isn't it?'

'Shut-up, Rag Doll.'

'Ah yes, Rag Doll,' repeated Ell, remembering the man in his car. 'He was great, wasn't he? I gave him one of those liquorice allsorts with the blue bobbles all over it. Kind of went with his mood, I thought.'

'A blue-bobble mood,' said Berry. 'I think I might be in one of those right now.'

'Really?' said Ell. 'Well, now. In that case, there is really only one cure known to man.'

'Oh yes?' said Berry. 'What's that then?'

Ell stood up and held out his hand.

'Berry Benjamin,' he said, 'let's go *shopping*!'

The security guard looked at Ell suspiciously as he pulled Berry through the entrance to the store, grasping her firmly by the hand in an effort to overcome her reluctance.

'So many clothes,' he said, looking around, 'and so little time.'

'Remind me,' said Berry. 'Why are we doing this again?'

Ell put his hands on her shoulders and steered her past a rack of evening dresses until she was standing in front of a full-length mirror.

'Exhibit A,' he said. 'Need I say more?'

Berry stared at her reflection.

Her green canvas jacket was covered in patches of mud which had dried to a crisp, pale brown, like camouflage paint applied by a five-year-old. Beneath it, her faded yellow T-shirt was flecked with specks of dirt thrown up from the bike tyres and her green corduroy jeans — which had already ripped in several places when she fell off – now had a tidemark of mud ending just below the knee.

'Oh,' she said. 'I see what you mean. Perhaps we should have washed before we dried.'

'Never mind that,' said Ell enthusiastically. 'This is your chance for a makeover!'

'But I don't want a makeover,' said Berry. 'Why would I want a makeover?'

'Because,' replied Ell, lowering his voice, 'you stand out like a pig on a pogo stick.'

'Thank you, Ell,' said Berry. 'You say the nicest things.'

'It's for your own good,' said Ell. 'If those guys are anywhere around, they'll spot you a mile off. You just need a new look for a while, that's all. At least until we've put the Atlantic Ocean between them and us. Besides, we don't want to draw attention to ourselves at the airport, do we? We need to blend in.'

Berry looked at Ell standing next to her in his multi-coloured jumper, his purple trousers and his green leather boots. The rain had smudged his blue eyeshadow and his mascara had run, leaving strange dark tracks across his cheeks.

She stepped sideways so that he could gaze upon his own reflection.

'Yes,' she said pointedly. '*We* do.'

Ell gazed at himself for a few seconds before pressing

his hands against his cheeks in horror.

'The situation', he said gravely, 'is worse than I thought.'

Twenty minutes later, Berry emerged nervously from the changing room. Ell had picked her out a pair of stonewashed trousers ('I know how you love your cords, but I think these have got a bit more to say') and she had chosen a short-sleeved, conker-coloured top to go with them. It had tiny yellow flowers embroidered around the neck which reminded her of the poached-egg plants she had once grown in a broken teapot.

'What do you think?' she asked. 'Do you like it?'

'*Like*', replied Ell, 'does not do justice to the emotions I am experiencing at this moment in time.'

Berry giggled. 'Do you really like it?'

'No,' replied Ell, beckoning her over. 'I hate it. I'm just trying to spare your feelings.' He stood her in front of the mirror again and pulled her hair back from her face. 'Look,' he said. 'You see? An angel walks among us.'

Berry stared at her reflection and realized that she hadn't looked at herself properly in months. It felt strange, as though she had just bumped into an old friend. But the clothes felt good; like the start of something new.

'OK,' said Ell, 'and now for the finishing touch.' He

stepped across to a nearby clothes rack and unhooked a jacket from the rail. '*Voilà!*' he said, holding the jacket out for Berry to inspect. 'Go ahead. Try it on.'

The jacket was grey-blue velvet with buttoned sleeves and a small toggle clasp at the front. It fitted perfectly and Berry felt as though it had been made just for her. She turned sideways to look at the back and noticed, to her delight, that the pleats were delicately edged with a fine silver thread.

'Well?' asked Ell. 'You like?'

Berry felt suddenly as though she were setting sail, casting off her chains into the waters behind.

'Yes,' she said. 'I like very much.'

'Wait there,' instructed Ell sternly. 'And no peeking.'

Berry sat on a chair outside the men's changing room and began to imagine what clothes Ell might have selected. Despite her protests, he had flatly refused to allow her to accompany him on what he called his 'styling expedition'.

'Surprises are more fun,' he said. 'You wait. It'll be just like Christmas.'

Berry guessed the only reason for him wanting to shop without her was that he intended to surprise her with the most outrageous outfit he could possibly find. She made up her mind that, whatever he came out wearing, she would not allow herself to be shocked.

Even if he flounced out in thigh-length boots and a gingham frock, she wouldn't bat an eyelid.

'OK!' Ell called down the corridor. 'Are you ready for this?'

'Yes,' Berry called back. 'Ready as I'll ever be.'

'Shut your eyes then.'

'Why?'

'For me?'

'OK, OK.' Berry put a hand over her eyes and heard him pad down the carpet towards her. He stopped a little way off and cleared his throat.

'Can I open them yet?' asked Berry.

'Only if you promise not to laugh,' said Ell.

'I promise,' said Berry, thinking, *This is going to be even worse than I imagined.*

'OK,' said Ell. 'Open them.'

As Berry took her hand away, her eyes widened and she gasped in astonishment. Then she clapped a hand over her mouth and gave a little squeak of delight.

'What?' asked Ell. 'Too much, you think?'

And as Berry stared at the beautifully cut charcoal and blue flannel suit, the pressed cotton shirt and the Italian leather shoes, the sight of it quite took her breath away, and all she could say was, 'Ell, you look fantastic.'

20

A Change of Clothes

The blood-orange sun was sinking behind the city as they abandoned the bike in the airport car-park and took the courtesy bus to Terminal One. Berry's feet were aching as she took her bags into the toilets and washed beneath the harsh neon glare of the strip lights. Grimacing at her matted, unkempt hair in the mirror, she hung her head over the basin and used liquid soap from the dispenser to wash out the mud before crouching beneath the hand dryer and blasting it dry again. That done, she locked herself in a cubicle and removed her old clothes for the second time that day, changing into the new trousers, top and jacket. Last of all, she pulled on some fresh white socks and slipped her feet into a pair of shiny black lace-up shoes. Then she picked up her old clothes, stuffed them into a carrier bag and unlocked the door again.

The toilets were quite busy now, but everyone seemed intent upon their own business, washing their hands or fixing their make-up. With a quick glance to check that no one was looking, Berry dropped the bag into the waste basket and walked briskly out through the swing door without looking back. As she emerged into the main concourse she spotted a sharply dressed Ell standing next to the duty-free shop in his new clothes.

'You', he said, pointing a finger at her with his thumb cocked back like a pistol, 'have got it goin' *on.*'

'Feeling in need of a drink, are we?' she asked, looking up at the duty-free sign.

'Feeling in need of a bag actually,' said Ell, tapping his fingers on the top of Berry's mud-spattered ruck-sack. 'Doesn't quite go with the new image.'

Berry pulled the rucksack from her shoulder and examined it.

'I see what you mean,' she agreed. 'Are you going to get one too?'

'No need,' said Ell. He opened his hands and turned them over, like a magician proving there was nothing up his sleeves. 'As you can see, I'm travelling light.'

'Maybe this'll weigh you down a bit,' said Berry, pulling out a wad of dollar bills and stuffing them into his top pocket.

'Hey!' said Ell. 'What's this for?'

'I don't like carrying all that money about,' said

Berry. 'It makes me feel uncomfortable.'

'Really?' asked Ell, patting his pocket and grinning. 'That's the kind of discomfort I could definitely learn to live with.'

Berry chose a green canvas shoulder bag with zipped pockets. Then she squirted herself with a perfume tester before paying the checkout woman in cash.

'You smell like a flower,' said Ell. 'Makes me want to chop your head off and put you in a vase.'

'You're so lovely, Ell,' said Berry.

They sat down while Berry transferred the contents of her rucksack to her new bag.

'How much English have you got left?' asked Ell.

'Money, you mean?' said Berry who had paid for Ell's ticket in cash. 'Probably enough for a couple of croissants and a coffee.'

'Ah,' said Ell. 'Exactly the right amount, then.'

He watched Berry put her ticket in her mouth, remove a small, neatly wrapped blue package from her rucksack and place it quickly into her canvas bag.

'Is that it?' he asked.

'What?'

'Is that the thing we're supposed to be delivering?'

'Yes,' said Berry quietly. 'That's it.'

Ell raised his eyebrows. 'Not much to look at, is it?'

'I don't know,' said Berry. 'I haven't opened it.'

'What, not even a little bit? Not even a tiny peek?'

'No,' said Berry. 'Joseph warned me not to.'

'Of course,' said Ell. 'I remember.'

'Come on,' said Berry. 'Let's go and get something to eat.' She picked up her old rucksack and looked around. 'Can you see a rubbish bin anywhere?'

'They don't have them at airports any more,' said Ell. 'Security, you see – in case someone puts a bomb in them. Nowadays, you're supposed to swallow all your own rubbish. Full of fibre, apparently.'

As they headed off in search of a coffee bar, Ell said, 'Aren't you even tempted?'

'To do what?' asked Berry, stuffing her empty rucksack behind a vending machine.

'You know. To see what's inside.'

'I told you before. Whether I'm tempted or not doesn't come into it.'

'So you *are* tempted then.'

'No. Well, yes. A little bit. Of course I am. But that's not the point.'

'I don't see that it can hurt,' said Ell. 'What if it's drugs or something?'

'It isn't drugs,' said Berry.

'How do you know?'

Berry thought of the strange, beautiful sounds that she had heard in the tent and found herself longing to hear them again.

'I just know, that's all. Look, Ell, if you're worried,

you don't have to do this. I can go on my own.'

'Do me a favour,' said Ell, 'and shut your face.'

Berry awoke to the warning beep of a luggage cart as it trundled past the seats where they had been sleeping. Opening one eye, she looked up at the departure board and saw that it was seven minutes to six.

'Come on, Ell,' she said, shaking him awake. 'It's time to go.'

21
THROWING AWAY THE GLASSES

BERRY WATCHED ELL hold up his hands as a female security official performed a brisk body search on him. 'Oh baby,' he murmured, 'that feels *good* . . .', which earned him a stern look of disapproval before she finally waved him through. Taking a deep breath, Berry placed her bag on the conveyor belt and watched it disappear into the X-ray machine. She caught sight of Ell on the other side, looking at the screen monitor. He seemed worried, and Berry felt her stomach flip.

What if they made her open the package?

The security woman waved her through the metal detector and she hesitantly removed her bag from the conveyor belt, half expecting a tap on the shoulder and a request to empty the contents for inspection. But, to her relief, no one said anything and she quickly joined

Ell at the entrance to the departure lounge.

'What's up?' she asked. 'You look worried.'

'I just want to know what's going on, that's all,' said Ell, and when Berry looked at him she was shocked at how angry he looked.

'What do you mean?' asked Berry.

'You know what I mean,' said Ell.

'No. I don't. Look, Ell. Please, tell me. What is it?'

Ell looked at her for a moment or two, as if trying to decide whether or not she was being sincere. Then he seemed to soften a little.

'You really don't know?' he asked.

'No,' said Berry, trying desperately to think what could possibly have changed between them in the last few minutes. 'I honestly have no idea what you're talking about.'

'You know what?' said Ell. 'It's nothing. Forget it. It's just – oh, I don't know. Maybe I'm getting cold feet.'

Although Berry could see that something was still troubling Ell, right now she didn't want to know what it was. As she looked at him, standing there in his smart suit and shiny shoes, she already felt a sadness for the future, a feeling that these strange days of danger and excitement would soon be gone. Their lives would become ordinary again, just like everyone else's. But now . . . now was their chance to live, to stand on the edge of things and throw away the glasses that Ell had talked about. Berry felt too scared, too excited by the whole prospect to think about anything else. And as they made their way in silence towards the boarding gate, Berry realized that somewhere, beyond the clouds that gathered above the grey runway, a new life was waiting to begin.

William Kruger sat stony-faced in the back of the blue Ford Estate and watched a small green dot flash on the screen of a hand-held computer. They had lost the signal somewhere on the M4 just outside London, but while the others had vented their frustration in a series of angry exchanges, he had remained calm, knowing that in such moments of crisis, a cool head was a definite advantage. Now it seemed that his patience had paid off. After driving around all night they had picked up the signal again about half an hour ago. And the even better news was that, during the whole of that time, the green dot hadn't moved at all. It had stayed exactly where it was. And the red dot, pinpointing their own position, was moving closer with every minute that passed.

But it wasn't time for celebration yet.

Kruger looked at his watch and saw that it was 6.22.

'I think perhaps we should go a little faster,' he told

the driver, his voice still giving an impression of calm that was no longer entirely accurate. And as they accelerated past an illuminated sign that said: 'Heathrow Airport 3' he had to remind himself that emotion was a sign of weakness.

But it was no good pretending.

He was excited.

Elbowing his way through the queues around the check-in desks, Kruger quickened his pace until the others were striding to keep up. 'This is it,' he said as they entered the departure lounge. 'They're here.' As the green and red dots merged on the hand-held computer screen, Kruger attached a thin white plastic lead and pushed a small earphone into his ear. Flicking the switch to *Audible Find*, he listened intently for a few seconds, hearing a continuous, mid-pitched whine. As he walked forward, it dropped in pitch to a lower note and he stepped back again, returning the note to its original pitch. Turning to the right, he moved forward once more and this time the sound in his ear began to climb, rising in pitch with every step until it was a continuous high-pitched whine. His eyes bright with anticipation, Kruger looked up expectantly to be met with a colourful display of crisps and chocolate bars.

'What', he hissed, 'is going on?'

'Look,' said the man in the tracksuit, cupping his hands around his eyes and peering behind the vending machine. 'Down here.'

Angrily, Kruger pushed him out of the way and thrust his arm into the space between the machine and the wall. Even as he pulled out the pink, mud-spattered rucksack and struggled to open the buckles with his shaking fingers, he knew that he would find it empty.

'They were here!' he spat. 'They were *here*!'

And as he flung the rucksack to the floor, the announcement came loud and clear across the tannoy:

'This is the final call for Mrs Benjamin, travelling on British Airways flight 9–5–7–0 to New York. I repeat, this is the final call for Mrs Benjamin. Would Mrs Benjamin please make her way to Gate 47 where the aircraft is preparing for take off. Thank you.'

Kruger took a deep breath and calmed himself.

'All right,' he said. 'Give me the phone.'

22
Into the Blue

As the engines roared and the plane lifted from the end of the runway, Berry looked out of the window and saw the ground drop away beneath her. A white vapour trail streamed from the wingtip and, below, all the cars, houses and sheep turned quickly into tiny, inconsequential models of themselves. Berry watched a small green bus crawl along a toy-town road and imagined all the little people sitting inside, reading their tiny newspapers or staring out at the rain through misted windows.

Is that all we are? she wondered. She felt sorry for them then, all those miniature people going about their business, moving from place to place, none of them realizing that they were just little dots, shifting from one small piece of the earth to another. All keeping busy, trying not to think about the time when they would stop moving altogether.

'Are you OK?' asked Ell.

Berry nodded.

'Just thinking,' she said.

'In that case,' said Ell, holding out a bag of Maltesers, 'you'd better have some brain food.'

Berry took a chocolate between finger and thumb.

'I thought fish was brain food.'

'Ah well. Fish. Maltesers. Same difference.'

'Remind me never to come fishing with you,' said Berry. She nudged him with her elbow. 'Look. Isn't it beautiful?'

Ell leaned over and together they peered out of the small oval window at the bed of white clouds below them and the impossibly blue sky above. 'All those people down there, walking around in the rain,' said Berry. 'They can't see, can they? They don't know that it's summer up here.'

'There's a lot of things people can't see,' said Ell, leaning back in his seat. He popped another Malteser into his mouth and looked thoughtful. 'In fact, when you come to think about it, most people don't even see the things that they *could* see. Things that are right in front of their noses.'

'What do you mean?' asked Berry.

'Well, take the inside of this aeroplane for instance. Even in a small space like this, there must be a million things that you could notice, but probably never would.'

'Like what?'

'Oh, I don't know, the broken buckle on the sandal of the lady in seat 37A, the loose thread on the hem of the steward's jacket, the lipstick on the captain's collar . . .'

Berry raised her eyebrows in surprise.

'You *noticed* all that stuff?'

'No,' replied Ell, 'I made it up. But the point is, we only see the things that we care about, the things we're interested in. Ninety-nine per cent of what goes on around us doesn't even register. OK. Try this. I'm going to say a word, then you look around.'

'What do you mean?'

'Yellow.'

'What?'

'*Yell—ow.*'

'I don't —'

'Go on. Just look around.'

Berry knelt up on her seat and noticed: a lady peeling a banana three rows back, a boy in a yellow baseball cap with '*Coleman's Motors*' written on the front, a bright yellow packet of cheesy crisps and a girl wearing a lemon-coloured sweatshirt.

'Wow,' said Berry as she sat down again. 'I see what you mean.'

'There you go then.' Ell smiled. 'It's all about focus.

The more you focus on something, the more you see it. Stands to reason really.'

'Good game, Ell,' said Berry appreciatively. 'I like it. So tell me. What are *you* focusing on right now?'

'Don't ask,' said Ell. 'My focus is all over the place.'

'Why?'

Ell checked to see that the woman next to him was still wearing her earphones, then turned back to Berry.

'OK, well there's my drastic change of plan, for starters. One minute I'm set to go selling ice-creams on a beach in St Tropez, the next I'm wearing a sharp suit and sitting on a flight that's heading all the way to the US of A.'

'It's a very nice suit,' said Berry.

'Thank you,' said Ell. 'Even so.' He lowered his voice. 'Then there's that whole thing with the creepy men and the dead body. I mean, come on. Doesn't that still freak you out?'

'The whole thing freaks me out,' said Berry. 'That's why I'm sitting here. Trying to get away from it all.'

'Which brings me to my next point,' said Ell. 'Because that isn't the only reason you're sitting here, is it?'

'What do you mean?' asked Berry.

'I'm worried,' said Ell. 'You're delivering this package to a guy you've never heard of in a *place* you've never heard of and you don't even know what's in it. I'm worried that it's become some kind of weird mission for you. Why do you have to do this?'

'After everything that happened, I realized the world isn't safe and it isn't predictable,' Berry replied. 'It's weird, it's scary and it's random. And I'm somewhere in the middle of it, thinking all I've got is a small blue package and a promise to myself that I'll take it back to wherever it belongs.'

She looked at Ell and shook her head. 'You're right, Ell. It's not normal and I don't know what's in the package. I'm not sure I even *want* to know. But taking it back just feels like the right thing to me. And if somehow that gives me the chance to start my life again then – whether it makes any sense or not – that's what I'm going to do.'

Ell nodded. 'OK,' he said. He put his hand on her arm. 'But I wish life could have turned out differently for you.'

Berry looked at the sun on the clouds.

'Life's what it is,' she said. 'It's up to us to make it better.'

23
SHERBET CRYSTALS

'DID YOU SEE THAT WOMAN at the gate?' asked Berry as they strode across the arrivals hall at San Francisco International Airport. 'She was really staring at us.'

'Which one?' asked Ell, looking back over his shoulder. 'I didn't see anyone.'

'The one with the dark hair. Wearing a green sweater.'

'Show me,' said Ell.

But when Berry turned round to look for her, she had gone.

'Maybe she just liked your outfit,' said Ell, pulling a hair from Berry's sleeve. 'I mean, it is to *die* for.'

'Not funny, Ell,' said Berry. 'Not funny at all.'

There had been a slight delay with the connecting flight in New York and Ell had been all for setting out on another shopping expedition, but Berry had managed to distract him with a cup of hot chocolate and a plate of fries. Now that they were finally here, Berry could hardly believe it. She stared across the concourse at all the people, shopping, eating, leaning against luggage trolleys, killing time until someone took them to the places they wanted to go. Then she tilted her head back and looked up at the elegant roof structure, all clear glass and shining steel. It fanned out like five symmetrical leaves above her, lit by the intense blue of the summer sky. Sunlight streamed from the high windows, creating a pathway of dappled blue light all the way to the exit doors. Berry thought of the ocean that separated them from all that had gone before and relief swept over her like a wave.

'We made it, Ell,' she said, feeling as though she had travelled a million miles. 'We made it!'

Then she took him by the hand and they walked through the doors to the other side of the world.

'Whereabouts you headed?' asked the cab driver, switching off his 'For Hire' light as Berry jumped in beside Ell.

'We want to stay a night in San Francisco,' said Ell. 'Do you know of any hotels?'

The cab driver laughed. 'Only a million,' he said.

'We're after somewhere quite big,' said Berry. 'Somewhere in the middle of town. The sort of place a person might get lost.'

'Don't tell me,' said the driver as he pulled out into the line of traffic. 'You're Bonnie and Clyde, right?'

He dropped them off in Union Square, opposite the cable-car turnaround and only a short walk from Chinatown. 'Hotels everywhere,' he said as a cable car trundled past with its bell ringing. 'Take your pick.'

Ell paid him and then stood with Berry in the shade of a large palm tree, watching people clutching bags from 'Saks Fifth Avenue' and 'Macy's' and listening to the shout and roar of the city.

'Do you think we can afford one of those?' asked Ell, gazing around at the impressive array of hotels surrounding the square.

'Well, I guess we're not staying long,' said Berry, 'and we've still got all the money Joseph gave me.'

'Oh yeah,' said Ell, patting his top pocket. 'God *bless* the man.' He pointed at a huge, rectangular white building with a fancy covered walkway jutting out from the lobby. 'How about that one over there? The "Grand Hyatt". Place like that, you just know they're going to call you "sir" and have those little chocolates on the pillow.'

'I don't want to be called "sir",' said Berry.

'Well, they wouldn't call *you* "sir",' replied Ell. 'Obviously.'

'I like that one better,' said Berry. It's got more character.' She pointed at a tall, creamy-coloured building with French windows and wrought-iron balconies. 'I bet you'd get a fantastic view of the city from up there.'

'Possibly,' said Ell. 'But do you get chocolates on your pillow?'

The room was $170 a night and came with a couple of double beds, a complimentary fruit basket and an assortment of pre-packed cookies.

'You were right about the view,' said Ell, chewing on a mouthful of Oreos. He pushed open the French windows and a warm breeze wafted in through the floor-length muslin curtains. Berry joined him on the balcony and, as she looked out across the square, she was suddenly struck by how neat everything was. The carefully planted palm trees, the colourful flowerbeds, the tall white memorial column in the centre of the square and the geometrical blocks of shops and offices; down in the street, everything had seemed so busy and chaotic but now, observing it from a distance, Berry could see patterns that she hadn't seen before.

'Ell,' she said, watching a tramcar rattle down a side street beneath a criss-cross of wires, 'you know what you were saying earlier? About the more you focus on something, the more you see it?'

'Uh-huh,' said Ell, tearing open another pack of cookies. 'What about it?'

'Well, if we really focus on getting to New Mexico and finding this Eddy Chaves, do you think that we can do it?'

Ell shrugged. 'I guess so.'

'You want to though, don't you?' asked Berry, suddenly finding herself in need of reassurance. 'Now that we're here, I mean?'

'Sure,' said Ell. 'Of course. But right now, there's something I want even more.'

Berry sensed that he was deliberately changing the subject, but she was too tired to push it.

'Let me guess,' she said. 'Chocolate?'

'No,' said Ell. 'That would be childish.'

Berry shrugged. 'Well, what then?'

Ell smiled. 'Ice-cream,' he said.

Milly's Ice-Cream Parlour was shiny and spotless, with a gleaming steel counter and red check tablecloths in every booth. Elvis records boomed from a multi-coloured jukebox and every wall was covered with black-and-white posters of film stars from the 1950s.

'It's like stepping back in time, isn't it?' said Berry, still excited by the newness of everything. They squeezed into opposite sides of a booth and began to study the menus.

'Right then,' said Ell. 'Down to business. What are you having?'

Berry chewed her lip thoughtfully.

'I think maybe I'll just have a couple of scoops of vanilla.'

'What?' said Ell. 'No *way*, missy.'

He waved at a waitress who was busy wiping down a nearby table. 'Excuse me? Could we get a couple of ice-creams over here?'

The waitress put down her cloth and reached for her pad from her top pocket.

'Sure. What can I get you?'

'We'll have two Knickerbocker Glories, please,' Ell told her. 'With maple syrup and extra cream.'

'Thank you, sir,' said the waitress. 'Will there be anything else?'

'Almost certainly,' Ell told her. 'Can we get back to you?'

'Of course, sir.' The waitress collected the menus and made her way back up towards the counter.

'Do you think that "sir" was ironic?' asked Ell. 'Her heart didn't seem in it.'

'Ell,' said Berry. 'I don't want a Knickerbocker Glory.'

'Ever had one?'

'No, but —'

'Then you may not think you want one, but you do.' He pointed at her across the table. 'You know your trouble, don't you? Too much vanilla and not enough Knickerbocker.'

'Well,' said Berry, 'thanks for the advice. I'll try and remember it.' She looked at him for a while, still trying to figure him out.

'What?' asked Ell.

'Tell me some more about yourself,' she said. 'I want to know.'

'No, you don't.'

'Yes, I do.'

'Well, maybe I don't want to tell you.'

'Well, maybe I didn't want a Knickerbocker Glory.'

Ell sighed and stared at a red-faced woman jogging past the window.

'All right. Well, I told you about my mum running off and leaving us. Which, you know, wasn't great. Having your own mother prefer the company of a guy from the betting shop. Do you know what she said to me before she left?'

Berry shook her head.

'No. What?'

'She said, "Be a good boy for your dad."'

Ell laughed, but his eyes gave him away. 'Be a good boy for your dad! Yeah, of course, Mum. Because, you know, you showed me how important it was not to let people down.'

'There we are,' said the waitress. 'Two Knickerbocker Glories.'

'Thank you,' said Ell. 'That's very nice of you.'

Berry stared at the tall glasses packed with fruit, chocolate and layers of coloured ice-cream.

'Enjoy,' said the waitress.

'I'm sorry, Ell,' said Berry when the waitress had gone. 'I don't know what to say.'

'Then eat your ice-cream,' said Ell.

Berry picked up her long spoon, took a scoop of ice-cream with the cherry on top and popped it into her mouth.

'How is it?' asked Ell.

Berry nodded appreciatively. 'Lovely. Try some.'

Ell excavated a lump of chocolate ice-cream from halfway down the glass.

'Now that's what this world needs,' he said. 'Less talk and more chocolate.'

Berry smiled, allowing him to change the subject for a while.

'You've got a sweet tooth,' she said, 'I'll say that for you.'

'Blame my gran,' said Ell. 'It's her fault.'

'Your *gran?*' said Berry. 'How do you work that one out?'

Ell licked his spoon and examined his own reflection in the back of it. 'I look like Mr Magoo when I do that,' he said.

'Ell,' said Berry, touching his hand. 'Please.'

Ell put his spoon down and looked at her across the top of his ice-cream.

'When I was little,' he said, 'five or six, maybe, I got really sick with a fever. My mum and dad sent me to school, of course, like they always did, but the school wouldn't take me because I was too ill. So they phoned my gran and she took me home. My mum and dad were really angry because they'd fallen out and we'd stopped seeing her. But because they didn't want time off work, I stayed with her for three days until I got better. And on the fourth day, when my fever had gone, she took me to the seaside. She said the sea air would do me good.'

'And did it?'

'Oh yes,' said Ell. 'I can still remember it. It was a baking hot day, and when we got to the beach she let me take my shoes and socks off and paddle in the sea. Then she bought me some ice-cream, said it would help my throat get better. We walked along the pier and threw bread to the seagulls. Then, just before it was time to go home, she took me to a sweet shop. There were these whole shelves of bottles, all filled with different coloured sweets. It was fantastic, the prettiest sight I'd ever seen. I was allowed to choose anything I wanted. I chose some tiny yellow sherbet crystals and the woman wrapped them up in a paper bag for me to take home.'

Ell picked up his spoon again and took a big scoop of ice-cream.

'And you know something? That was the best day of my life. For the first time ever, I was with someone who was happy to be with me. When she dropped me home again, I cried so much that my mum put me to bed. "Don't be such a baby," she said. "You can cry all you want, but you're going back to school tomorrow." But I wasn't crying about that. I was crying because I saw how my life could have been.'

Ell threw his spoon on to his plate again and leaned back against the velvet-covered booth. 'Sorry. I'm boring you, aren't I?'

'Not at all,' said Berry, nonchalantly taking a scoop of ice-cream so that Ell wouldn't see how much she still longed to know. 'I'm waiting to hear how your gran gave you a sweet tooth.'

Ell shrugged. 'That was it. You heard it all right there.'

'The bag of sherbet?'

'Yup. After that, whenever my dad hit me or had big rows with Mum about money, I would just take my bag of sherbet and crawl under my bed. And I would lick the end of my finger and dip it in the sherbet so that I just got the tiniest little bit on the tip. Then I would screw my eyes tight shut and think about that day at the seaside. And just at the moment when I could picture everything – the seagulls and the blue sky and the pier and the waves and my gran holding my hand – that's when I would put the sherbet in my mouth. And it would dissolve on my tongue and all of a sudden it would be like I was there all over again. Just me and my gran and the sound of the sea.'

Ell drummed a little rhythm on the tabletop with his fingers and dug out some more ice-cream. He sucked it off the spoon and went cross-eyed.

'Uh-oh,' he said. 'Brain freeze.'

'When did you see her again?' asked Berry.

'Who? My gran?'

Berry nodded.

Ell rested his chin on his hand and stared at the tiger-stripe shadows that fell from the railings on to the sun-washed pavement outside.

'Well now, you see, that's the best part. Because when they saw how I was when I came back, they decided that she must have *unsettled* me. They decided it was best for everyone if I didn't see her any more.'

'What, never?' Berry shook her head, stunned by such ordinary, everyday cruelty.

'No. Whenever I asked, they told me she'd moved away. So in the end I just stopped asking. But she hadn't moved away, of course. I found out recently that she never gave up trying to make contact, but they just wouldn't let her see me again. Too disruptive for everyone, apparently.'

Ell smiled sadly.

'Crazy, isn't it? And you want to know the craziest thing of all?'

'Go on.'

Ell reached inside his jacket pocket and pulled out a small paper bag, ripped, torn and stained, but still recognizable as a paper bag.

'Oh, Ell,' said Berry.

'Kept it all these years.' Ell opened it and inside, Berry could see the tiniest trail of faded yellow crystals.

'Still enough for emergencies,' he said.

Later, in their twin-bedded room with its crisp folded towels, trouser press and little sachets of shampoo, Berry stood at the window and looked at the lights shining above the dark streets of the city. She wondered how many people were out there, lost and alone, trapped in lives they couldn't escape from.

She was one of the lucky ones.

She had loved and been loved.

Now she knew she must take what strength remained from those lost, beautiful days and try to make a difference in the days still left to her.

She had been given a chance.

A chance to do the right thing.

24
An Argument

'So what's the plan then?' asked Ell the next morning after they had showered and dressed. He lay next to Berry with his hands behind his head, staring at the ceiling. 'Tell me some more about this package. I need details.'

Berry turned her head and felt the pillow soft against her cheek.

'You didn't want to talk about it yesterday.'

'Yesterday's yesterday,' said Ell. 'Today's today.'

'OK, all right. Well, I think you know most of it. Joseph saved my life, and when I told him about the plane ticket he asked if I would deliver the package.'

'Why couldn't he deliver it himself?'

'Too old, apparently. Too old and too ill.'

'He can't have been that ill. He saved your life, didn't he?'

'I know. That was the weird part. He must have been so quick when he pulled me away from the bus. But afterwards, when we got back to his house, it was as if saving me had taken all his strength away.'

'And then the bad guys turned up.' Ell looked at her and narrowed his eyes. 'Do you really think it's the package they're after?'

'It has to be,' said Berry. 'Why else would they come after me?'

'Maybe it's an antique box or something,' suggested Ell, his eyes widening again as if the thought had only just occurred to him. 'Maybe it's the package itself that's valuable. Maybe it's worth a fortune!'

'Maybe,' said Berry. 'But I don't think it's just for money that people want it. I think it's more special than that.'

'More special?' asked Ell, turning to face her. 'What could be more special than a couple of million bucks?'

'Money's not everything, Ell,' replied Berry.

'My mum thought it was,' said Ell. 'Maybe she was right. Maybe money is everything.'

'You don't really believe that,' said Berry, sitting up and leaning against the quilted headboard. 'Please tell me you don't.'

'Listen,' said Ell. 'All I'm saying is, I've seen what having no money can do to people. It can tear them apart. That's why . . .'

Ell trailed off.

'That's why what?' asked Berry.

'Nothing,' said Ell. He looked away awkwardly. 'Look, without money, we wouldn't be here, would we?'

'No,' said Berry. 'So?'

'So it gives us a chance to change things, doesn't it? You know, when I was a kid, I used to lie in bed and think, if only I could make lots of money, then maybe my mum would come back and we'd all be happy again. She'd love me, because I'd *be* somebody.'

'You're already somebody,' said Berry. 'Having lots of money doesn't make you any better inside.'

'Inside?' replied Ell dismissively. 'What's inside? People are always going on about it. But it doesn't mean anything. When you open someone up, there's no magical fairy comes flying out. There's nothing in there but blood, guts and bones. It's the outside that's who you are. It's what people see and, as far as I'm concerned, it's the only thing that counts.'

'I can't believe you're saying this, Ell,' said Berry. 'What about that poem you wrote?'

Ell shrugged. 'It was just a poem.'

Berry felt shocked, as though she had been ambushed. Ell had changed from gentle and sweet to angry and bitter in a matter of seconds. She had seen a flash of it at the airport and now it was happening again. It suddenly seemed that he wasn't who she thought he was at all.

'What about the good things people do just for the sake of it?' she asked. 'What about your gran, for instance, taking you to the seaside?'

Ell's eyes flashed angrily. 'What's that got to do with anything?'

'Well, she wasn't just worried about how things looked. She *cared* for you, Ell. Don't you think that was because of something inside her, something more than just blood and bones?'

Ell said nothing. Instead he swung his feet off the bed and went over to the window. He pulled the curtains back a little way and, over his shoulder, Berry could see a plane climbing steeply above the city into the morning sky.

'Say something, Ell,' she said to his back. 'Speak to me.'

'It's always a disappointment,' he said softly. 'Every single time, it's a disappointment.'

'What?' asked Berry. 'What's a disappointment?'

Ell turned back from the window to look at her.

'Life,' he said simply. 'Just when you think that there might just be something worth believing in, life comes along and lets you down.'

Confused, Berry shook her head.

'Look, I don't know where all this is coming from.

I'm sorry I mentioned your gran if that's what's upset you. But you asked me about the package and all I said was, I think there's more to it than just money. Actually, I think there's a lot more to it than that.'

'Oh, yeah?' said Ell. 'How do you figure that then, exactly?'

Berry was alarmed by the coldness of Ell's tone, but she was determined to explain what she meant.

'Well, firstly, Joseph told me how important it was. And, before you say anything, I know he could have been lying to me, but the thing is I don't think that he was, OK?'

'You don't *think* that he was?'

'No, I don't.'

'So you don't *know*.'

'No, I don't know. But I choose to believe that he was telling the truth. And with all the things that have happened since, I think I was right to believe that.'

'That's it?'

Berry looked at Ell, uncertain whether to trust him any more. But maybe she could convince him, make him see that — in spite of what had happened to him in the past — there was more to life than just what was on the surface of things.

'Sometimes,' she said slowly, 'when I listen to it, I hear strange sounds, beautiful sounds. Like music from somewhere far away. It's not like anything I ever heard before. I don't understand it, but it makes me feel as though I want to follow wherever it leads me. Does that make any sense?'

'No, it doesn't,' said Ell. 'And shall I tell you why?'

'Yes,' said Berry. 'Go ahead. Please. Tell me.'

'Because the old man lied, Berry. He lied to you, and I guess maybe I've been playing along because, like you, part of me wanted it to be true.'

'What?' said Berry, shocked. 'Don't be ridiculous, Ell. How on earth can you possibly know that?'

'The package is empty,' said Ell. 'I didn't want to tell you yesterday because you seemed so happy and everything. But I saw it on the airport scanner, Berry. There's nothing in it. It's just a box.'

Berry felt as though an electric current had just been passed through her.

'That's not true!' she protested. 'It can't be. If it were true, then why would all those people be after us?'

'Who knows? Maybe I'm right and the box itself is worth a lot of money. Maybe the old man was just using you as a decoy to throw them off the scent of whatever it is they're really after. But I'm telling you what I saw. And what I saw was an empty package. So you know, spare me all that stuff about the strange music, Berry. I've had one too many disappointments to be taken in again, OK?'

'Look,' said Berry, jumping off the bed and standing

in front of him with her hands on her hips. 'I'm not making this up, Ell, I swear. Why would I make it up?'

'I don't know. Maybe because you just really want to believe it?'

'Oh-wuh!' In her exasperation, Berry clenched her fists and glared angrily at Ell. 'Do *not* treat me as though I am stupid, OK? It has absolutely nothing to do with what I do or don't want to believe! I know what I heard and, whatever you may or may not have seen at the airport, I know that there is something in there.'

'OK,' said Ell, folding his arms. 'Prove it.'

'What?'

'Prove it.'

He walked across to Berry's bag and unzipped the top.

'Hey!' shouted Berry. 'Give me that!'

Ell jumped on to the bed and held the bag up out of reach.

'What's the matter?' he taunted. 'Afraid of the truth?'

He thrust his hand into her bag and pulled out the brightly wrapped package.

'Ell!' Berry shouted angrily. 'Give me that NOW!' Leaping forward, she grabbed him around the legs and caught him off balance, knocking him to the floor. As the package flew from his grasp and bounced across the carpet, Berry untangled herself from his legs and crawled across to where it had landed. Picking it up, she retrieved her bag from the bed and put the package back inside.

Ell sat up, red-faced and angry.

'What the hell was that for?' he asked, rubbing his head.

'You were going to open it,' said Berry.

'So?' Ell rubbed his head some more. 'What if I was?'

'I told you. Joseph said we shouldn't open it.'

'Joseph said we shouldn't open it,' Ell repeated in a whiny voice. 'No, actually, he didn't. He said *you* shouldn't open it. He never said anything about *me*.'

'Now you're just being ridiculous.'

Ell stood up and brushed himself down.

'*I'm* being ridiculous? Well, excuse me, but I don't think I was the one who said I'd risk my life to take an empty package thousands of miles across the ocean just because some crazy old guy asked me to.'

'No, you're right,' said Berry angrily. 'You weren't. And you know what? I don't even know why you're here. Unless, you know, it was for the free ride and the new clothes. I mean, I know how important money is to you.'

Ell stared at her and froze. He put a hand up to his cheek as though he had been slapped.

'*What* did you say?' he whispered.

Berry looked at him and immediately wished that she could take it back.

'Look, Ell, I'm just saying –'

'So that's what you think. You think I only came with you for the money?'

'No, look, I'm sorry, I didn't mean it. I was –'

'Yes, you did mean it,' said Ell, pulling on his jacket. 'But you're wrong. Do you want to know why I came with you? Shall I tell you?'

'Ell, listen –'

'I came because it was exciting, and I'm all for doing exciting things. I also came because I saw that you were sad and in trouble and I thought you needed help. But the money? No. Not at all.'

Slipping on his shoes, he walked towards the door and then turned back to face Berry.

'There was another reason too,' he said. 'Wanna hear it?'

Berry shrugged and bit her lip.

'I came because I thought we were friends. But like I said. Life is full of disappointments.'

He opened the door and Berry could see beyond him to the stretch of blue carpet outside.

'Where are you going?' she asked.

'I don't know,' said Ell. Then he stepped out into the hallway and closed the door.

Berry stared at the door for several moments, wait-

ing for Ell to come back. When the door remained
closed, she pulled it open and peered out into the corridor, half expecting to find him still standing there.

But the corridor was empty.

Ell was nowhere to be seen.

25
Hiding

Berry went back into the room and shut the door. Why had she spoken that way to him? Why had she been so careless with his feelings when he had come all this way to help her?

She felt tired and wretched.

Sitting alone on the bed, she reached inside her jacket and took out the crumpled birthday card that her mother had given to her. She stared for a few moments at the picture of the blue house with the cherry tree in the garden and remembered then that she had dreamed of it again last night. She had been running towards it through a field of golden corn, and beyond the cliffs, stretching all the way to the horizon, was the sea. As she returned the card to her pocket she was suddenly filled with a fierce, terrible longing which made her feel further away from home than she had ever felt before.

She was a stranger in a big city on the other side of the world and the only person who might have cared something about her had walked out. Walked out because of a stupid argument over a package, a package that now seemed likely to be nothing more than cardboard and paper.

Wiping away the tears that welled in her eyes, Berry unzipped her bag and stared at the cube of shiny blue paper at the bottom. Would it *really* matter if she opened it? At least she would know one way or the other.

Several times, she put her hand into the bag only to remove it again. It still felt wrong. But with Ell gone, what was there left to lose?

She was about to take the package out again when she remembered what Ell had said. *I thought we were friends.* She couldn't just give up on him now.

Hurriedly, she put the bag back on the bed and ran across to the French windows. Pulling back the curtains, she twisted the handle and stepped out on to the balcony. The morning air was warm and still, and the sound of traffic floated up from the city below. Leaning over the railing, she saw Ell disappearing into an alley across the street.

'Ell!' she called. 'Ell, wait!'

But she realized he couldn't possibly hear her from so far away and, as she lost sight of him, she banged the top of the railing with frustration.

She was about to go inside again when she saw a dark-blue Ford pull up outside the hotel and three men got out. As they walked up the hotel steps, one of the men looked up at her. Not possible, she thought.

It *couldn't* be.

But then she noticed the white stripes across his shoulders.

With a cry of terror, she ran back into the room and grabbed her jacket from the bed. Thrusting her arms into the sleeves, she wrenched open the top drawer of the bedside cabinet and shook the contents out on to the bed. Throwing the drawer back on to the pillow, she scooped up her passport together with the rest of the money and thrust it into her bag. She tried to pull the zipper shut but her hands were shaking so much that it took her several attempts before she got a grip on it. She caught a glimpse of her terrified expression in the mirror and guessed they would already be checking her room number.

Checking the number and tipping the lady on reception.

Thank you, ma'am. You've been a big help.

Slinging her bag over her shoulder, Berry opened the door a little and peered through the crack. As there didn't appear to be anyone directly outside, she opened it wider and looked both ways, but the corridor was empty.

Closing the door behind her, Berry walked quickly along the hallway towards the lift. But when she got there she noticed that one of the white buttons was already lit.

The lift was coming up from the ground floor. She could hear the cables creak and rattle as it approached.

Her heart thudding, she turned and ran back up the corridor, her legs weak at the thought of the men and their guns.

Behind her, the lift bell chimed and the doors clunked open just as she reached the end of the corridor and skidded around the corner. Pressing herself against the dark-red wallpaper she heard footsteps and then the sound of men's voices, low and urgent.

A knock at the door.

'Hello? This is room service. We have a complimentary meal for you.'

Berry put her hand up to her mouth, stifling the sob that rose from her throat.

She knew there was no complimentary meal.

Only men with fists and bullets.

She ran down the next corridor, looking for lifts, stairs, anything. As the adrenalin pumped, her mind searched desperately for a way out. But every door had a number, every door was a locked room –

Then, to her right, a set of double doors.

Beyond them a stairway.

Shoulder-charging her way through the doors, Berry took the steps three at a time, gripping the polished banister rail and flying out of each turn like a stone from a slingshot. Reaching the ground floor in less than a minute, she bent over and put her hands on her knees while she caught her breath, her eyes flicking upwards every couple of seconds to check the stairway.

'Come on!' she told herself. 'Just do it!'

Still breathing heavily, she approached the elegant wood and glass doors that led into the lobby. The hotel entrance was only a short distance across the patterned carpet. Berry imagined the men breaking into her room upstairs and finding it empty.

She had to move now.

Placing her fingertips on the brass doorplates, she was about to push her way into the lobby when she stopped and took a step backwards. Sitting on a brown leather sofa, reading a newspaper, was a man in a khaki-coloured suit. Only he *wasn't* reading the newspaper. He was peering over the top of it, scanning the lobby. As Berry watched, he took out his phone, put it to his ear and nodded. Then he flipped it shut and put down his paper. As he turned, he looked at Berry and she saw that he was blond, and that he was smiling.

He got up from the sofa and began to walk across the lobby towards her.

Berry turned and ran, just as a waitress came out of the kitchen pushing a trolley in front of her. Berry fell headlong into it, sending a tray of desserts splattering up the wall.

'Hey!' protested the waitress. 'Watch where you're going!' But Berry was already on the other side of the swing doors, running past amazed kitchen staff through a world of steam and stainless steel until she burst through the far door into a restaurant where a surprised waiter with a tray of drinks stepped back just in time to avoid a collision. The neatly set tables with their linen tablecloths and quiet couples disappeared in a blur as Berry hit the double doors on the far side and fell into another corridor that seemed identical to all the others.

Looking frantically both ways, she saw a sign for 'rest rooms'. An arrow pointed down the corridor and Berry followed it until she came to the door of the Ladies. Pushing it open she saw, to her relief, that the rest room was empty.

Her shoes echoing across the tiled floor, Berry walked past the polished mirrors and gleaming wash-basins until she reached the far cubicle. Once inside, she locked the door and heard her ragged breath cut through the sterile silence. Her stomach churned and her hands were shaking. The world seemed so terrifying now, so fraught with danger that she felt she wanted to stay locked in here for ever. Alone in this small space, she could see the boundaries of her world and feel, for the moment at least, that she was safe.

Gradually, her breathing became quieter, more regular.

Closing the toilet lid, she sat down and unzipped her bag. She took out the package and cupped it gently in her hands. It felt heavier than before, more solid. She stared at it for a long time, uncertain of her next move. If they found her, they would find the package too. They could hardly miss it; all wrapped up in bright blue paper like some expensive birthday gift. But what if she took out whatever was inside and hid it somewhere? Perhaps then they would think they had made a mistake. She could say . . . she could say that she ran away because she had thought that they were school inspectors . . .

Berry suddenly felt the panic rise in her chest.

Ran away to America? They wouldn't believe her.

She had to think of something. She just *had* to.

Closing her eyes she leaned forward and pressed the cool, shiny paper of the package against her forehead.

Immediately she heard the strange music again. Fingers of sound twisted through her mind, unearthly notes tumbling from the shadows and weaving sad patterns around her heart before fluttering and falling like warm summer rain. Berry gasped as the music sparkled and sang inside of her, swelling, blossoming and flaming through her blood in an explosion of sweetness that made her fingers dance.

'Oh,' cried Berry. '*Oh!*'

With a sound like ice cracking, the music stopped and Berry looked down to see the floor covered with shredded blue paper and her fingers fumbling with the lid of the box.

'No,' she whispered. 'I mustn't.'

But she knew that she would.

26
SECRETS OF THE PACKAGE

SLOWLY, CAREFULLY, TERRIFIED and excited by what she might see, Berry lifted the lid to find a layer of tissue paper covering whatever lay beneath. With her finger and thumb she plucked at the centre and then gazed in silent wonder at what had been revealed. For there, nestling on a bed of cotton wool, was a perfect circle of gold, fashioned into a beautiful shining bracelet.

Five bright colours, spaced at regular intervals, sparkled beneath its surface like precious jewels. As Berry looked more closely she saw that four of the colours – blue, violet, green and yellow – were constantly moving within their own space, rippling like miniature cornfields in the breeze. At the very centre of the bracelet, a tiny ball of fire appeared to burn brightly beneath its golden skin, softening the metal above so that it wrinkled and shimmered like the waters of a sunlit lake.

It was the strangest, most beautiful thing that Berry had ever seen.

She was about to touch it when she heard the rest-room door swing open and the sound of footsteps, regular and precise, ticking across the floor like a metronome.

Instantly, her fear returned and she fought the urge to scream. But although she was afraid, she was also determined that these people would not get their hands on what she had found. Pulling up her left sleeve, she snatched up the bracelet and slid it on to her arm. Immediately a violent spasm ripped through her muscles and she had the sensation of hot liquid burning through her skin, shooting up her arm and swirling around her head before it cascaded down over her shoulders and surged like a wave down into her fingers and toes. As it reached the soles of her feet, her skin seemed to freeze and become solid so that, for a brief second, she was completely paralysed. At the same moment the strange music returned, whirling through her mind until all the notes merged together and then – like dust sucked into a vacuum – they were gone again, leaving only silence in their place. Berry stared at the floor in bewilderment, unable to compre-hend what had happened.

Then a noise outside brought her to her senses.

It was the sound of running water; someone was washing their hands and humming – a soft, tuneful melody. Berry realized then, to her utter relief, that it was a woman. Of course it was! No one had seen her come in, had they? Perhaps the woman would be able to help her.

But Berry wasn't about to take any chances. Stuffing the torn packaging behind the toilet cistern, she pulled down the sleeve of her jacket, dropped to her knees and peered beneath the toilet door. She saw the hem of a beige raincoat above a pair of dark tights with a seam along the calf, leading down to a pair of shiny black, patent-leather shoes.

No doubt about it. Definitely a woman.

She stood up, opened the door and saw that the woman was watching her in the mirror. She was young, mid-twenties, with dark hair and brown eyes. She looked kind and quite pretty, Berry thought.

'Excuse me?' Berry ran her thumb nervously beneath the strap of her bag where it rested on her shoulder. 'I was just wondering if you could help me with something?'

As the woman turned and smiled, Berry felt there was something familiar about her.

'I'll do my best,' said the woman. 'What's the problem?'

'Well,' said Berry, glancing nervously across at the door. 'I know this is hard to believe, but there are some men out there who are trying to kill me.'

The woman looked at Berry doubtfully for a moment or two. 'Are you sure about this?' she asked.

Berry nodded and as she spoke her lower lip began to tremble. 'Look, I know it sounds crazy, but I absolutely swear I'm not making it up. They've got guns and everything and I'm really, really scared. You've got to help me. *Please.*'

To her relief, the woman put a hand on her shoulder.

'OK,' she said. 'I can see that you're very frightened. I'll tell you what. If you like, I'll take you up to my room where you'll be safe for a while. Then, if you want me to, I'll call the police and we can try and get your problem sorted out for you.'

'Oh, *thank* you,' said Berry. She wasn't sure about the police part but was just happy to have found an ally. 'That would be brilliant. But, where is your room?'

'It's on the seventh floor,' said the woman. 'It'll only take a moment in the lift.'

'OK,' said Berry. 'That sounds great. Only thing is, they're out there looking for me right now. If they see me, I've had it.'

The woman thought for a moment.

'Well, there's a lift just outside, a little bit further

along the corridor. Do you want me to pop out and have a look, make sure there's no one there?'

'Would you?' asked Berry gratefully.

'No problem,' replied the woman. 'You wait here.' As she disappeared off into the corridor, Berry chewed her lip anxiously, waiting for her to return. A few seconds later, the woman put her head around the door and smiled reassuringly.

'All clear,' she said. 'Come on.'

With her heart in her mouth, Berry followed her out into the corridor and was relieved to see that it was empty, just as the woman had said. Berry wondered whether she actually believed her story or whether she just felt sorry for her, maybe thinking her a bit mad. Either way, Berry was grateful to have met her. At that moment she seemed to be her best chance of escape.

The doors of the lift slid together and as the woman pressed the button for the seventh floor, Berry leaned back against the cool steel wall and let out the breath she had been holding since they walked out of the rest room.

The woman winked at her. 'Nearly there,' she said kindly. 'Don't you worry. If these people really are threatening you, we'll have the police on to them in no time.'

Berry watched the number 7 light up. The lift

stopped with a clunk and the doors slid open. Stepping out into the corridor, the woman looked both ways and then nodded.

'OK,' she said. 'Coast's clear.'

Her legs shaking, Berry walked out of the lift and followed her quickly across the soft blue carpet until, a few seconds later, they reached the door of the woman's room. She pushed her keycard into the slot and the green light on the door lock flashed. There was a click and then she pushed the door open.

'In you go, sweetheart,' she said. As Berry walked in she saw, with a dreadful sick feeling in her stomach, that the curtains were drawn and that three men were standing around a chair with their arms folded.

Berry turned to run, but the woman leaned back against the door and closed it again. And as she smiled and began unbuttoning her coat, Berry saw the green sweater and remembered, too late, why she had seemed so familiar. She was the woman from the airport.

'Hello, my dear,' said the blond man, gesturing towards the seat. 'Please, sit down.'

He smiled.

'We have been expecting you.'

27

OPENING THE OYSTER

IN SPITE OF HER FEAR — or perhaps because of it — Berry took in a lot of detail before she reached the chair, her mind soaking up any information that might help her. The men were the same men who had chased her back in England. The woman was the same one who had watched them walk through the arrivals gate. Berry guessed that the men must have somehow found out what flight she was on and told the woman to follow her.

The room was virtually identical to the one that she and Ell were staying in. She decided that beyond the curtains there was probably a balcony. The fact that the curtains were moving slightly told her that the French windows were open a little. But, she remembered, this was the seventh floor.

She sat down, facing the door. As the woman folded her arms and smiled at her, Berry thought of what Ell had said earlier: *It's the outside that's who you are.* Well, if that was true, then the outside of this woman was pretty misleading.

The woman looked past Berry at the man standing behind her. 'There is something I have to check,' she said. 'I'll be back shortly.'

As she left the room, Berry felt a cool breeze blowing through the curtains. Somewhere in the distance, a dog barked above the sound of the traffic.

Hands touched her lightly on the shoulders and she flinched.

'Oh, come now,' whispered a voice in her ear and as its owner removed his hands from her shoulders and walked around in front of her, she saw that it was the blond man from the lobby.

'There's really no need to be nervous,' he said.

Berry squeezed her hands together to stop them from shaking and stared at the swirly patterns in the carpet.

'If we have frightened you,' he continued, 'then I am sorry. But you know, we mean you no harm.'

He was lying of course. Berry knew what they had done to Joseph and she had seen what had happened to the security guard at Glastonbury. But she needed to buy some time, to give herself a chance to think.

'I don't understand,' she said. 'I'd like to help you, but I don't know what it is that you want.'

She saw right away that he didn't believe her, saw how he sucked in his cheeks and stared at her, trying to control his temper.

'Don't play games with me, Miss Benjamin.'

Berry swallowed nervously. The fact that he knew her name seemed to make everything worse.

'I'm not playing games,' she said. She spoke quietly, careful not to make eye contact. She didn't want to do anything that might antagonize him. 'I just need to know what it is you want from me. If you tell me then I can try and help.'

Berry noticed that one of the men was emptying the contents of her bag on to the dressing table. There was the half-eaten packet of mints she had bought at the airport, her boarding pass, a small packet of tissues and her passport. She was relieved to remember that Ell still had the phone and the money in his jacket.

The blond man raised his eyebrows hopefully at the man with the bag, but he just shook his head.

'Nothing,' he said.

'All right then,' said the blond man. 'Perhaps you'd like to tell me about Joseph Mitchell.'

'Who?' asked Berry innocently.

'The old man who pulled you out of the way of the bus. The man who saved your life.'

'Oh,' said Berry, wondering how they knew. '*Him.*'

'Yes. Him.'

'What do you want to know? He saved my life. I said thank you very much. That was it, really.'

'He gave you something, didn't he?'

'I don't think so,' said Berry. 'But wait a minute, let me just . . .'

'All right,' said the man, losing his patience. 'I thought we might be able to do this in a sensible and civilized manner, but it would seem not. So. Take off your jacket, please.'

Berry thought of the bracelet pushed high on her wrist and her terrified mind searched desperately for a way of protecting it.

'Wait,' she said. 'He did give me something, now that I come to think about it.'

'Good,' said the blond man. 'Now perhaps we're getting somewhere.' He stroked the stubble on his face and, when Berry did not immediately continue, he smiled. But it was a cool, thin smile and its only purpose was to mask his impatience for a while longer. 'Are you going to tell me what it was?'

'It was a package,' said Berry. 'A blue one. He said that it was a present for a friend.'

'I see,' said the man. 'A present for a friend. How thoughtful. So tell me – why did he give it to you?'

'Because I told him I was going to America,' said Berry, 'and that's where his friend lives. He wanted someone to deliver it personally, you see.'

'And what was in the package?'

'I don't know,' said Berry. 'He didn't tell me.'

'Ah,' said the man. 'Well, that all makes perfect sense then.'

Berry could tell from his tone that perfect sense was the last thing he thought it made.

She also guessed what was coming next.

'Where is the package now, Berry?' His tone was harder now. Time to stop the nonsense.

'Well, that's the problem,' said Berry with a sudden flash of inspiration. 'The boy I was with. He stole it from me.'

The man's face changed at once, all pretence at reasonableness disappearing in the space of a moment.

'What?' he snapped. 'When?'

'Just before I saw you,' replied Berry, sensing from his reaction that this might be a useful avenue to lead him down. 'He left about an hour ago. He said he was going out to get some fresh air, but then I saw that the package had gone. I was just going to see if I could find him when I saw you in the lobby. I was frightened because of what happened last time, so I tried to run away. But I don't know what's in the package and I don't know where he's taken it.'

Berry stole a glance at the man and saw that he was hesitating. This, she thought, was a good sign. If she could just persuade him to take her out of the building, she might get a chance to escape and find Ell.

'I could help you look for him, if you like.'

The man stared at her, still undecided.

Then the door opened and the woman walked in. As she closed the door behind her, Berry saw that she was holding some blue paper and a crumpled cardboard box.

'I found this,' she said, 'in the cubicle where she was hiding.'

At once the fear was back, crackling through Berry's veins like an electrical storm. They knew she was lying now. There was no way out.

'Take off her jacket,' instructed the blond man.

The Tracksuit stepped forward from beside the dressing table, grabbed her by the lapels and pulled her to her feet. He yanked the front of the jacket so hard that a button flew off and hit the mirror. Berry cried out as he grasped her collar and tugged the jacket off backwards. As he ripped out the lining, Berry clamped her hand over the place on her arm where the bracelet should have been. But she couldn't feel it. All she could feel was a curious warmth, as though that part of her arm had been resting on a hot radiator.

'Look,' said the woman. 'She's hiding something.'

'I'm not!' cried Berry. 'I don't know anything! Leave me alone!'

But as the Tracksuit seized her roughly by the wrist and pulled her hand away, a hush descended on the room and everyone stared at Berry's arm.

There, glowing beneath the surface of Berry's skin, were five distinct colours – blue, green, red, violet and yellow. It was as though the bracelet had somehow melted into her arm and now its strange lights shone through her skin like headlamps underwater.

As Berry moaned with fear and turned her head away, she saw the wild excitement in the blond man's eyes and knew that this was what he had been searching for.

'Oh,' he whispered, sinking to his knees and clasping his hands together. 'It is here! We have found it!' He turned and looked at the others, his eyes shining with a fierce passion. 'Now at last we can begin to undo the wrongs our enemies have visited upon us. But first . . . first we must free this precious pearl from its unworthy carrier.'

Berry's eyes widened with horror as she watched him pull something small and shiny from his pocket. He pressed a button and with a click, a silver blade sprang from his hand.

'It is time', he said, 'to open the oyster.'

The sight of the knife slashed terror into Berry's mind and before she knew what she was doing she had spun out of the chair and made a break for the windows. A shout came from behind her and as she burst out on to the balcony she heard a sound like firecrackers and realized that they were shooting at her. In blind, unthinking panic, she saw the fire escape over to her right, scrambled over the balcony rail and jumped.

If the stairs had been a little closer, she might have made it. As it was, the fire escape had been positioned to allow for exit further along the corridor, and the distance was too great.

'No!' she shrieked. 'NO!'

Her fingers slipping from the iron railings, Berry saw the city streets far below her, distant and unreal, like a tiny model. Then the wind whipped through her hair and as she hurtled towards the ground she was aware of the sounds from the street becoming louder and louder. As she screamed in terror she put her hands out to shield herself from the inevitable impact and then the pavement rushed up to meet her and she hit it with a loud, sickening crack.

Somewhere far away, a woman screamed.

Darkness came, followed by silence.

Am I dead? Berry wondered. *I must be dead.*

Then, after a moment or two:

Do dead people think?

Slowly, carefully, Berry tried to open her eyes but something pressed against her face. Fearful of the pain, she tentatively flexed her fingers and was astonished to discover that they seemed undamaged. She shifted her weight on to her hands and – to her amazement – she still felt no pain.

Then she heard a woman's voice.

'My God,' it said. 'Oh, my God!'

Berry pushed herself up into a sitting position, rubbed her eyes and then opened them. The face of a middle-aged lady was staring into her own.

'Are you all right?' she asked.

'Yes,' said Berry, confused. 'At least, I think I am.'

As the woman continued to stare, Berry turned back to check herself over for injuries and then let out a little cry of shock. Radiating out in all directions from where she sat were cracks in the paving stones, splitting the pavement and snaking out across the road. Where seconds earlier she had been lying face down, there was a shallow impression in the smashed paving stones. As she staggered to her feet, she saw the shape of her body imprinted in the pavement.

But there was still no pain. No blood. No broken bones.

Only waves of panic and confusion, swirling and breaking inside of her.

'I'm sorry,' she said. 'I – I've got to go.'

And as she walked away, faster and faster, she glanced briefly over her shoulder and saw the woman looking down at the broken pavement, then lifting her head and staring after her, for all the world as if she had seen a ghost.

28
POLLY

POLICE SERGEANT POLLY WASHINGTON sat alone on the terrace of her new house in the Central Coast district of California, looking out over the sea and wondering where her life had gone. At the end of the month she would be taking advantage of the retirement package offered to her by Otero County Police Department. In a couple of days she would drive back to her house in New Mexico, pack up the last of her stuff and then – when her working life was finally over – move out here to the coast for the next phase of her life. But the trouble was, thinking about the next phase of her life was keeping her up at night. She was already starting to think that moving out here might be a big mistake.

It had always been her dream to live out by the sea. The other police officers didn't think too much about the future; most of them spent their salaries on cars and holidays, maybe even a pool in the backyard for the kids.

But not Polly.

Polly lived alone, and she lived frugally. Carefully, year after year, she saved her money, putting most of her monthly pay check into stocks and shares or high-interest accounts. And over the years, her money had grown. Slowly at first, with decent but unremarkable returns. But then, in the 1980s, the stockmarket had gone crazy. All of a sudden, Polly had found that she was a rich woman who never needed to work again. But she had liked her job, and wanted to keep it. So she kept on working and saving, always keeping her dream a little way in the distance; something good to look forward to at the end of the road.

Now, after all these years, the dream had become reality. She had cashed in her savings and bought an old farmhouse by the sea.

But the reality was: California was for the young. If you were seventeen, blond and beautiful, then the beaches and bars welcomed you with open arms. But if you were old, then the place simply shook its head and turned its back.

She had spent two weeks' holiday here in the late spring, just to get a feel of what her new life would be like.

It had certainly been an eye-opener.

Mornings were spent at the local store, checking out the special offers and talking to the counter girls, always for just a little bit longer than they were comfortable with. She could see it in their glazed expressions, the way they looked past her and disappeared into their own thoughts, leaving her standing on the outside like a ghost at a window. And so she would leave the shop ashamed, telling herself that the next time she would stop talking before they got tired of her. But the next day it was always the same; they would nod and smile thinly and she would end up hating herself just a little more.

And so it went.

The hot blue days merged, one into another.

She knew the truth, of course: she was lonely. There had been a boy once, Sidney, a pilot from the military base at White Sands in New Mexico. She had pulled him over on the highway one hot afternoon in late summer. Told him that one of his tail lights was out and that he should get it fixed.

'Are you gonna give me a ticket?' he'd said, with a smile that went nearly all the way to his ears. 'Cos if you are, it was worth it just to make your acquaintance.'

It had sounded like a line. A corny one at that. But

there had been something about the way his eyes sparkled that shot straight through her police badge all the way to her heart.

'How about we just call it advice,' she had replied, 'and you buy me a drink tonight instead?'

'Ma'am,' he had said, 'you just got yourself a deal.'

And that had been the start of it.

Thirteen months of going to movies, eating at Dot's Diner and planning a future together.

Thirteen months of happiness.

Then it had happened.

The thing that changed everything.

It was nearly forty years ago now, but she still remembered it like it was yesterday.

1969

Late afternoon, about five thirty; the sun starting to redden and the shadows growing longer. She was taking a shortcut home, driving along the desert road south of Dexter when she saw it: something unusual in the sky. It was silver, moving fast, and at first she thought it was a jet. But something wasn't right. It was travelling too fast, flying too smoothly and there was something else too, though she didn't realize it until she wound her window down.

There was no sound.

Instead of the expected roar of jet engines that she had grown accustomed to over the years, there was only silence.

And yet it was moving at incredible speeds, changing direction every few seconds, hovering, turning and swooping in a way that was unlike anything she had ever seen.

Pulling her patrol car off the highway, she jumped out and shielded her eyes against the sun. As light glinted off the smooth, metallic surface she saw that it was a large circular disc and that it was coming straight towards her. She ducked instinctively and it swept overhead, hovering for a few moments before landing several hundred metres away in the shade of a windswept thorn tree.

Polly had heard the stories of course — who hadn't? Stories about Unidentified Flying Objects seen in the skies over New Mexico, about the one that was supposed to have crashed back in 1947. Stories of how the government had supposedly hushed it all up. But like most people on the force, she had believed the stories to be foolish imaginings.

Which only made what she saw now all the harder to understand.

Two figures, dressed in white coveralls, crouching in the dirt.

Looking for something.

Polly swallowing, taking a few more steps towards them. A figure looking round, pointing at her. The other figure turning. Polly walking backwards, keeping her eyes fixed firmly on what she couldn't believe she was seeing.

A flash of silver against the blue sky.

Then nothing.

Nothing but an empty landscape; the shadows of clouds moving across the dry earth and the chirping of cicadas.

Polly running back to her car and snatching up the radio, calling urgent, urgent, get me some back-up . . .

There had been an investigation, naturally. After the Roswell Incident, the government was keen to give the impression that, officially at least, it wasn't covering anything up. But unofficially, the story got buried and, at the same time, so did Polly's career.

She was sent for psychological testing, diagnosed as suffering from stress and given six months' leave on full pay. When she returned, she found the job that she loved had become a job behind a desk. Her days were spent filling in forms and making cups of coffee.

Worst of all, Sidney was discouraged from seeing her any more. Unofficially, of course. But the military made it plain that it didn't want one of its future pilots mixing with some crazy woman who imagined she had seen a UFO. Sidney fought it of course – they both did. But what the military wants, the military gets. Sidney was sent to Vietnam and, six months later, his helicopter was shot down over the jungles of My Khe.

Her heart broken, Polly knew that if she were to carry on living she would have to draw a line under the whole thing. So she threw herself into her work and never mentioned the incident again. She tucked it away somewhere, deep down at the back of her mind, desperate to forget about the life she might have had and the children she would never see.

Through determination and hard work, she quickly made sergeant and, over the years, helped to pull a few hundred criminals off the streets. But some nights, when the sky was clear and the stars were bright, she would look up and wonder if she had ever really seen what she thought she had seen.

Polly never dated again and she never married. And now, after all these years, she was still weighed down by the burden of a love that had nowhere to go.

29
A SPECIAL PURCHASE

BERRY HAD WALKED ABOUT a block from the hotel when she spotted Ell emerging from Starbucks on the corner of Sutter Street. He was carrying a brown paper bag and looking pretty pleased with himself. The 'Walk' sign illuminated and he strolled across the road, heading in the direction of the hotel.

Spinning on her heel, Berry sprinted back along the street, caught up with him and grabbed him by the elbow.

'Oh, hi,' he said, smiling and holding up the paper bag. 'I bought some bagels. A peace offering.'

'Don't go that way,' Berry warned, tugging at his arm. 'We can't go back there now.'

Ell furrowed his brow. 'Is everything all right?'

'No,' said Berry. 'It isn't.'

She steered Ell into a 180-degree turn and pushed him in the back to make him go faster.

'Are you going to tell me what's going on?' he asked as they crossed the road again.

Berry pulled him into the doorway of Lori's Diner and said, 'It's them. They've found us.'

'What?' Ell sounded incredulous. 'How?'

Berry shrugged. 'You tell me. But the woman I saw at the airport is one of them.'

'Did they see you?'

'Oh, they saw me all right. They wanted the package, Ell. If I hadn't have got out of there they'd have killed me. No question.'

'So what did they do when they found the package was empty? Did they think you'd taken it or something?'

'Like I told you, Ell. The package wasn't empty.'

'But I saw it on the air—'

'Ell, will you just shut up about the airport scanner? It wasn't empty, OK? Look!' Berry pulled up her shirt sleeve to show Ell the lights glowing beneath her skin. But, to her surprise, the bracelet had reappeared now and was resting on her arm again.

'Hey!' exclaimed Ell, impressed. 'That's beautiful. Where'd you get it?'

'That's what I'm trying to tell you,' said Berry. 'This is what they're after. If I hadn't jumped out of the window, I wouldn't be here talking to you.'

Ell looked at her suspiciously. 'Are you winding me up again?'

'No,' said Berry. She could tell he didn't believe the part about the window, but now wasn't the time to try and explain. She didn't even understand it herself. 'Look, if these people have come halfway round the world looking for me, they're not going to give up now, are they? So the sooner we can get this thing to New Mexico, the better. Any suggestions?'

'Apart from ditching it, you mean?'

'Yes, Ell. Apart from ditching it.'

Ell shrugged.

'Bus?'

'Too obvious. If they were watching the airport, they'll be watching the bus terminals too.'

'Maybe we could find another hotel somewhere. Lie low for a while.'

Berry thought about the $10,000 that Joseph had given her. 'We could. But the money won't last for ever. And if we hang around it'll give them more chance to find us. I say we move now.'

'OK,' said Ell. 'But I'm all out of ideas. Unless . . .'

He wagged a finger as if trying to marshal his thoughts in her direction. 'Unless . . .'

'Unless *what?*' said Berry, glancing around anxiously to check that she hadn't been followed.

'A motorbike,' he said. 'We could buy ourselves a motorbike.'

They bought a couple of $3 tickets at the cable-car turnaround and rode the Powell–Mason line towards Mason. As they rattled up and down the hills, a boy of about six pointed to a tall red lever and asked the gripman, 'Is that the brake?'

The gripman looked at the lever and scratched his head as if he was seeing it for the very first time.

'Gee, I guess so,' he said, winking at Berry. 'This is my first day.'

Berry smiled, but inside she was still in turmoil. Her stomach turned over as she desperately tried to make sense of what had happened back there. And as for those people in the hotel room – they would be after her again now, she was sure of it. What would they do if they caught up with her?

'Look,' said Ell, interrupting her thoughts. 'Over there.'

Bob's Bargain Bikes was just off Mason, halfway between Green and Filbert. Berry followed Ell into the shop and, after looking at the price tag on a gleaming Harley Davidson, concluded that Bob's idea of a bargain was different from her own.

'Come on, Ell,' she whispered. 'There's no way we can afford one of these.'

Ell turned to face the shop owner, a straggly-haired man in a denim jacket and sunglasses. He looked as though he had enjoyed the 1970s immensely and was still wondering where they had gone.

'Have you got any used ones?' Ell asked breezily, moving away from the rows of shiny new machines that stood in the shop window. 'We're on a bit of an economy drive at the moment.'

Berry was amazed at Ell's laid-back attitude. She was still on edge and constantly felt the need to look over her shoulder. But he seemed quite relaxed about the whole thing and she wasn't convinced that he really appreciated the seriousness of the situation. He seemed able to put the Glastonbury episode behind him and almost pretend that the whole thing was some kind of game. Thinking about it, she supposed he hadn't actually had to deal with any of the really bad stuff yet. He hadn't fallen out of any windows, been shot at, or worn a bracelet that filled him with sweet music and kept him from dying. But the few minutes she had spent in the hotel room with those people had reminded Berry that this particular game was deadly serious. She knew they had to get away from here now, before it was too late.

'How about this one?' asked the man. 'This baby came in last Tuesday. Sure, she's got a few miles on her, but she's still got plenty of grunt.'

Ell stroked the thick padded seat.

'Looks comfy,' he said. 'And, more importantly,

extremely cool.'

'Oh yeah, she's cool all right. A real 'Cisco cruiser. Want to sit on her?'

'Yeah,' said Berry, still thinking about the hotel room and the bracelet. 'OK.' The man looked from Ell to Berry, but if he was at all surprised, he managed to hide it pretty well.

'Sure,' he said. 'Why not? Climb aboard, little lady.'

Berry put one hand on the polished silver tank and the other on the twist grip of the handlebars which curved down to meet her. It was a big, heavy bike, but it was low slung and the large four-cylinder motor kept the centre of gravity close to the ground. Throwing one leg over the seat, Berry sat back and tipped it off its side-stand, balancing the bike with the tips of her toes and feeling it bounce gently up and down on its suspension.

'You've ridden before, ain't ya?' said the man. He sounded impressed.

'Once or twice,' said Berry. 'But never one quite as big as this.'

'Oh, she's a pussycat,' the man assured her. 'Least-ways, she is right up until the moment you pull that throttle right back. Then she turns into a bit of a wild-cat.'

'Hear that?' said Ell. He held up his hands like claws. 'Mee-*ow*!'

'Is the engine fairly reliable?' asked Berry, starting to get interested. 'We were planning on maybe taking a bit of a trip.'

'Oh yeah,' said the man. 'I'm tellin' you, these things just keep going for ever. They're bullet proof.'

'Now that,' said Ell, 'could come in *very* handy.'

'OK,' said Berry, ignoring Ell. 'How much?'

'For this little beauty? Let's call it three thousand dollars.'

Berry narrowed her eyes.

'I'll give you two thousand five hundred.'

'Ouch,' said the man. 'I can see you're a hard one. How about we split the difference. Say, two seven fifty.'

'Two thousand six hundred with a couple of helmets,' said Berry 'We'll pay cash.'

She held out her hand to Ell who took the wad of dollars from his top pocket and began counting them out. 'I don't know,' he said, shaking his head like a weary parent. 'Buy me this, buy me that.'

Berry glanced at the bike-shop owner and guessed he had never come across a pair of customers quite like them before. But he was staring at the money and smiling, which was a good sign.

'You two', he sighed, 'are going to put me out of business.' But when he reached for the money Berry knew they had themselves a deal.

Maybe, she thought, they could do this after all.

Ell chose a bright blue helmet with glossy pictures of surfboards and palm trees all over it.

'What was it you said?' asked Berry. 'About not drawing attention to ourselves?'

'Yeah, but this is different,' said Ell, holding up the helmet and beaming. 'This is *class*.'

Berry went for a dark red, slightly more restrained, helmet and they picked up some panniers, sleeping bags, a couple of leather jackets and a two-man tent for an extra $500.

'You guys really are planning a trip,' said the man. 'Where are you headed?'

'New Mexico,' said Berry. 'Somewhere down south. At least, that's the plan.'

'New Mexico, huh? You must really like your desert. You got friends out there?'

'Think so,' said Ell. 'We just need to find out who he is and where he lives.' He winked at Berry and she shook her head disapprovingly, but the man didn't seem to notice.

'Whereabouts in England you from?'

'Somerset,' said Berry.

'Is that anywhere near London?'

'Not really,' said Berry. 'About a hundred and fifty miles away I guess.'

'A hundred and fifty miles?' said the man. 'I don't

wanna worry you or nothing, but in New Mexico they got neighbours who live further away than that.'

'Big place, huh?' said Ell.

'Big place,' said the man. 'Big 'n' empty.' He took a road map down off the shelf and handed it to Berry. 'Reckon you're gonna need this,' he said.

Berry whispered something to Ell and he shook his head so she whispered it again more insistently while the man poured a can of petrol into the tank.

'That'll get you as far as your first gas station at least,' he said.

Berry pushed Ell in the back and he stumbled forward, turning to scowl at Berry before regaining his composure and shaking the man by the hand.

'Right then, well, thank you very much. I guess we'll be off now then.'

Ell sat on the motorcycle and as he began to push it outside the man smiled and shook his head at Berry.

'For a moment there, I thought *you* were going to be riding it,' he said with a chuckle.

Berry laughed along with him. 'Imagine!' she said.

'I bet you'd like to one day though, wouldn't you?' asked the man.

'Oh, I don't know,' said Berry doubtfully. 'It seems awfully powerful.'

'Well, you know, when you're ready, come back and see me. I do a nice little scooter which would be right up your street.'

'A scooter,' said Berry. 'Now that does sound nice.'

Then, as Ell slid back on the seat and held on to the rear grab rail, she jumped on the bike, fired up the motor and, with a little wave, roared off down the street in a cloud of smoke and dust, leaving the bike-shop owner gazing after her with a look of utter surprise on his face.

'Well, I'll be damned,' he said.

30

BENEATH THE WAVES

ALTHOUGH THE BIKE WAS BIG, Berry quickly got used to the feel of it. Once they were on the move, it was just as easy to ride as the smaller bike and a good deal more comfortable. The main thing was remembering to drive on the right instead of the left, but apart from one close call at an intersection (where they were nearly flattened by a tram as it appeared over the top of a steep hill), Berry soon felt totally at home on it. They drove through Pacific Heights towards the Marina District, past thrift shops, parks and coloured murals where groups of children gathered on the steps of tenement buildings and a graffiti message advised its readers to 'Drink more and think less.' Trams buzzed up and down the wires and as they passed beneath a green sign which read 'San Jose', Ell cried, 'Now I know the way!'

As they rode over the rise, Berry saw the waters of

the bay laid out below them and the famous Golden Gate bridge towering above the blanket of white mist that tumbled in from the sea. She watched a tiny yacht tacking its way back and forth across the waves and as it struggled against the choppy sea she imagined her mother standing here, all those years ago.

'Look at that,' said Ell. 'That's quite something, isn't it?'

'Yes,' said Berry. 'It really is quite something.' Then, pushing her visor shut, she accelerated smoothly away down the hill, not wanting Ell or anyone else to see that she was crying.

They took the Pacific Coast Highway through Santa Cruz, the ocean sparkling blue and magnificent below them as they leaned through the sweeping turns above Monterey Bay, following the Big Sur road through Carmel and all the way down to San Simeon. Six hours later – after only one comfort stop – Berry turned down a sandy road and pulled into a small, deserted car-park next to the beach.

'Aaarghhh,' cried Ell, staggering off and rubbing his thigh muscles. 'My legs have turned to concrete!'

'Mine too,' said Berry, kicking out the side-stand and flexing the numbness out of her fingers. 'But just look at it, Ell! What do you think?'

They both stared at the ocean, listening to the roar

of the breakers as they thundered down and hissed across the sand.

'Now that', said Ell, removing his helmet, 'was definitely worth coming for.' He unzipped his jacket, hung it on the handlebars and began removing his suit trousers which, Berry noticed, had patches of dirt and oil spattered across them.

'Ell,' she said. 'What are you doing?'

'What do you think I'm doing?' replied Ell.

'I think you're taking all your clothes off,' said Berry. 'Which, I have to say, is a bit weird.'

'*I*', said Ell, ignoring her, 'am going swimming.' He folded his trousers neatly over the seat of the bike and stood there, pale and white in his red stripy boxer shorts. He held out a hand. 'Coming?'

'No,' said Berry, taking off her jacket and hanging it on the other handlebar. 'That would just be stupid.' She took off her boots and placed them side by side next to the front wheel, then unbuttoned her trousers and draped them over the seat next to Ell's. 'I mean, there are people out there who want to kill us and we have to get to New Mexico as soon as we possibly can.' She took off her socks and pushed them into the tops of her shoes. 'So we really haven't got time for swimming.'

'No, you're right,' said Ell, looking at her standing there, smiling, in her shirt and knickers. 'We really should be going.'

'OK,' said Berry. 'That's settled then.'

She held out her hand and together they ran squealing across the soft white sand towards the surf that foamed up the beach to meet them. Beyond the breakers, pelicans folded their wings and dived into the blue waters, fishing for their dinner. Two young seals popped their heads out of the water and watched as Berry and Ell splashed noisily into the shallows.

'Last one to Hawaii's a cissy!' shouted Ell, striking out towards deeper waters with a surprisingly powerful front crawl.

As the cool water washed away the day's heat and dust, Berry tasted salt on her tongue and felt her tiredness slip away with the tide. She suddenly felt fresh and alive again, her spirits washed clean by the sea.

'Come on!' called Ell. 'Swim out!'

'No, I'm fine here!' Berry shouted back, lying in the shallows and feeling the sand shuffle between her fingers. 'I don't want to go out of my depth! I'm not as strong a swimmer as you!'

Suddenly remembering the bracelet, she clamped her hand to her wrist and was relieved to find it still in place. But as she took her hand away again, she noticed that the blue light was glowing more strongly than the others. A large wave knocked her backwards and, as she struggled to her feet, she saw that Ell was now quite a long way from the shore.

'Don't go out too far!' she shouted, finding it hard to make herself heard above the booming surf. She felt the undertow drag shingle past her legs and although her breaststroke wasn't bad, she knew that she wasn't a strong swimmer.

'Ell!' she called again, worried now. 'Come in a bit!'

She caught sight of him briefly before another large wave broke and she turned sideways to avoid its full force. She was knocked into a froth of white water and when she regained her footing she saw that Ell was even further out than he had been before. He was waving frantically and seemed to be shouting something. Suddenly, Berry realized that he was in trouble.

He's caught in a riptide, she thought. *He'll be swept out to sea.*

Blue music flashed through her mind and she saw pictures of bright fish, darting through shadowy caves. Dolphins trailed silver bubbles up to patterns of light that danced like stars above the ocean floor.

'Yes,' she answered as another wave sent her tumbling down into the churning sand. '*Yes.*' Her fingers fumbled through the turbulent water, seeking out the blue light that sang so brightly under the bracelet's golden skin. Then she touched it and it exploded inside her, cold and powerful, like a glacier crackling into the sea.

As she opened her mouth, the seawater roared in

and filled her with such fierce energy that it snapped her body straight and thrust her forward beneath the surface of the ocean. She hurtled at high speed over wave-patterned sand, twisting through swaying forests of sea-kelp and soaring above barnacle-encrusted rocks, searching the underwater landscape for Ell. As she burst through a glittering shoal of mackerel they scattered in all directions. Sunlight bounced off their shining scales, tracing patterns of shimmering silver across the ocean floor.

Another incredible surge of power shot through her veins and suddenly she felt capable of anything.

What was happening to her?

Feeling the whole of her left side shiver and tremble, she thrust her arm forward and curved her fingers around in the same direction. Instantly, her whole body veered around to the left and with a flick of her feet she shot forward like a torpedo.

Ahead of her she saw Ell's legs kicking uselessly against the strength of the tide that was pulling him out to sea. Finding herself strangely unafraid, Berry curved her arms above her head and swept quickly up towards the light. As her head broke the surface she saw Ell struggling to stay afloat, his face tipping backwards in a desperate attempt to breathe.

'Go back!' he cried. 'The current's too strong! Go back!' He splashed his arms frantically in an effort to stay afloat, but only succeeded in sinking further beneath the surface. With a quick flick of her feet, Berry was beside him, slipping an arm beneath his flailing body. Using her free hand she pulled him firmly on to his back and tipped his head so that he was staring up at the sky. 'Just look up at the clouds,' she told him. 'It'll help you stay afloat.'

Her muscles singing with new strength, she dug into the waves with her free hand and rocketed backwards, bubbles erupting in her wake as she kicked back hard and powered through the water. Another flick of her legs sent the two of them shooting back across the surface, skimming over the tops of the waves and crashing down into the troughs, each powerful kick propelling them up on to the crest of the next one.

The water was shallower now; Berry could hear the drag of the shingle and the waves breaking on the beach behind her. Tipping her legs forward, she felt the sand shift beneath her toes as seawater swirled and foamed around her waist.

Setting Ell down, she pushed him back towards the beach. 'Go,' she told him. 'Go and get warm.' Exhausted, Ell looked into her eyes and saw that something had changed, something was different. Without a word he splashed away through the shallows, too shocked to try and understand.

Berry turned back, felt the pulse and thunder of the waves and for a moment, as her mind drifted through chambers of seashells and underwater caverns, the ocean's secrets were no longer hidden from her. She was part of the whole pattern; no longer separate, but the same. Tipping her head back, she stared at the thin wisps of cloud striping the very edges of space and heard the music again, caught somewhere between the sky and the sea.

Wading back through the swirling tide, she stood at last on the wet sand, staring at the shivering figure of Ell like someone waking from a half-remembered dream.

31
MAGIC AND MEANING

'THAT', SHE SAID BREATHLESSLY as they walked back up the beach, 'was just incredible!'

'Yeah,' said Ell shakily, still recovering. 'That was some riptide, eh?'

Berry glanced over at him and realized that he still hadn't seen the things she had seen; he still didn't understand.

When she was sitting on the sand again, resting her back against the front wheel of the bike, she held up her arm so that the evening sun reflected off the bracelet. 'It's this, Ell. It's so powerful. I can feel it.'

'You can feel it?' asked Ell, sitting cross-legged on the sand opposite her. 'What do you mean, you can feel it?'

'I don't know,' replied Berry. 'It just seems that whenever bad things happen, the bracelet helps me deal with them.'

She picked up a handful of sand and let it trickle through her fingers.

'Like back at the hotel, for instance. I fell seven floors, Ell. Seven floors and there wasn't a scratch on me. It has to be the bracelet. This bracelet is protecting me, somehow.'

Ell picked up a small stone and flicked it away down the beach.

'You serious?' he asked.

'Yes!' said Berry emphatically. She shivered. 'It scares me, Ell. The whole thing scares me. I can see now why people want it so badly. When I'm wearing it, I feel as though I could do anything. And it makes me realize that they're not going to give up until they get it.'

'It does look pretty valuable,' said Ell, staring at the bracelet. 'How much do you think it's worth?'

Berry frowned. 'I told you, Ell, it's not the money. Don't you see? That's not why they want it. They want it because of what it can *do*.' She glanced at him and was horrified to see from his expression that he still didn't believe her.

'You think I'm crazy, don't you?' she said. 'You *still* think I'm making all of this up!'

'I don't think you're making it up,' said Ell. 'I think it's fantastic that you swam out and helped me just now. But, you know, people can do amazing things when they have to. I read about a guy once who lifted up a heavy truck because his son was trapped beneath the wheel.'

'But it's not *like* that,' said Berry. 'It's not like that at all. I'm telling you, this is different. *Really* different.'

'OK then,' said Ell. 'Make it do something.'

'What?'

'Show me. Make it do something amazing.'

'No,' said Berry.

'Why not?'

'Because . . . because it doesn't work like that. You can't just make it happen. You have to wait for it. It sort of . . . tingles.'

'Tingles, huh?' said Ell.

'All right, look, I know it sounds stupid, but why else do you think these people want it?'

Ell shrugged. 'Like I said. Maybe it's worth big bucks.'

'OK,' said Berry. 'You know what? If that's what you want to believe, then go right ahead. I know what I feel, that's all.'

'Look, I don't want to fight about it,' said Ell gently. 'I just think, you know, sometimes we believe what we want to believe because it helps us get through. And I understand that. God, absolutely I understand it. I've done it enough times myself.'

'What do you mean?' asked Berry.

'I used to tell myself that my gran would come back

for me one day. That she'd take me home to live with her. You know, I wanted it so badly that I really started to believe that it was true. And then, one day, I just woke up and realized that she was never coming back. And I don't want you to feel the way I did that day, Berry. That's all. I don't want you to be disappointed.'

Berry saw how sad Ell looked and suddenly remembered Joseph's words: *Don't tell anyone and don't open it.*

Well, she'd already blown the second part. Now here she was trying to tell Ell everything about it. Maybe it was a good thing that he didn't believe her, after all. Perhaps she should let him carry on thinking that everyone wanted it for the money and keep the truth to herself, just as Joseph had wanted.

She put a hand on Ell's arm.

'You're right,' she said. 'I'm sorry.'

'No,' said Ell. 'Don't you dare apologize. You've got absolutely nothing to be sorry about. Look, I know how important this whole delivery thing is to you. So even though I think it's crazy, I'll help you get through it, OK? I'm your friend and I'm going to stick with you. The way I see it, the sooner you do what the old guy asked you to do, the sooner you can forget about it and start getting on with the rest of your life.'

'Thank you, Ell,' said Berry. 'You're a good person.'

'Well, I don't know about that,' said Ell, looking at her with a new determination in his eyes. 'But what I do know is, if it's the bracelet they're after, then once we've taken it to where it has to go, they should leave us alone, right?'

He rummaged in the motorcycle panniers and retrieved the road map, which was already looking rather crumpled.

'How long do you think it'll take us to get there?' asked Berry. 'New Mexico, I mean.'

'Well, let's see,' said Ell, spreading the map out on the sand. 'At the moment we're here, look, just outside San Simeon.' He glanced at his watch. 'It's already half past four. How much driving do you think you've got left in you?'

'Reckon I'm still good for a few hours,' said Berry. 'How about you?'

Ell shrugged. 'All I have to do is sit there.' He looked back at the map and traced along a route with his finger. 'Maybe we should aim to get somewhere near Barstow before we stop for the night.'

Berry sat up and looked over his shoulder. 'Looks as though it's in the middle of a desert,' she said. 'That's probably a good thing, actually. I think we should try and stay away from towns and cities as much as possible. At least until we get to New Mexico.'

'Makes sense,' agreed Ell. 'If we get some rest tonight, there's no reason why we shouldn't be somewhere in the middle of Arizona by tomorrow night.

We can take the road south of Phoenix and skirt around it. If we do that tomorrow, we should be in New Mexico the day after, no problem.'

'Sounds good,' said Berry. She brushed sand from the map and ran her finger east of the border along Route 10. 'Joseph said something about working down in the south, so perhaps we should start here at Las Cruces, look. It seems to be about the biggest place in that area. What do you think?'

Ell nodded. 'Probably as good a place as any. And once we get there we have to track down this Eddy Chaves guy, right? Take him the package?'

'Eddy Chaves and the Eunice Vaughn Anthony Centre. Sounds like a hospital, doesn't it? Wouldn't have thought there were too many around with a name like that.'

'Well, let's hope not,' said Ell. 'Maybe this Eddy Chaves guy works there. Should be able to look it up in a phone book or something.'

'Maybe we'll try your little focusing trick when we get there,' said Berry with a smile. 'Seemed to work pretty well on the plane.'

Ell was silent and Berry sensed an air of unhappiness about him.

'What's the matter, Ell?' she asked gently. 'Are you all right?'

'Oh, it's nothing,' replied Ell, but Berry could tell

that it was something, and she waited. 'You'll think I'm stupid.'

'No, I won't,' said Berry. 'Tell me.'

'Well, it's just that, for a moment back there, a very small part of me wanted to believe that it was true. That maybe there was a little bit of magic in the world after all.'

Berry watched Ell smooth the sand over with the palm of his hand and suddenly the temptation to tell him everything was overwhelming. But she remembered Joseph's words and was afraid that any more mistakes would put both their lives in danger. So she listened and said nothing.

'When my mum left, I realized that the world wasn't the way I thought it was at all. Everything I believed in just walked out of the door. Fairies, Father Christmas, happy families, the whole lot went with her. And I knew then that nothing is really worth anything. There's no order in the world at all. Everyone spends their lives doing their little jobs, pretending that everything's all right. But in the end, it's all just meaningless, isn't it? There's no magic. Nothing means anything at all.'

There was a long silence, broken only by the sound of the waves crashing down upon the sand. Then Berry touched his hand and said:

'We can make our own meaning, Ell.'

'How?' asked Ell. 'How can we possibly do that?'

'By not giving up,' said Berry. 'By doing the right thing.'

32

GETTING WARMER

BILL HORTON HAD ALREADY had one shock that day.
He had sent the image of Joseph Mitchell to the British
police, telling them he thought it was the same man
shown on the CCTV tape of the bus accident. They had
come back with the news that Mitchell had been found
murdered a few days earlier and that they were now
trying to establish the whereabouts of the young girl
on the tape. She had been observed by a police officer
near the scene of Mitchell's murder and later in the
vicinity of another unexplained murder at a music festival in Somerset. The British police had identified her
as Berry Benjamin, fourteen, and established that she
had caught a flight to San Francisco that same morning.
CCTV pictures from both airports showed her with a
sixteen-year-old accomplice, one Elliott Watts.

Horton had already booked himself on to the next

internal flight when the news came in. A shooting in downtown San Francisco. Nothing unusual about that of course, but when he heard the report about some girl jumping off a seven-storey balcony and disappearing without trace, Horton was out the door like his lottery numbers had just come up.

'I think this is it, Andy,' he whispered as he headed along the freeway in the direction of Albuquerque airport, steering wheel in one hand and a half-eaten ham roll in the other. 'Whatever it was you were looking for, buddy, I'm gonna find it.'

Later that afternoon in San Francisco, he showed his pass to the uniformed guy standing outside the hotel room and walked through to where a couple of forensic guys in blue nylon jumpsuits were doing their thing with tweezers and test tubes.

'What've you got so far?' he asked the nearest one, watching him pull a strand of hair off the bedspread. 'Anything?'

'Bit early to tell,' replied the man, placing the hair inside a collection tube and pressing on the cap with gloved fingers. 'You might want to take a look out there on the balcony, though. It's got us scratching our heads, that's for sure.'

Horton raised one eyebrow and made his way across to the French windows where the other man was dusting the glass for fingerprints.

'Excuse me,' he said. 'May I?'

The man stopped doing what he was doing with his little brush and took a step backwards. 'Watch where you're putting your feet,' he said. 'It's still a scene of crime out there.'

Horton stared at him, unable to hide his irritation. He'd been visiting crime scenes when this guy was still filling his diaper and crayoning on his mother's walls. But some things just weren't worth the effort and Horton decided to let it go.

Stepping out on to the balcony, his attention was immediately taken by three chalk circles on the ground. In the middle of each one was something small and shiny. Crouching down for a closer look, he saw that they were flat, brass-coloured pieces of metal, each about the same diameter as a cent. Horton frowned and turned back to face the room.

'Any ideas?' he asked.

The man nodded. 'They're bullets.'

'*Bullets?*' repeated Horton. 'Are you sure?'

'Uh-huh. If you look closely at the flat edges you can make out the friction marks from the barrel. Don't quote me, but I'd say they were from a Walther PK automatic.'

Horton glanced back at the flat discs of metal glinting in the sunlight and shook his head. 'But how did they get to be that way?' he asked.

'Beats me,' said the man. 'We found traces of explosive from the gun cartridge on the wall, which suggests the gun was fired from inside this room. So whatever was out there on the balcony just took all the sting out of those bullets and stopped 'em dead. Can't say I ever saw anything like it. How about you?'

'No,' said Horton. 'Never.'

Deciding he had better take a look around the hotel, Horton was just heading out the door when he spotted a plastic evidence bag on the dressing table. Inside were some pieces of shredded blue paper.

'What's this?' he asked.

The forensic guy shrugged. 'It's paper,' he said. 'We found it on the floor.' He gave Horton a look to suggest he didn't have time for any more stupid questions. Then he went back to work with his tweezers.

Knowing that it was pointless asking if he could borrow a sample, Horton pulled out his phone, lined up the built-in camera and took a quick picture.

Look out for the unusual.

'Hey,' said Tweezer Man, alerted by the sound of the camera. 'What are you doing?'

Horton smiled and held up his phone. 'Just wanted to remind myself of the good times we had together,' he said.

He waited until he reached the end of the corridor,

then made an international call to New Scotland Yard in London. 'Yeah, you heard right,' he said. 'I want to send you a photo message.'

33
A Bag of Bones

It was dark by the time they pitched camp between clumps of brittle bush and sage brush. They were on the western fringes of the Mojave desert and a crescent moon cast long shadows beneath the giant cacti dotted across the barren landscape.

'My clothes are completely dry now,' said Berry contentedly. The evening breeze was warm against her face and the sky seemed huge, stretching from horizon to horizon in a bright, star-scattered curve.

'That's the thing about deserts,' said Ell, knocking in a tent peg with a mallet. 'They dry your washing in a flash.'

'Fancy some soup?' asked Berry, rummaging around in the panniers. They had stopped off at a small grocery store in Paso Robles and picked up a few provisions, including an assortment of sweets for Ell.

'No, thanks,' said Ell. 'I'm happy with chocolate.'

'You can't survive on just chocolate,' said Berry disapprovingly, unpacking the small gas stove from the panniers. 'Look.' She waved a packet at him. 'Tomato. It's good for you.'

'If I only stuck with what's good for me,' said Ell, 'then I wouldn't be here, would I?' He pointed the mallet at her. 'Ha. Think about it.'

Berry shrugged. 'If you want all your teeth to fall out, then that's your business.'

'Yes, it is,' agreed Ell, popping four chunks of chocolate into his mouth at once. 'It *is* my business.'

He finished knocking the last of the pegs in, sat back on his haunches and looked across at Berry. 'How are you feeling, anyway?'

Berry lit the gas and it roared into life.

'Oh, you know,' she said. 'Bit tired. I'm all right though.' She poured the soup powder into a pan of water and balanced it on top of the little stove.

Ell threw the sleeping bags into the tent and zipped it up again before sitting next to Berry by the fire.

Berry stirred the soup and watched a shooting star trail silver across the sky.

'Did you see that?' asked Ell excitedly.

'Look,' said Berry, pointing towards the west. 'There's another one.'

For the next few minutes, they lay next to the fire

and watched a succession of shooting stars flare and sparkle above their heads before disappearing into the darkness.

'What makes them do that?' asked Ell.

'They're bits of dust and rock from space,' said Berry, remembering the project she had done about the solar system with her mother. 'When they enter the earth's atmosphere, they burn up and that makes the light that we see.'

'Are you sure?' asked Ell. 'They seem far too glamorous just to be dust and rocks.'

Berry turned to look at him as he lay on the hard ground with his hands behind his head, gazing up at the heavens.

'There's more to things than just what they're made of,' she said. 'Take the sun, for instance. It's made up of flaming gases, burning away in outer space. But that's not all it is.'

Ell turned his face to look at her by the light of the fire. 'No? What is it then?'

'Well, it's something that makes the plants grow. It's something that turns winter into spring and spring into summer.'

Berry closed her eyes and remembered. She thought of the days when she would wake early to find the light hard and clear. Days when she would dress quickly and walk alone by the old canal, watching the mist hang above the water and feeling her sadness mix with light and colour until her heart flew so high and fast that she felt fragile and empty, as if she were made of glass. Sometimes, in the silence of those sunlit mornings, it was hard to know where she stopped and the world began.

'But it's still just a ball of burning gas, isn't it?' said Ell.

'No,' replied Berry patiently. 'It's not just a ball of burning gas, any more than you're just a bagful of blood and bones.'

'But that *is* what I am,' said Ell. 'That's exactly what I am.'

'No, you're not,' said Berry, sitting up and stirring the soup again. 'That's what you're *made* of. It's not what you are.'

'OK,' said Ell. 'If I'm not a bag of blood and bones, then what am I?'

'I don't want to say,' said Berry quietly.

'Why not?' asked Ell.

'Because', she replied, 'you'll laugh at me. And I don't want to be laughed at. Not tonight.'

'I won't laugh,' said Ell. 'Why would I laugh?'

'Because you're unhappy,' replied Berry, 'and so you laugh at serious things. It stops you having to think about them.'

Ell stopped smiling then and Berry felt bad, as

though she had slapped him for no reason. But although part of her wanted to apologize and take it back, she didn't, because it was true.

'Is that so bad?' he asked. 'Does that make me a bad person?'

'No,' said Berry, banging the spoon on the side of the saucepan and laying it on a dry stone. 'It doesn't make you a bad person at all. Look, maybe I'm just doing it again, Ell. Maybe I just believe these things because I want them to be true. Maybe I should just stop talking.'

'No,' said Ell, propping himself up on one elbow. 'Go on. Tell me what you think.'

Berry looked at the distant mountains, silhouetted against the sky. 'I just hope that somewhere, mixed up with all that blood and muscle, is something else; something they would never find even if they cut the bag of bones right open and examined it with the most powerful microscope in the world.'

'Oh yeah. And what's that?'

'It's what makes you *you*, Ell. And what I'm trying to say is, you might be just a bag of blood and bones, but there isn't another bag like it in the whole universe. And the thing is . . .'

Berry's voice trailed off in the darkness.

'What is the thing, Berry?' asked Ell quietly.

Berry looked at him in the firelight and saw the vast

spaces surrounding them, the dust and sky and the empty road stretching away beneath the stars. She saw how, like her, Ell was alone in the middle of it all and suddenly she didn't want the world to be meaningless for him any more. She wanted to close the gap and show him that he mattered.

'If I could choose any bag of bones to travel across America with,' she said, 'then yours is the bag of bones I would choose.'

Ell scratched at the dust with the end of his mallet and Berry saw that he was embarrassed, and that he was pleased.

'Really?' he said. 'Do you mean it?'

'Yes,' said Berry. 'I do.'

'In that case,' said Ell quietly, 'will you promise me something?'

'What?' asked Berry.

'When all of this is over, just promise me we won't forget, OK? Promise that we'll remember how it feels to be living like this, on the outside of everything. That somehow we'll find a way of living right.'

He took her hand then, and as they huddled together beneath the stars she nodded and whispered, 'That's what we'll do, Ell, I promise. That's what we'll do.'

34
CLOSING THE NET

OVER THE YEARS, Kruger had found two excellent ways of making people do the things he wanted them to do. The first was with money. If you paid them enough, most people would do anything.

The second was through fear.

If you hurt them, or threatened their families, the effect was akin to some kind of dark magic: they would cower in the corner like whipped puppies, pathetic and anxious to please.

But the best discovery of all was that the two were actually linked in a neat circle of violence. You could use fear to create money, and once you had enough money you could pay people to create more fear and that would make you even more money.

And so on and so forth.

When Kruger had left school at fifteen, he had

dreamed of finding what his father had lost. Of becoming someone with the power to rebuild the Fatherland and hit back at the country which had never wanted him.

But with no money, no job and no prospects – the dream had seemed an impossible one. He soon discovered, however, that if you want something badly enough, you will often find a way.

And Kruger's way was violence.

It had started with some of the younger kids. He would smoke a cigarette at the bottom of the lane by the park, waiting for them on their way home from school. Whenever Kruger saw a boy on his own, he would watch him averting his eyes – looking anywhere but at Kruger – wait until he was nearly level with him and then step out and grab his shirt, pulling him in close. He would listen patiently to the squeals, the protests, watch the eyes wildly searching around for someone to help. Then he would knock him to the ground, kneel on his arms and pull out his hunting knife.

'You owe me money,' he would say, running the blade along the terrified boy's cheek. 'Lots of money.'

By the time the parents got wise to it, Kruger had fleeced seven kids of their pocket money and collected enough to buy himself a Smith & Wesson .45-calibre pistol from an ex-con who wasn't asking any questions.

But after cleaning out some tills in a few late-night

hold-ups, he decided that there had to be an easier way. It wasn't long before he found it.

Over the next few years Kruger built up a protection racket, paying a few muscle-men to put the frighteners on local store-owners while he sat back and creamed off a fat profit in return for a guarantee that they could carry on their businesses in peace. Naturally, in the early days, he had to break a few heads and burn down some premises, but it wasn't long before they got the message: it was easier to pay up than suffer the consequences.

The local gangs didn't like it, of course, but once in a while they got their heads blown off and they didn't like that either.

So everything had settled down just fine.

Once the money was flooding in, Kruger had turned his attention to creating the network of people who would help him achieve his dream. On his visits to several extremist neo-Nazi groups, he soon discovered that there was no shortage of angry, alienated people who were willing to listen to a man with money and a dream of power.

Now, forty years on, it was all coming together. He had everyone he needed and they had finally located the item that would unlock the door to unlimited power. Yet somehow – inexplicably – they had allowed a fourteen-year-old girl to steal it. He already had his people checking the main bus depots and hotels but, so far, nothing.

Then, suddenly, another possibility had occurred to him. Taking a deep breath he had calmed himself, reminding himself that emotion was strictly for the weak. There was, after all, a solution to every problem and he knew he would find the solution to this one.

But he was going to need some help.

Pulling the two-year-old hire car into the empty parking lot, Kruger turned off the motor and waited. He could have afforded any car he wanted, of course, but he had learned his lessons well: Don't draw attention to yourself, watch from the sidelines and bide your time.

He got out of the car, leaned against the door and checked his watch.

9.27. Three minutes and they'd be here.

Kruger knew these people had a fearsome reputation for violence. But he also knew that they weren't foolish enough to bite the hand that fed them. And if they did exactly as he asked, he would feed them like they'd never been fed before.

In the distance, he heard the rumble and growl of powerful four-stroke engines. Calm and unruffled, he lit a cigarette, drawing deeply as the tip glowed red hot in the darkness. Then, as a dozen motorcycles entered the parking lot and roared around him in a circle of smoke and noise, he calmly removed the cigarette from his mouth and studied the end of it, giving the impression that he had not even noticed the gang's arrival.

The man at the front of the pack kicked out the side-stand of his custom-chromed Harley and, as he walked slowly towards Kruger's car, Kruger noticed the skull and wing emblem of the Oakland Hells Angels on the leather waistcoat. He also saw that, below the closely shaved bullet head, the guy was two hundred pounds of hard muscle.

'Are you Kruger?'

Kruger flicked ash from his cigarette.

'*Mr* Kruger,' he corrected him. 'And who am I talking to?'

'The name's Jackson.'

'Well then, Mr Jackson. I take it you've spoken to Snyder?'

Snyder ran the Hells Angels Chapter in Albuquerque and Kruger had used his services for over twenty years. If Kruger wanted a place smashed up, Snyder and his boys were always his first port of call. Brutal maybe. But always effective.

'Yeah, I've spoken to him. Says you wanna make a donation to me and the boys.' Jackson laughed nastily. 'Is that right? You wanna make a donation?'

Kruger dropped his cigarette and squashed it with a twist of his shoe. Then he looked up and held the gang leader's gaze with a cold, unwavering stare. 'No,' he said. 'I don't want to make a donation. Shall I tell you what I want?'

Jackson stared back, but said nothing.

'I want you to save your smart-ass comments for your little babysitters here. And then I want you to tell me whether you want to do business or not. Because if you don't, then I'll find someone else who does.'

A couple of Hells Angels dismounted from their bikes and moved forward, squeezing their knuckles until they cracked. But Jackson held up his hand, signalling for them to stop.

'Let's say I do wanna do business,' he said. 'What exactly are you offering?'

'What I'm offering', said Kruger, 'is fifty thousand dollars in cash. Interested?'

Jackson nodded slowly and the corner of his mouth turned up in a half-smile.

'Sure,' he said. 'Who wouldn't be? But if we ain't talking about a donation, then what are we talking about?'

'All I want', said Kruger, unlocking the trunk of his car and removing a zipped brown holdall, 'is for you and your friends to take a little road trip.'

'A road trip?' Jackson was unable to hide his surprise. 'To where?'

'I want you to travel the main road – Route 10 – between here and southern New Mexico. Maybe put a few guys on 8, but that's it. All you need do is look out for any lone motorcycles. The one you're after will be ridden by a fourteen-year-old girl, black shoulder-length hair. Possibly with a sixteen-year-old boy riding pillion.'

'What do you want 'em for?'

'That', said Kruger, 'does not concern you.'

He dropped the holdall and slid it along in the dust with his toe.

'Twenty thousand dollars,' he said. 'Cash. Do we have a deal?'

Jackson frowned. 'You said fifty.'

Kruger took a piece of paper from his pocket and handed it to Jackson between two forefingers. 'I think we both know that twenty thousand dollars for riding around on a motorcycle is a more than generous offer. However. Should you find the girl, then call this number immediately. If it's her, you'll get the rest of the money.'

Kruger opened his car door and then turned back. 'By the way, you should probably know that I have friends watching the border in New Mexico. They would be extremely disappointed to discover you had taken the money without completing your journey.'

Jackson curled his lip. 'I hope you're not threatening me,' he said.

Kruger smiled.

'I'm sure you do,' he said.

As the red tail-lights of Kruger's car faded into the distance, Jackson spat into the dust, picked up the holdall and threw it to one of the other Angels.

'OK,' he said. 'Fill your tanks. Looks like we're going on a trip.'

35
Alone

Berry woke early and gathered the sleeping bag under her chin. She listened in silence, wondering nervously if there were any dangerous animals out here in the desert. She remembered once reading a true story about a hiker being attacked by mountain lions. This had taken her completely by surprise. She had always thought that lions were confined to Africa. The idea that they might share the same space as the White House and McDonald's made her realize what a huge, wild place America must be. She wondered what other secrets lay buried here, waiting for the light to reflect their strange truths back into the world.

Shivering, she curled herself up into a ball and thought of the winter mornings when, as a little girl, she would wake early and creep across the floor of the old bus to her mother's bed. She would slip beneath the blankets and huddle against the warm slab of her mother's back, listening to the slow rise and fall of her breathing. Most nights her mother would stay asleep until morning and Berry would drift in and out of dreams until the winter sun sparkled through frosted windows. Then, throwing on a thick jumper, her mother would clatter about, making tea and talking about the day ahead of them. But sometimes, very occasionally, she would wake and whisper softly, 'What's the matter, my precious? Can't you sleep?' And Berry would lie in the cradle of her arms, imagining herself a jewel, polished and flawless, shining at the centre of the turning world.

Dawn was breaking.

The darkness was less solid now. Berry saw how objects began to shrug off their shadows, revealing their shapes once more. Above her, the smooth cylinder of the ridge pole split the dark canvas sky in two and ripe droplets of condensation hung like tiny, translucent pears, poised to rain their harvest down upon the stitched green fields of her sleeping bag. She watched her breath form mist clouds in the half-light and listened for the sound of Ell's breathing. But all she could hear was a gentle breeze flapping the fly sheet on the outside of the tent.

She held her breath and listened harder.

Nothing.

Strange, she thought.

Twisting around, she propped herself up on one elbow and stared at Ell's flat, empty sleeping bag. Unwilling at first to believe what her eyes were telling her, she shifted her gaze and scanned the inside of the tent, hoping perhaps to find him huddled in some dark corner. But it was a very small tent and there was no sign of him.

'Ell?' she called, quietly at first, then louder. 'Ell!'

Kicking off her sleeping bag, Berry pulled on her jacket and unzipped the tent. As the first rays of sunshine crept over the distant mountains, she looked desperately around and saw what she already knew; that she was surrounded on all sides by flat, featureless desert and that she was completely and utterly alone. Watching the morning sun light up the landscape she felt detached, like a spectator, watching the day unfold from some distant planet. Above her, the shrill cry of a buzzard scratched a warning across the early-morning sky.

As she stared at the vast space surrounding her, Berry suddenly remembered. Pulling up her sleeve, she ran her hand across her wrist and it was only then that she realized the truth; that not only had Ell left her, but that he had also taken the bracelet.

36
ELL'S TEMPTATION

HE HAD NEVER INTENDED TO TAKE IT. He had simply been
curious. He had dreamed of walking through ice caves, sliding
down bright tunnels and hearing his footsteps ring like iron as
they whirled and shattered into music of starlight and stones.
'Help me,' he had pleaded and as his eyes opened in the darkness he had seen the bracelet glowing on Berry's wrist in front
of him. The colours had fascinated him, drawn him into the
music with invisible fingers that hooked themselves into his
mind and sent his hands fluttering noiselessly through the
gloom to alight upon the golden bracelet. But Berry had
stirred, uttering strange sounds that came frothing up from the
depths of sleep to bubble and burst upon the surface of her con-
sciousness. Ell had frozen then, poised on the threshold as his
heart cried out for the light. But the prize was too precious to
be lost through haste and he had waited in the darkness until
Berry returned to sleep. Then, as his hands leapt the gap and

slid the bracelet from her arm, she had sighed, a soft whisper of regret.

But she had not woken.

With trembling fingers, Ell had taken the bracelet and, pausing only to relish the delicious moments between wanting and possessing, he had slipped his fingers through the golden band and pushed it on to his wrist.

Instantly, the music had become liquid, rushing up his arm and pouring its notes into his veins, coating his skin and hardening all around him like mud baking in the midday sun. He had gasped, staring at the bracelet, which seemed now to be a living thing, touching his innermost thoughts and desires. His eyes had been drawn to the coloured lights that shone so brightly on his wrist and he moved his fingers towards them with a mixture of fear and excitement, feeling like a child reaching out for forbidden sweets. His fingers caressed the light that glowed — purple as plums beneath a stormy sky — and then the world shimmered and called to him and he walked out into the darkness, breathless with wonder at the patterns that twisted and shone beyond the borders of his imagination.

Berry knew that there was no point in staying here any longer. Ell was gone and the sun was already climbing above the horizon. Its pleasant warmth would soon become unbearable, sending the air temperature soaring above 120 degrees. She would need to get the bike moving into a cooling wind until she could find the next town with some shade and an icebox.

Still reeling from Ell's sudden disappearance, she pulled back the tent flap, dropped to her knees and began rolling up her sleeping bag. Her mind swarmed with questions, buzzing and humming like flies at a window.

Where was Ell? Had he taken the bracelet? If so, why? If not, had someone else taken it?

This last question frightened Berry the most. She had already experienced enough of the bracelet's power to appreciate how destructive it could be in the wrong hands. Like everything else in the world, it could be used to make things better or worse, to save or destroy. And the few terrifying seconds she had spent looking into the blond man's eyes had told her all she needed to know about his intentions. From that moment on she had promised herself that, while she still had breath in her body, she would never let him get his hands on it. But what if he had come and taken the bracelet while she slept? And what if Ell had tried to stop him . . . ?

There were no answers, Berry realized. Just the sound of her breathing and the beating of her heart. As she knelt on the rolled-up sleeping bag and pulled the nylon cover over the end, she began to understand what Ell had meant. The world was not, after all, the neat, ordered place she had once believed it to be. It was not a place where if you multiplied x by y then you always got z. Sometimes you got music. Sometimes you got two people on a motorbike riding across America, searching for an answer to a question they did not understand.

And sometimes . . . sometimes you got nothing at all.

Just empty skies and the wind caressing a billion faces; faces that allowed the earth to look upon itself in new ways for a while, until at last it grew tired of them, and returned them to dust.

Ell wandered across the dry ground as if in a dream, listening to the sweet music that sung through his mind. As he walked further he saw the shapes and patterns of the earth and the trees, and the sky and the stars, and he saw that they were also the shapes and patterns of his heart.

Berry pulled the cord tight on the sleeping-bag case and threw it out of the tent. She picked up the bike keys and then pulled on her boots, tucking her trousers into the tops to prevent them from flapping about once she was on the road. The temperature in the tent was already becoming unbearable and she knew that she really should be on her way. But, for the first time since she had arrived in America, she had lost all sense of purpose. While her mind had been focused on taking the bracelet to New Mexico, there had been little time to think about anything else. Caught up in the danger and excitement of the situation, she had given little thought to life beyond it. But now there seemed no reason to carry on. Without Ell, without the bracelet, her life no longer had any direction.

What would she do now? Where would she go?

She looked at Ell's empty sleeping bag and felt a pang of loss as she caught sight of the small square of paper folded neatly on the floor beside it. He had left so quickly, he hadn't even had time to take his bag of sherbet. But the world had surprised her so often in the last few days that she was already becoming immune to its twists and turns. She was starting to accept the fact that her life could no longer be explained. In some ways, this made everything easier; she was able to adapt more quickly to things that a few weeks ago she would have thought impossible.

But none of this altered the fact that her only friend in the world had left her alone in the middle of the desert. She was afraid for him and she was afraid for herself. But there was another fear, too — a fear that if she had lost the bracelet then the whole world would suffer the consequences.

She couldn't go back. Not now.

She must keep on moving, keep going forward into whatever future was left for her. Perhaps she would find an answer; or perhaps, more likely, there were no answers to be found. But she would keep going anyway – not looking back – and perhaps, one day, she would understand what it was that she was searching for.

She turned and picked up the corner of Ell's sleeping bag, ready to fold it away for the last time.

And that was when she heard him.

37
Patterns

ELL HAD WALKED BACK to the tent in a daze and now, as he watched Berry rolling up his sleeping bag, he couldn't understand why she seemed to be in such a hurry.

'What are you doing?' he asked. 'Why are you packing all my stuff away?'

Berry turned and stared at him, but her eyes were distant, as though she was focusing on something a long way off. She seemed troubled, puzzled almost. Was she annoyed with him for wandering off, he wondered? He hadn't gone far. Surely she could easily have seen him from the tent.

'What is it?' he asked. 'Why are you staring at me like that?'

Berry didn't say anything. She just kept right on staring. Then, after a few moments, she stood up and looked around.

'Ell?' she said uncertainly. 'Ell? Is that you?'

Berry could hear his voice. She could definitely hear his voice. But where was he?

Something wasn't right. She was starting to scare him now.

'What do you mean?' he asked. 'Of course it's me.'

He reached out and touched her arm.

Then, as she screamed and pulled away from him as if she had been burned, he stepped backwards in shock. Watching her hold her arm and stare past him in bewilderment, he was suddenly afraid.

'What's the matter?' he asked. 'What's the matter with you?'

But Berry just shook her head and whispered, 'There's nothing the matter with me, Ell. It's you. I can't see you. You've disappeared.'

At first he hadn't believed her, but as she watched little puffs of dust scuff up all the way to the bike and then heard the sudden cry as he looked in the mirror, she knew that he realized the truth.

'Help me!' he pleaded, sounding like a small, lost child. 'Please, Berry. Find me. Find me!'

'Shush, Ell,' said Berry reassuringly. 'Don't worry. It'll be all right. I'll work it out.'

She ran her fingers anxiously through her hair and began to think. It was almost certainly something to do with the bracelet. Could it be that Ell had taken the bracelet and pressed one of the colours? Could they be like some kind of switch?

'Ell,' she asked. 'Do you have the bracelet?'

'Yes,' replied Ell, sounding a little ashamed. 'What should I do?'

'Press it again,' said Berry. 'Whatever colour it was you pressed, press it again!'

A moment later Ell was standing in front of her, looking pale and extremely frightened.

'Can you see me now?' he asked.

'Yes,' said Berry. 'I can see you.'

Ell stared, transfixed, at the bracelet on his wrist, and Berry held out her hand.

'Give me the bracelet, Ell,' she said gently. 'Give it to me now.'

'What?' Ell glanced up at her, confused.

'Give me the bracelet,' Berry repeated.

Slowly, Ell looked back at his wrist.

'Oh no,' he said, realizing the truth. 'No, no, no.'

'It's all right Ell,' said Berry. 'It's perfectly safe. Nothing else is going to happen to you as long as you give me the bracelet.'

Slowly, tentatively, like someone in the last delicate stages of defusing a bomb, Ell moved his hand towards the bracelet.

'Hold it by the sides,' Ell warned him.

'I can't,' replied Ell, losing his nerve and turning his head away as if half expecting it to explode. 'I don't want to touch it.'

'All right,' said Berry calmly. She could see that he was terrified. 'Just hold out your arm.'

Ell stretched his arm towards Berry and as she pulled the bracelet from his wrist he cried out softly, as if in pain. Berry quickly slipped the bracelet on to her own wrist and felt the familiar surge of power sparkle up her arm, wrapping itself around her like a blanket.

'Ohhh,' she sighed, feeling that, somehow, some kind of order had been restored.

'You were telling the truth,' whispered Ell, staring in wonder at the bracelet as it glowed on Ell's wrist. 'My God. You were telling the *truth*!'

Berry nodded. 'Yes,' she said. She watched Ell sink to the ground and wrap his arms around his legs, resting his chin on his knees. His eyes had a frightened look and she saw that he was shaking. 'What's the matter?' she asked. 'It can't hurt you now, Ell.'

'It's not that,' said Ell.

'What is it then?' asked Berry.

'You remember what I was saying earlier? About how, when my mum left, all the magic went with her?'

'Yes. Of course I remember.'

'Well I'd learned to deal with it. And now, all of a sudden, I've discovered that there is magic in the world — scary, frightening magic — and it just knocks everything sideways.'

'How come?'

'Well, because – because yesterday it was just me playing along with some crazy idea that you had.'

'You thought I was crazy?'

'Yeah, in a way. Why wouldn't I? I mean, yeah, I saw what happened at Glastonbury and I believed those people wanted the package. But all that talk about falling out of buildings and being shot at. Like I said yesterday, I thought you were just trying to invent something to believe in. But, hey, don't get me wrong, Berry. I was glad to be playing the game. Really glad. It made no less sense than the rest of my life up until that point. It was fun and it was exciting. Suddenly my life was full of the colours I had dreamed of as a kid.'

'So what's changed?'

'Before I put on the bracelet, I thought I had life sussed. You're born, you die, and you just do whatever you can to enjoy the bit in between. In the end, nothing really matters. But when I was wearing the bracelet, I felt things, saw patterns that I didn't understand. But there were patterns, Berry. There were *patterns*. And I realized two things. Firstly, that everything is far more complicated than I thought. And secondly . . .'

For a long time, Ell just stared at the bracelet, as if trying to search for the words that eluded him. Finally, when he looked up, Berry saw that beyond the fear in his eyes, something burned brighter and stronger than before.

'What was secondly?' she asked.

'That things matter,' said Ell. 'That everything matters. Which makes life much, much harder than I thought.'

'That's what scares you?' asked Berry.

'Yes,' said Ell. 'And it makes me feel that everything I've done with my life so far has been a complete waste of time.'

'It brought you here though, didn't it?' Berry reminded him. 'I'd say you've lived your life exactly as it should have been lived. It brought us together at exactly the right moment. And that matters. It matters a lot.'

'Why?' asked Ell.

'Because', said Berry, '*we* matter.' And with that, she kissed him lightly on the cheek, grabbed him by the hand and pulled him to his feet.

'Well, if that's true,' said Ell, moving away a little, 'then there's probably something else you should know.'

'What?' asked Berry.

'I wanted to tell you back at the hotel,' said Ell, 'when we were having that argument. But in the end I couldn't. You hated me too much already.'

'I didn't hate you, Ell,' said Berry in surprise. 'I was

annoyed, but I didn't hate you. Why on earth would you think that?'

Ell shrugged. 'Everybody does in the end. I never dressed the right way, never fitted anyone's idea of who they thought I should be. But the thing that saved me, the thing that stopped me from going under, was thinking, well, at least I'm true to myself. At least I'm a good person. But then I did something that made me realize I was just like the rest of them. That I wasn't a good person at all.'

Berry saw that Ell seemed diminished by his words, as if speaking them had sapped all his energy away.

'What did you do, Ell?' she asked.

And as Ell lifted his gaze from the dry, stony ground and looked into Berry's eyes she saw that, in spite of all the years of hurt and neglect at the hands of others, the only person he really hated was himself.

'I stole the last of my dad's savings,' he said. 'Three hundred pounds from a washbag under his bed.'

'Why?' asked Berry, shocked. 'Why would you do that?'

'Because it bought me a train fare and I thought my freedom. But what I didn't realize is, when I took it, I also took away the only part of me that was still worth something.'

'That's not true,' said Berry, shaking her head. 'That's not true at all.'

'Yes, it is,' replied Ell. 'When you talked about doing the right thing, you made me feel that there was something precious out there, something worth doing for its own sake. But I can't get past what I did, Berry. It keeps coming back to me and all I can think is, how can I do the right thing when it was a wrong thing that got me here in the first place?'

'Things don't have to stay wrong for ever,' said Berry. She walked across to the bike, unbuckled one of the panniers and reached inside. 'How much did you say it was?'

'What?'

'How much did you steal from your dad? Three hundred pounds?'

'Yes, but —'

'OK then.' Berry took out a wad of money and began counting it on to the seat.

'One hundred, two hundred, two hundred and fifty . . .'

'What are you doing?'

' . . . three hundred, four hundred, four hundred and fifty, five hundred . . .'

'Berry —'

' . . . six hundred. There.' Berry slapped her hand on top of the small pile of dollar bills, folded the rest up and replaced it in the panniers. 'Six hundred dollars should cover it.'

'Look,' said Ell. 'I know what you're doing, but I can't take it. That's your money.'

'No,' said Berry. 'It's Joseph's money.'

'But he gave it to you. So that makes it your money.'

'Well then, now I'm giving it to you,' said Berry, scooping it off the seat and holding it out to Ell. 'So that makes it your money, doesn't it?'

'I told you,' said Ell. 'I didn't come with you for the money.'

'I *know* that,' said Berry. 'And it's *because* I know it that I'm happy to give it to you.'

'I don't want it,' said Ell.

'All right,' said Berry. 'Fine.'

She reached back inside the panniers and took out a box of matches.

'My money, right?'

'Right.'

'Right.'

Berry held up a fifty-dollar bill and struck a match.

Ell frowned. 'Berry,' he said. 'What are you doing?'

'What do you care?' replied Berry. 'It's not your money.'

'You *wouldn't*,' said Ell.

'Watch me,' said Berry. She held the match to the corner of the bill until it caught and then, as an orange flame licked up through the centre of the paper, she dropped it on to the ground where it flared into a grey rectangle of ash. Then she peeled off another fifty and prepared to light another match.

'Stop!' shouted Ell. 'Don't be stupid!'

'Then let me in, OK?' said Berry angrily as the match flared. Tossing it away, she flung the rest of the money into the dirt and stomped across to the bike. 'I don't understand it. You've come halfway across the world with me and yet, somehow, you still seem to think you have to walk through it alone. But it's not true, Ell. You don't. Not any more. Not unless you want to.'

She shut her eyes and felt the sun's heat burning the back of her neck. Suddenly she just wanted to be somewhere cool and dark, out of the heat, away from everything.

'I never met anyone like you,' said Ell quietly. 'Never.'

'Well, snap,' said Berry. She folded her arms and leaned back against the warm leather saddle. She looked at the blue sky reflected in the chrome fuel cap, breathed in the smell of dust and petrol and listened to the silence. Then, from the corner of her eye, she saw Ell bend down and start to pick up the money.

'Well, now,' he said. 'Look what I found. Reckon I could use some of this. Unless . . .'

Berry turned to look at him.

'Unless what?' she asked.

Ell smiled shyly.

'Unless you want to start any more fires,' he said.

Berry watched him stuff the money into his pocket and felt that, somewhere, a gap was closing.

'In this heat?' she said. 'You have got to be kidding.'

38
RICKY'S BAR & GRILL

AFTER STOPPING AT THE border town of Blythe, where
Ell bought some stamps and posted off the money,
they spent another night camping under cold, clear
skies. The following day they crossed the plains of Arizona, its flat expanse of rock and scrubland shimmering in the endless heat.

As the bike tyres hummed along the grey, dusty
road, Berry watched the warm summer wind blow
tumbleweed across the dry ground and saw the
bleached, white bones of cattle long dead, lying like
strange sculptures in the ditches where they had fallen.
She thought then about the strangeness of everything,
of all the magical things she had seen and it was as
though she had lifted a corner of the world's surface
and, just for a moment, caught a glimpse of something
hidden beyond all imagination. And, as she thought

these things, she began to wonder if, in fact, she had been hit by the bus after all. The life she lived now was so unlike her life before the accident. Could everything that had happened since be some strange new reality, a place through which her spirit wandered, not knowing that its old life was at an end?

But as she caught the sweet aroma of silver-leaved shrubs that dotted the prairie, saw how they burst through the dry ground like tiny miracles to spill their oily perfume upon the warm air, her heart sang and she felt certain that now, in this moment, she was warm and alive and nothing that happened before or afterwards could take that away from her.

At first they appeared as no more than a dot in her rear-view mirrors, but after a while the dot formed itself into two motorcycles, chrome shining silver on the road behind them. As they drew level, Berry just had time to register beards, sunglasses and cut-off leather jackets before they cut in front of her, pointed to a building up ahead and signalled for her to pull off the road.

As she killed the engine and kicked out the side-stand next to half a dozen other bikes that stood gleaming in the sunshine, the man who had signalled to her walked across and smiled.

'Hope I didn't scare ya too much back there,' he

said. 'But when we get visitin' bikers down our way, we like to show 'em a little hospitality.'

As he pointed up at the flaking sign that said: '*Ricky's Bar & Grill*', Berry felt relieved. She remembered hearing that there was a kind of fraternity between fellow motorcyclists and guessed these guys just wanted to buy them a drink or something. She could tell from the sound of Country-and-Western music and the smell of stale beer leaking beneath the heavy oak door that it wasn't exactly a high-class establishment. But they had been travelling all day and she was hungry and thirsty. They wouldn't be crossing the state line into New Mexico for a couple of hours and there wouldn't be too much else in between.

'Are you sure about this?' whispered Ell.

'It'll be fine,' Berry replied as the two men pushed open the door. 'We'll get something to eat, have a quiet drink with them, then move on.'

But as they walked into the smoky bar, Berry knew it was the wrong decision. There was something about the way the atmosphere changed, the way the group of men around the pool table stared at them, that told her they should have just kept right on going.

She had become used to the strange looks at gas stations whenever they stopped to fill up. After she'd spoken to the pump attendants she could always see them thinking, *Is it me, or was that girl too young to be driving a big motorbike?* She had taken to keeping her helmet on, watching in her rear-view mirror as they stared after her, trying to figure it out.

But this felt different. This felt like trouble. In the five seconds or so that it took her to reach the bar, Berry's mind had taken in the whole scene: the juke-box in the corner, dark wood panelling on the walls, sawdust on the floor and a red-and-white Confederate flag tacked on to the ceiling. There was even a stuffed deer head on the wall, looking vaguely surprised at finding itself in Ricky's place instead of the forest.

The two men left them and joined the others by the pool table; all late twenties, dressed in jeans, leather jackets and frayed denim cut-offs. Berry knew then that the hospitality they had in mind was not of the drinks variety.

'Look what we found,' said the one who had spoken to Berry. They all wore dark sunglasses except for the biggest guy, the bald guy with the skull and wing emblem of the Oakland Hells Angels on his jacket. His sunglasses were mirrored, and Berry caught sight of her own reflection as she walked past him.

'Looking good,' she heard him say. 'But first we got some other business to attend to.'

'Hi,' said Berry to the bartender, trying not to show that she was afraid. He continued to polish a glass with a towel and she leaned against the counter. 'Do you think we could get a drink and something to eat?'

The bartender stopped his polishing and regarded her suspiciously.

'Got any ID?'

'ID?' asked Berry, puzzled. 'What for?'

'Can't sell alcohol to minors,' replied the bartender. 'That'd be against the law.'

'But I don't want alcohol,' Berry explained politely. 'I just want two orange juices and something to eat. Is that OK?'

'I guess.' As the bartender pushed a couple of menus at her, Berry saw that gas-station look again and noticed him glance nervously across at the men by the pool table. He seemed unnerved by them, as if he too sensed trouble in the air. He poured two tall glasses of orange juice and set them on the counter, ice clinking against the sides.

'That'll be four dollars, please,' he said.

Berry watched Ell take out a thick wad of dollar bills and pull out a five.

'There you go,' he said. 'And could I have a couple of bars of chocolate as well, please?'

'Jeez,' hissed the bartender as one leatherjacket nudged another and pointed in Ell's direction. 'I wouldn't wave that around if I were you.'

'Sorry,' said Ell and as Berry watched him smile

apologetically she realized that, for all his troubled life, there was an innocence about him that she hadn't fully appreciated until now.

'Can you tell me where the loos are?' Ell asked. 'I'm busting.'

'The *what* now?'

'The loos.'

'I think he means the bathroom,' Berry explained helpfully.

'No, I don't,' said Ell indignantly. 'Why would I want the b—'

'He does,' Berry assured the bartender. She turned to Ell. 'That's what they *call* them, Ell.'

'Men's bathroom's through that door on the left,' said the bartender, pointing to a door at the end of the bar beyond the pool table. 'But watch yourself buddy, OK?'

'Let me come with you,' said Berry.

'Now you're just being weird,' said Ell. 'Or should I say weird*er*.'

'Ell, I mean it,' said Berry quietly, putting a hand on his arm.

'Berry,' said Ell, misunderstanding her meaning. 'I haven't got the bracelet any more, remember? So relax. Drink. Order food. Have a dance if you like. I'll be back in two ticks.'

As Berry carried the drinks to a table in the corner, she saw the men turn their heads and follow Ell's progress across the room. Then the hard-muscled man with the mirrored shades picked up a snooker cue and walked towards the bar, bringing two other men with him.

'I'd like a round of beers,' he said to the bartender, 'if that's all right with you.'

Berry saw that the bartender was worried, but he was no pushover.

'That's fine,' he said, 'but you need to pay for the other drinks first.'

The big man remained impassive behind his mirrored shades.

'Other drinks?' he asked.

The bartender swallowed nervously but held his ground. He nodded towards the glass that the man was holding.

'Yes,' he said. 'The drinks you had out of those glasses. Remember?'

The man held up the glass in front of his face and stared at it for a few moments, as if seeing it for the very first time. He looked back at the bartender and smiled.

'No,' he said. 'Can't say I do.'

Then he opened his hand and the glass shattered into a thousand pieces on the hard stone floor.

The barman's face was white now.

'Look, buddy,' he said. 'I don't want any trouble. Why don't you just give me the money for the drinks and hit the road?'

'Well, I'd like to,' replied the man, 'I really would. But, you see, there's some business I really need to discuss with you.'

'Business?' asked the bartender. 'What kind of business?'

'Well, you know, it's kind of a coincidence when you think about it,' said the man. 'I mean, there's you saying that you don't want any trouble, and here's me wanting to make sure you don't get any.'

'I'm not sure I understand what you're saying,' said the bartender.

'It's very simple,' said the man. 'I'm saying that, for a very reasonable rate, me and my *associates* can provide you with complete protection and peace of mind. We can make sure that you and your establishment remain trouble free at all times.'

'But I don't need protection,' replied the bartender. 'I've been here nearly twenty years and I've never had any trouble.'

'Well, that's good,' said the man. 'I'm glad to hear it. But, you know, the world can be a very dangerous place.'

'That's as maybe,' replied the bartender. 'But I guess I'll just have to take my chances.'

'Fair enough,' said the man. 'But don't say I didn't warn you.' He nodded and as Berry watched in horror, the other two men took up their snooker cues, leapt over the bar and began systematically smashing up the rows of drinks bottles lined up at the back. The terrified bartender threw his arms over his head and, as the glass shattered and flew in all directions, the man in the mirrored shades picked up a heavy wooden table and brought it crashing down into the jukebox. Berry saw the top crystallize like sugar before disintegrating in a crackle of sparks and broken records.

Then, as suddenly as the violence had started, it stopped again. The silence that followed was almost as shocking, punctuated only by the dripping bottles and the crunch of the man's boots as he walked back towards the bar across a glittering carpet of broken glass.

The bartender, who had been cowering in a corner, slowly uncovered his face and stared around at the damage, unable to quite believe what he was seeing.

'Why are you doing this?' he asked in a voice that was shaken and cracked with emotion.

'It's nothing personal,' said the man. 'As I said, we're here to help. I think you'll find our rates are very competitive.'

'How much?' asked the bartender nervously.

'Five hundred a month,' said the man. 'Cash.'

'Five hundred?' exclaimed the bartender. 'But that's nearly all my profit!'

'I know,' said the man, sounding almost sympathetic. 'Times are hard. But I guess we all have to make sacrifices one way or another.'

Berry — who had looked on in horrified fascination as the violence erupted — suddenly remembered Ell. She turned just in time to see the two other men emerging from the toilets. They were smiling and one of them was rubbing his knuckles.

'Oh no,' she whispered. '*Ell.*'

39
Slow Motion

THE DOOR BEHIND the two men swung open to reveal Ell standing in the doorway, a scrunched-up tissue pressed against his nose. His shirt was ripped and covered in blood. Even from where she was sitting, Berry could see that he was trembling.

'Give it back!' Ell demanded, his voice shaking with rage. 'Give me my money back!' As he moved slowly and purposefully across the room towards the two men, Berry saw one of them reach for a snooker cue.

'You see?' smiled the man in the mirrored shades. 'Looks like you've got a troublemaker in here already.' Worried for Ell's safety, Berry jumped out of her seat and stood between him and the man with the snooker cue.

'Get out of the way, Berry,' said Ell. 'I'm going to get my money back.'

'Well now,' said the man, tapping the snooker cue against the palm of his hand and running his tongue across his top lip. 'Seems like Kruger's girlies are looking for some action. Maybe we'll have ourselves a little fun before we call him.'

'Hate to say it, Jed,' chuckled the other man, pointing at Ell. 'But yours is looking pretty rough, wouldn't y'say?'

'Not as rough as she's gonna look,' said Jed. 'Come on then, ladies. Let's see what you've got.'

'It's all right,' said Berry, struggling to keep the emotion out of her voice. 'We were just leaving. Weren't we, Ell?'

But Ell, it seemed, had other ideas. 'Give me my money back!' he screamed, and before Berry knew what was happening he had pushed past her and launched himself at Jed.

At first, Jed seemed taken aback by the speed with which Ell hit him and he took a couple of paces backwards. But Ell was no fighter and Jed knew it. As Ell pummelled at his chest, he lifted a thick, powerful arm and swatted him sideways into a table, scattering the chairs like skittles as Ell crashed heavily to the floor.

'I'm gonna teach you a lesson, boy,' he said, lifting his snooker cue. 'There ain't no one takes a swing at Jed McClaverty and gets away with it.'

'Go on, Jed,' sneered the other man. 'Let him have it.'

The fear that Berry had felt up until that point had left her shaking; it had been as much as she could do to walk across the bar and step in front of Ell. But now that he was in real danger she found her eyes drawn once more towards her wrist. And when she saw that the green light was glowing more brightly than before, she placed the ball of her thumb on it and pressed, lightly at first, then harder until she felt the fear move, shifting and changing into something that seethed and boiled like hot lava.

'Don't touch him,' she said, stepping forward. 'Leave him alone.'

Jed turned to face her and when he smiled she could see his yellow, tobacco-stained teeth.

'Excuse me?' he asked. 'Did you say something?'

'You heard me,' said Berry, her voice clear and confident. 'Leave him alone.'

The man's smile grew wider. 'Or what?' He put on a mock-frightened face and said in a baby voice, 'You'll hit me with your make-up bag?'

'Come on, Ell,' said Berry firmly. 'Let's go.'

'Oh, he ain't going nowhere,' said Jed, nodding at his friend who stepped forward and seized Berry roughly by the arms. 'Now how about you shut your mouth while I deal with your little girlfriend?'

As Jed turned back to face Ell and lifted up his snooker cue, Berry felt the power surge so strongly through her veins that it made her gasp out loud.

'What's the matter?' sneered the man holding her arms. 'Scared or sumpen?'

'No,' said Berry. 'Not any more.' And with that she reached back, grabbed him by the front of his jacket and flipped him so hard over her head that he couldn't think what was happening until his face slammed into the green baize of the pool table. At which point, he could no longer think at all.

'What the — ?' exclaimed Jed, spinning around as the coloured balls bounced and clattered to the floor.

'Give me the cue, Jed,' said Berry calmly, holding out her hand. 'Give it to me now.'

'Sure,' said Jed, pulling his arm back. 'I'll give it to you all right.' As he swung it with all his strength towards the side of her head there was a swoosh of air and then time crackled and froze.

Berry flicked her eyes sideways and wondered why the world had stopped moving. Then she realized that it *was* moving, but incredibly slowly. As the snooker cue crept through the air towards her, she glanced across at the bar and saw that the man in the mirrored shades and his two buddies were heading in her direction, but the air seemed to hold them like insects in treacle and their movements were heavy and slow.

Berry considered her options. Ell was staring open-mouthed at the guy on the snooker table, but Berry knew that he was safely out of action for the moment.

She decided to deal with Jed first and think about the others afterwards.

Decision made, she held up her left hand and suddenly the world shrieked back into action. As the snooker cue smacked into the palm of her hand she grabbed it and pulled so hard that Jed flew towards her as though he had been shot from a cannon. Thrusting her right arm forward, Berry halted his progress with the heel of her palm and, with a yelp of surprise, he thumped to the floor and lay still.

Berry breathed deeply and felt as though she was performing some strange, ritualistic dance in which every step, every movement was already written into her bones. Everything was easy and natural, and as the two men rushed forward and raised their snooker cues above their heads she stepped quickly between them, holding her arms at exactly the right angle so that their blows deflected into one another, leaving them groaning on the floor next to the splintered table and the broken glass.

Berry felt almost sorry for the man with the mirrored shades as he ran towards her with a bellow of rage, his heavy muscular bulk intent on steamrollering her into the wall. She could tell he was used to winning and getting his own way, used to breaking people into pieces and taking whatever he wanted from them.

But not this time.

This time he was way out of his league.

Berry watched him run, waited until he was nearly upon her. Then, transferring her weight slightly on to her back foot, she caught him by the front of his jacket and spun herself around like a hammer thrower, swinging him faster and faster until finally she released him with such force that he smashed clean through the window and bounced across the parking lot, rolling into a pile of trash cans with a loud crash.

Berry glanced left and right to check for further threats. Satisfied that there were none, she stepped carefully over one of the men, retrieved the money and held out her hand to Ell.

'OK?' she asked calmly, as though she had just returned from paying the bill. 'Ready to go?'

The bartender, who had been watching all this from behind the bar, now stared at Berry as she helped Ell to his feet and asked, 'How the hell d'you do that?'

Berry smiled sweetly. 'I've been working out,' she said. Then, as the bartender picked up the phone, she asked, 'Are you calling the police?'

The bartender nodded nervously. 'Yeah. Is that OK with you?'

'Would you mind just giving it a minute or two?' Berry asked. 'It's just, I'd rather not get involved – if it's all the same to you.'

The man stared at her for a few moments and Berry

could see that he was trying to find some category to fit her into, looking for an explanation that might make some sense of the whole thing. But he couldn't do it, and in the end he just said, 'OK. Sure. Whatever.'

'Thanks,' said Berry. 'I appreciate it.'

As they walked out into the hot sunshine, Ell put the money back in his top pocket and asked, 'Was it the bracelet?'

'Uh-huh,' said Berry.

Ell seemed worried. 'You look as though you enjoyed that,' he said. 'Am I right?'

And when Berry smiled and said, 'No', they both knew she didn't mean it. For a while she had felt like the most powerful person in the whole world and it was addictive and exciting. So much so, in fact, that when the big man suddenly came staggering out of the trash cans and pointed a sawn-off shotgun at her, she didn't hesitate to step forward — cool and detached — and push a finger down each barrel. But as the gun blew apart in his hands and he ran down the road hollering like a baby, the noise of the explosion seemed to do something to her. She stared at the powder burns on her jacket, at the smoking remains of the shotgun and rubbed her eyes as if she had just woken from a dream.

'What's happening to me, Ell?' she whispered. 'What have I done?'

'Nothing that can't be mended,' said Ell, looking nervously over his shoulder before taking her firmly by the arm. 'But let's go before that changes, eh?'

Berry allowed herself to be steered gently towards the bike. The ease and ferocity of the violence she had unleashed only served to strengthen her determination that the bracelet should not fall into the wrong hands. But at the same time she felt as though she had trampled upon something that could not be mended. Her mother had once told her that the way for the world to solve its problems was not through violence, but through love. Now she felt lost, as though a gate had been closed and locked behind her for ever. Without a word, she fired up the motor and soon Ricky's Bar & Grill was just a small black speck in her rearview mirror.

By the time they passed the sign that said 'Welcome to New Mexico' a few hours later, Berry's mood had lightened a little. She had made a silent promise that she would never again use the bracelet to hurt anyone and the very act of doing so had lifted her spirits. The road was fairly quiet with only a few cars and the occasional long-haul tanker, but the bike's powerful acceleration meant Berry was able to make short work of overtaking, clicking the gear lever down and revving the engine so that they flew past other vehicles in a matter of seconds. Berry soon found herself settling back into the rhythm of the motor, content to hum along at speeds of sixty or seventy until a car appeared on the horizon. Then she would hunt it down, twisting the throttle until the exhausts howled before scorching past and flipping back on to the right side of the road again, a clear highway stretching away between fields of ripening corn.

As they followed the main Interstate through the town of Lordsburg, Berry spotted an old red-and-white bus at the side of the road, with a sign saying '*Taco Locos*' on the roof. Outside were a couple of brightly painted red tables and Berry realized that it was a roadside café.

'Couldn't resist,' she explained to Ell as they parked up and she led the way to the counter. 'Anyone selling hot food *and* living in an old bus gets my business any day of the week.'

She ordered two breakfast burritos and for $3 each the woman gave them warm, floury tortilla wraps filled with bacon, egg and hash brown potatoes shot through with a spicy flavour of salsa.

'I have got to say', Ell mumbled through a mouthful of burrito, 'that your choice of restaurant has certainly improved. These are *fabulous!*' He wiped his mouth and looked up at the sign which said: 'OPEN 7 am–9 pm 7 Days a week'.

'You must really love your job,' he said to the woman as she wiped down the counter. 'Have you been here long?'

The woman shook her head. 'Not long enough, I'm afraid. They sold the land here a couple of weeks ago and I've been told I gotta move on.'

'I'm sorry,' said Berry. 'Where will you go?'

'Oh, don't worry about me, honey,' said the woman. 'I'll just go wherever the road takes me. Things have always worked out so far. How about you? Where are you headed?'

'Same place as you, by the sound of it,' said Ell.

Just over an hour later, Berry saw '*Las Cruces 52*' on a road sign and knew that they would be there very soon. They still had enough money for a couple of nights in a decent hotel and she imagined soaking her aching muscles in a steaming hot bath before sliding dreamily between freshly laundered cotton sheets. She overtook an old brown Ford and settled down to a steady sixty-five, watching an eagle circle high above the plains. *We've made it*, she thought and a wave of happiness swept over her. She felt a new sense of optimism, a certainty that, from now on, everything would be all right. Against the odds, they had made it to New Mexico and now she felt confident that, some-how, they would find Eddy Chaves, and the bracelet would be restored to its proper place. Then they would find a way of living their lives the way they wanted to live them and nobody out there was going to stop them. Berry remembered her mother's words, etched across her heart:

'What did I tell you, my darling? You can do anything!'

Berry turned to Ell and put up her thumb.

'We did it, Ell!' she shouted triumphantly. 'We made it!'

Then the front wheel hit a patch of oil and as the handlebars snapped backwards and the bike slid out from under her, Berry just had time to see Ell hit the road before the tarmac flew up to meet her and everything went black.

☆ 40 ☆
An Invitation

'COME ON, HONEY, speak to me. Wake up! What's your name? Come on, sweet girl. Say something.'

The words sounded a long way off, as though they were floating up from the bottom of a deep well. Berry felt a warm hand on hers and as she opened one eye she saw the concerned face of a woman in her late fifties gazing down at her.

'Hello, my darlin',' she said and as Berry started to whimper she said, 'Sshh, honey, it's gonna be all right. I've phoned for the medics and they'll be here soon. Just you lie still now, sweetheart. We'll soon have you right.'

'Ell!' said Berry, trying to sit up. 'Where's Ell?'

The woman squeezed her hand and said, 'Just you worry about yourself, my darlin'. Your friend will be just fine.'

Berry stared past her at the blue sky and wondered if the truth was something different.

'Who are you?' she asked.

'My name is Polly,' said the woman, 'and I'm going to stay right here with you and make sure that everything is all right.'

In the ambulance, Berry held on tightly to Polly's hand as the medics clamped an oxygen mask over Ell's swollen face and thrust an IV line into his arm. Both paramedics were young: a pony-tailed girl and a crew-cut boy, neither of them long out of high school. But their calm, practised urgency gave nothing away and Berry guessed they must have seen it all before.

'He needs more fluids,' said the boy, flicking a syringe and squirting a jet of liquid from the needle before inserting it into the soft crook of Ell's arm. As the girl set up a second drip, Berry thought of a bag of bones, clinging to a life that was slipping away.

'Will he be all right?' she whispered.

'Yes, sweetheart,' said Polly, putting an arm around her shoulder. As Berry pressed her face into the swirling blue patterns of Polly's cotton blouse and began to cry, she heard her say, 'Of course he will', and this time she didn't care about the truth, because a lie was the only thing she wanted to hear.

The emergency team was ready and waiting. As the ambulance swung into the arrival bay with its sirens wailing, the doors flew open and Ell was hustled on to a gurney which rattled away up the corridor as the doors closed again.

'RTA,' shouted one of the paramedics as they ran with the gurney beneath the white glare of strip lights. 'Vital signs unstable, possible skull fracture. We need to check intercranial pressure.' Through the mass of sterile blue overalls, Berry caught sight of Ell's white, expressionless face beneath the ventilator and felt her heart fall farther and faster than it had ever fallen before.

'She is a very fortunate young lady,' the doctor told Polly Washington as Berry followed him out of the examination room into the corridor. Then, lowering his voice, he asked, 'Are you sure she was involved in the same accident?'

'Yes,' said Polly. 'I was the one that found her. Why? Is something wrong?'

'On the contrary,' said the doctor. 'There isn't a mark on her. I've seen worse injuries on people who've fallen out of bed.'

'I guess I was pretty lucky then,' said Berry, feeling the exact opposite.

'I'll say,' replied the doctor. 'In fact, with that kind

of luck, I should definitely have you pick out my lottery numbers.' He winked and then disappeared back into his room.

When he had gone, Berry asked, 'How's Ell?'

'I just spoke to the neurosurgeon,' Polly told her. 'He says they've managed to stabilize him for the moment.'

'Neurosurgeon?' repeated Berry, remembering her mother's illness. 'But that's to do with the brain, isn't it?'

'Yes,' said Polly gently, 'but don't go upsetting yourself. They've given him a CAT scan and discovered some swelling, that's all. They just need to keep an eye on him for a while.'

'Can I see him?'

'Not just now, honey. The body's a wonderful thing, but sometimes it just needs to rest in order to mend itself. And I reckon, right now, that's what you need to do too. You look about ready to drop.'

'But I can't leave him here on his own,' said Berry, her bottom lip trembling. 'I'm all he's got.'

'I understand how you feel,' said Polly, taking both Berry's hands in her own. 'But you're really not going to be much use to him at the moment. Besides, he's in the best place he can be right now. I'll make sure they tell us if there's any change. The question is, what are we going to do about you?'

'What do you mean?'

'The doctor tells me you won't give him the name of anyone they can contact. Says you told him there wasn't anyone. Is that true?'

'Yes,' said Berry, withdrawing her hands and folding her arms. 'It's just me and Ell. No one else.'

'Look, sweetheart, I don't mean to pry or anything, but how old are you exactly?'

'Does it matter?' asked Berry.

'Well, let's see,' said Polly. 'You crashed a motorbike on the state highway. That means at the very least that the police are going to want to talk to you and take a look at your licence. And it's just a hunch that I have, but I'm guessing that you probably aren't old enough to have one. Am I right?'

Berry didn't answer. Instead she asked, 'I'm in trouble, aren't I?'

'Not necessarily,' said Polly. 'But it wouldn't hurt to tell me a little bit about yourself, would it?' She smiled. 'For a start, I can tell that you're not exactly from around these parts.'

'That obvious, eh?' asked Berry.

'Well, it's a lovely accent,' said Polly, 'but New Mexico it ain't.' She thought for a moment, then said, 'All right, listen. Here's an idea. Why don't you come over and stay with me this evening? We'll get some good home cooking inside you and then when you've had a good night's sleep, I can help you sort this whole thing out. What do you say?'

Berry lifted her gaze up from the white tiled floor, grateful for the unexpected kindness; a lifeline thrown by a stranger.

'But what about the police?' she asked. 'Aren't they going to want to speak to me tonight?'

Polly smiled and winked at her.

'Don't worry,' she said. 'I *am* the police.'

☆ 41 ☆
POLLY'S STORY

POLLY'S HOUSE TURNED out to be in the suburbs of
Alamogordo, about an hour's drive from Las Cruces.
Although she had been determined not to fall asleep,
Berry found herself waking up in the dark and as the
car turned into the driveway she realized that she had
been asleep for most of the journey. Across the garden
she could see the gentle glow of fireflies, floating above
the fruit canes like burning embers.

'You'll have to excuse the mess,' said Polly as she
flicked the hall light on to reveal a trail of packing
cases. 'I'm retiring from the force at the end of the
month. Moving out to a place in California. That's
where I've been this weekend, trying to get everything
ready down there. But there are always more things to
do than there is time to do 'em in.'

As Polly boiled a saucepan of water on the stove

and busied herself in the kitchen, Berry took the plates and cutlery through to the dining room, setting them neatly on the table. She was still very tired, but the house seemed to have absorbed some of Polly's warmth over the years and – despite the packing cases – she felt quite at home.

'Hope you like pasta!' Polly called from the kitchen.

'Yes,' said Berry. 'I love it.'

She breathed in the rich aroma of tomato and basil and just for a moment she was back with her mother again, sitting at a fold-out table and sucking up spaghetti as the winter sunlight streamed in through the window of the old bus. She thought about the bracelet then; about how – for all its incredible powers – it could never bring back those things that had been lost.

'We all have the chance to make the world a better place before we leave it,' her mother once told her. 'In the end, it comes down to the choices we make.'

And when Berry had asked, 'What was the best thing you ever did for the world?' her mother had smiled and said, 'Bringing you into it.'

After supper, when Berry had helped Polly clear away the empty plates, the two of them sat together on the faded red sofa, Polly cradling a glass of white wine. The hospital had called to say that Ell was already sitting up in bed asking for chocolate, which had made Berry smile. Polly had promised that they'd go and see him first thing in the morning. As the cool breeze from the ceiling fan gently ruffled Berry's hair, Polly leaned back into the cushions and said, 'So tell me, honey. What's your story?'

'Well,' said Berry hesitantly, 'it's a bit of a long one.'

'So much the better,' replied Polly. 'I ain't got nothing else to do but smile. My packing's all but finished and I've only got a couple more days on the force before I retire. To be honest with you, I already retired in my mind a few months ago. All's I got left to do is fill in a form and collect my gold watch.'

'But you don't look old enough to retire,' said Berry and when Polly raised her eyebrows she added, 'Seriously. You don't.'

'Honey, you are so sweet I could eat you for breakfast. But I'm sixty this year. Should've gone years ago, but they couldn't bear to get rid of me.' She winked. 'Time to hang up my badge and live the easy life, I reckon.'

Berry saw the sad smile and guessed there was a story behind it. Despite the age difference and the fact that Polly was a police officer who could get Berry sent home at any time, there was a warmth that drew Berry towards her, made her feel able to say things she wouldn't say to anyone else.

'Polly,' she said. 'Do you believe in magic?'

Polly took a sip of wine and put her glass down on the wooden floor.

'You mean, like wizards and spells?'

'No. I mean like things happening that you can't explain. Weird things. Things that you wouldn't believe are possible.'

'Yes,' said Polly. 'Matter of fact I do.'

'Really?' asked Berry, surprised.

'Uh-huh,' said Polly. 'Why do you ask?'

'Because . . . because I've been carrying this secret around and it's just . . . it's getting too big for me. I feel like I need to tell someone. But the thing is . . .'

'What?' Polly asked gently, her brown eyes steady and serious. 'What is the thing, Berry?'

'It's just . . . it's just so strange and incredible that I don't know if anyone will believe it.'

Polly nodded.

'I know what that's like,' she said.

'You do? Really?'

'Oh yes,' said Polly. 'Like you wouldn't believe.'

She picked up her wine glass again, took a sip and put it down again.

'All right, honey. Listen. Here's what I'm going to do. I'm going to tell you something now that I haven't told anyone in nearly forty years. Then, when I've finished, you can decide whether or not you want to share your secret with me. OK?'

Berry smiled, her eyes shining with excitement.

'OK,' she whispered.

'What you need to bear in mind', said Polly, pushing a cushion behind her back, 'is that at the time this happened, I was a young police officer who was planning on going places. I'd done my time on traffic duty and spent a few years proving that I was a hard worker who was good at her job. I'd helped to nail a bunch of car thieves on my patch and there was some talk about me making detective the following year. Everything was looking rosy. On top of which, I also had a guy who I was getting pretty serious about.'

'Really?' Berry smiled. 'What was he like?'

'Oh, he was a cute one. Reckon we might have ended up going the distance.'

Berry saw a flicker of hurt in her eyes and guessed things hadn't worked out.

'So what happened?'

'I was driving home from work late one afternoon. Been over to Dexter checking out a stolen car and decided instead of driving all the way down to Artesia, I'd take a shortcut across the plains. There wasn't much in it really, but the scenery's beautiful, you know, very open and wild. I had nothing else to do that day and I was feeling pretty good about things so I thought, what the heck? But then, when I was about halfway across, that's when I saw it.'

Berry noticed that Polly's eyes had a faraway look in them, as if the years had fallen away and she was back in her old life again.

'What did you see?' she asked, her words bringing Polly back to the present.

'It was a spinning silver disc. Just appeared, suddenly, out of nowhere. One minute there was blue sky, the next there was this . . . this thing. And it moved so *fast*, faster than anything I'd ever seen before in my life.'

Polly sliced the air horizontally with the flat of her hand, demonstrating what she meant. 'One second it was *here*, the next it was *there* and yet it was impossible to say exactly how it had moved. It was just . . . amazing. Incredible.'

The last word hung in the air between them and Berry tried to imagine Polly as a young woman, driving across a deserted plain, staring up at something she didn't understand.

'While I was watching it through my side window, it suddenly came really close. It kind of hovered overhead for a few seconds then landed a couple of hundred yards away from my car. As I pulled over to take a closer look, I saw two figures, crouching next to it. They were wearing some kind of white coveralls. I couldn't see their faces, but I saw one of them turn and look in my direction. The next thing I remember is a bright flash and suddenly the thing was a tiny silver dot in the sky. I must have blinked, because when I looked again it was gone. It was as though it had never been there at all. I began to wonder then if I'd imagined the whole thing. But when I wandered across to where I thought I'd seen it, I saw a big circle in the dust. I knew then that what I'd seen was real.'

'That *is* amazing,' said Berry. 'Do you think it was a UFO?'

'An Unidentified Flying Object?' Polly shrugged. 'Well, it certainly flew, and I sure as heck couldn't identify it. So yeah, I guess it was.'

'Where do you think it came from?'

Polly sighed. 'I didn't know then and I don't know now. But what I do know is, the government didn't want me making a fuss about it.'

'Why not?'

'Who knows? There had been a lot of supposed sightings of UFOs over New Mexico in the forties and fifties and maybe the government was afraid that people were going to panic. Have you ever heard of the Roswell Incident?'

Berry shook her head. 'No,' she said. 'What was that?'

'Oh, it was front page news back in 1947. It was claimed that the wreckage of a flying saucer was found on a ranch near Roswell and some more debris was found on the edge of a top military base called White Sands.'

'Is that near where you were driving?'

'Same sort of area. Both the government and the military denied any knowledge of it at first, but some people thought that they were lying.'

'What about you?'

'I thought it was probably a hoax. I didn't believe in flying saucers and I thought that anyone who did was probably a bit crazy. But then my opinion changed.'

'Why?'

'Well, after I realized I *hadn't* imagined what I'd seen, I put in an urgent call for back-up, expecting a couple of cars from my squad to drive over. But instead, some guys I'd never heard of showed up. Said they were part of some special investigation team. So I took them over, showed them the marks in the dirt and they took a few photographs. Then they told me I should keep quiet about it for the time being. But I was young and feisty. I told them I wasn't about to be part of some government cover-up and that I would be putting in my report first thing in the morning, same as I always did. The next day I found myself suspended from duty.'

'But that's terrible!' said Berry. 'Why would they do a thing like that?'

'Because, for whatever reason, they didn't want the story to get out. Maybe it was some new aircraft they were testing in secret. Maybe it really was something from outer space. Who knows? What I do know is, from that day on, they set out to discredit me. I was off work for nearly six months, during which time I was sent to various places for psychometric testing. When they finally let me go back to work, I found they'd moved me out to some backwater, filing reports and making coffee. And the cute guy I told you about? He got posted to Vietnam and never came back. No happy endings there, I'm afraid.' Polly smiled sadly. 'So there it is. My strange secret. What do you think?'

'I think it's tragic,' said Berry.

'Tragic?'

'Yes. So many bad things happened to you just because you told the truth.'

'Yeah, well, I'm afraid that ain't too unusual. There's a lot of folks out there who only like the truth if it fits their idea of how the world is supposed to be,' said Polly. 'If it don't fit, they call it a lie.'

'Do you ever wish it hadn't happened?' asked Berry.

'Truthfully?' replied Polly. 'Yes. Many's the time I've wished I could have turned the clock back and taken another route home. Things might have turned out differently then: I might have got married, raised a family. But over the years I've come to realize you can only do what you believe is right at the time. You can't spend your life looking back, wishing things were different. Besides, other things happen which wouldn't have happened otherwise. Good things, some of them.'

'Like what?'

'Well, if I hadn't seen what I saw that day, I'd probably be settled down, maybe with a family. I probably
wouldn't be moving out to California. And if I hadn't
been moving out to California, I wouldn't have been
driving back along the number 10 Interstate this
weekend. And if I hadn't been driving along the number 10 Interstate, I wouldn't have met you, would I?'

Berry smiled. 'And that's a good thing?'

'That', said Polly, 'is a *very* good thing.' She picked
up her wine glass, took a sip and raised her eyebrows.
'Well?'

'Well, what?' asked Berry.

'I've told you mine,' said Polly and winked. 'Now
you've got to tell me yours.'

42

LOOKING FOR EDDY

BERRY TOLD THE STORY hesitantly at first, pausing every now and then to check Polly's expression. But gradually, as she saw that Polly was listening with an open mind, she became more and more confident until, by the time she reached the part about the fight in the bar, she was on her feet, acting it out.

'My Lord,' said Polly. 'Seriously? That was you at the Bar & Grill?'

'That was me,' said Berry. 'It was pretty frightening, actually.'

'I can imagine,' said Polly. 'I heard about it on the local radio news when we were driving home. But they said the damage was caused by a bunch of bikers.'

'Well, they did most of it,' Berry admitted. 'I think I only broke a window.' She paused before adding, 'And maybe someone's nose.'

When she had finished, Polly asked quietly, 'May I see this bracelet?'

'Of course,' said Berry. She pulled up her sleeve to reveal the band of bright colours, twisting and spinning, separated by golden space. She looked up and saw that Polly was sitting wide-eyed and speechless on the sofa, shaking her head as if unable to find any words to describe her feelings. 'The music,' she said at last. 'I'd forgotten about the music.'

Berry stared at her. 'You hear the music too?'

Polly nodded. 'Yes. I hear it.' She stared at the bracelet for a long time without saying anything else. Finally she turned to Berry and, when she spoke, her voice had a new urgency.

'You said the old man told you to return the bracelet to New Mexico. Did he give you the name of a place?'

'Yes.' Berry narrowed her eyes as she tried to remember. 'He left a weird message. Said I had to take it to a place called the Eunice Vaughn Anthony Centre.'

Polly shook her head. 'Can't say I've ever heard of it. Did he say anything else?'

'He mentioned someone called Eddy. Eddy Chaves.'

'Eddy Chaves?' Polly frowned. 'Are you sure?'

'Yes, I'm positive. That's what he said. Eddy Chaves. Why? Have you heard of him?'

'No,' said Polly. 'I haven't heard of *him*. But right now we're in Otero County, OK?'

'OK,' said Berry, not understanding where this was going.

'Right. Well Otero is bordered by the state of Texas to the south, Dona Ana and Sierra Counties to the west and Lincoln to the north. But to the east of Otero, there are two more counties. Guess what they're called.'

'No *way*,' said Berry excitedly as it began to dawn on her what Polly was saying.

'Yep,' said Polly. 'Chaves County and Eddy County. Eddy Chaves. It sounds as though your friend might have been talking about the border. What was the name of the other place?'

'The Eunice Vaughn Anthony Centre.'

'The Eunice Vaughn Anthony Centre,' Polly repeated. 'Sounds like it might be some kind of hospital, but I've never heard of it. Let's check it out on the web.'

Berry followed her as she made her way to a small study at the back of the house and turned on the computer. She typed *Eunice Vaughn Anthony Center* into the search engine and hit the return key. The screen was immediately filled with a list of near misses: *Civic Center ... Anthony Davis ...*

Polly scrolled through them and shook her head.

'Nothing there. Hang on though. Let's try again with quotation marks.'

She typed *"Eunice Vaughn Anthony Center"* and this time the screen came back with:

Your search *"Eunice Vaughn Anthony Center"* did not match any documents.

Suggestions:

Make sure all words are spelled correctly.

Try different keywords.

Try more general keywords.

'Darn it,' said Polly. 'Are you sure he said, "Center" and not "sent her"?'

'What's the difference?' asked Berry.

'You know. He might have been saying that this Eunice Vaughn Anthony person sent her.'

'Oh, *sent her*,' said Berry, finally understanding what Polly was getting at. 'Well, he might have done I suppose. But it doesn't make much sense, does it?'

'I s'pose not,' agreed Polly. 'Maybe if we just try the name. It might throw something up.'

'Worth a try,' said Berry, feeling tiredness catching up with her again. She watched as Polly typed *'Eunice Vaughn Anthony'* into the search engine and hit the return key again.

'Well, whaddaya know,' said Polly quietly. 'Can't

think why I didn't see it before. Look.'

Berry stared at the first entry on the screen. It read:

Area Codes and Maps

Anthony N.M. Dana Ana 505 . . . **Eunice** N.M.

'I don't get it,' said Berry. 'What am I looking at?'

'These are towns,' said Polly. 'Places in New Mexico.'
She pointed at the screen. 'See? Anthony, New Mexico.
Eunice, New Mexico. They're towns! Anthony is just a
few miles south of Las Cruces.'

'But what about Vaughn?' asked Berry with growing
excitement.

'Hang on,' said Polly. 'I'm sure I've heard of it.' She
typed in *'Vaughn, New Mexico'* and immediately the
computer came back with a whole list of entries, the
first of which read:

Map of **Vaughn**, N.M.

'Bingo!' said Polly. 'Now we're getting somewhere.'
She leapt out of her chair and began rummaging
through a packing case full of books.

'What are you doing?' Berry asked.

'I'm looking for a map,' said Polly, pulling out hand-
fuls of books and dumping them on the bare floorboards. 'Here we are. This is what I'm after.'

She held up a folded map decorated with the Stars
and Stripes and the words

AREA MAP:
ARIZONA & NEW MEXICO

printed on the front.

Berry followed Polly back into the dining room where she unfolded the map and spread it out on the table.

'All right,' she said, stabbing at the map with an index finger. 'There's Anthony, right there. Throw me that pen, Berry.'

Berry picked up a blue ballpoint and slid it across the table. As Polly drew a little circle around the town of Anthony, Berry shouted, 'Vaughn, I've got Vaughn!'

'All *right*!' said Polly, moving her pen across to circle Vaughn. 'Now all we need is Eunice for a full house . . .'

There was silence for a while as the two of them scanned the hundreds of small printed names.

'Are we sure it's definitely in New Mexico?' Berry asked.

'Definitely,' said Polly. 'It's got to be here somewhere.'

Berry's gaze slid along the edge of the map towards Texas and then suddenly she spotted it. 'Here it is!' she exclaimed triumphantly. 'Look. Just there. See?'

'Good girl!' said Polly, drawing a final circle on the map. 'That's all of them!'

She stared at the map for a moment, then took a

step backwards and frowned. 'OK. Three towns in New Mexico. Now what?'

Berry shook her head. 'I don't know. Centre, centre. Maybe there's something about the town centre of each?'

'Maybe,' said Polly. 'Let's give it a try.'

She typed *'Eunice NM Center'* and hit the return key, flooding the screen with results.

'OK. We've got Community Center, Youth Center, Wrecker and Service Center . . . any of 'em mean anything to you?'

'Nope,' said Berry. 'Not a thing.'

'Right, well, we'll keep on going.'

Polly brought up a New Mexico Tourist Department website and typed *'Vaughn'* into the search engine. Scrolling past photos of prairies and blue skies, she began to read:

> Established as a railroad community in 1919, Vaughn is the only town in New Mexico where the main lines of two railroads intersect: the Burlington Northern Santa Fe Railway (BNSF) and the Union Pacific (UP) Railway.

'What do you think?' asked Polly. 'Sound promising? X marks the spot and all that?'

'Maybe,' said Berry. 'Trouble is, there's probably a million things out there that cross or have got the word "center" in them. We need something that's common to all three.'

'Yeah, I guess you're right,' said Polly. 'Ever thought of becoming a police officer? I still got a few cases need solving before I leave.'

Berry smiled, but she could hardly keep her eyes open and Polly saw it.

'Hey, tired girl,' she said, switching off the computer. 'Time you were in bed. Let's do this tomorrow when you're fresh.'

Later, when she lay beneath cool cotton sheets watching Polly draw the curtains, Berry asked, 'What if we don't find the answer? What if I've come all this way for nothing?'

'Then at least you'll have done what you set out to do,' Polly told her, 'and there's not many people in this life can say that.'

She stroked Berry's hair in silence for a while until Berry felt her eyes grow heavy. Then she added, 'You know honey, over the years I've discovered that sometimes the journey is the best part of all. Folks don't often realize that until it's over.'

She kissed Berry lightly on the forehead and turned out the light. As Berry curled up beneath the duvet and watched the bracelet sparkle in the darkness, she realized that she felt genuinely loved for the first time since her mother had died. Tears pricked at her eyes, but they came from the unexpected happiness of discovering a small corner of the world that was glad simply because she was in it.

As the delicate lace curtains moved gently in the soft night breeze, Berry drifted in and out of sleep, clutching her mother's card and dreaming of a place where there would be no more danger and no more sadness.

Just a blue house and a cherry tree beneath a never-ending sky.

43
HORTON'S DISCOVERY

EARLIER THAT DAY, Bill Horton had driven up the long dirt track and parked next to the main entrance of Sid's Seed & Feed. It was the fifth farming whole-saler he had visited that day, and the last one within a hundred-mile radius. The car's air-conditioning had packed up and it was 105 degrees in the shade. To say that he'd had better days would be an understatement.

Horton wiped his forehead with a handkerchief and thought about what he had so far.

The British police had been quick to match the photo of the wrapping paper with paper found at Mitchell's house in England, which meant that at least one of the people at the hotel had to be connected with Mitchell. Mitchell's survival of the bus accident together with eye-witness reports of the girl's fall from the seventh floor − and the flattened bullets found at the scene – had left him convinced that she was in possession of the missing item Sampson had talked about.

But did all this mean there was a connection with Sampson's death, or was he just clutching at straws?

He was already beginning to wonder if his whole theory about the fertilizer bomb was flawed. All he really had to go on was the email, sent from downtown Albuquerque to Sampson before his death, and the fact that fertilizer had been used in the bomb. Even if the bomber was the same person who had sent the email to Sampson from Albuquerque, it didn't necessarily mean he would have purchased his bomb-making materials locally. In theory he could have bought them at any feed store in America. But then, Horton reasoned, he could have emailed Sampson from anywhere in America too. But he chose to do it from a few blocks down the street.

Call it gut instinct, but something told Horton that this guy wasn't too cautious. He hoped he was right. He hoped that the guy was cool and confident.

Because, in his experience, those kinds of people usually made mistakes.

'Hi, buddy,' said the man behind the counter. 'How can I help you?'

Horton flipped open his ID and said, 'Agent

Horton, FBI,' to save him the bother of reading it. 'I'm here about the sale of some ammonium nitrate.'

The man tugged on the back of his yellow baseball cap while he thought about that. 'Well, I guess you've come to the right place.'

Horton nodded. 'Do you sell a lot of it?'

'A fair amount. Mostly in the spring though, I'd say.'

'Would you have a record of who bought it?'

The man looked at him suspiciously. 'You did say the FBI, right? Not the IRS?'

Horton smiled. He guessed the man wasn't too keen on having a tax official turn up unannounced to look through his accounts.

'No,' he said. 'Definitely FBI. You got receipts?'

'Sure,' said the man, visibly relieved. 'I'll get them.'

As the man headed off into his office, Horton's mind wandered back to the incident with the girl at the hotel. Plane tickets found at the scene together with tapes from airport cameras had confirmed that she was the girl from the bus-accident tape. Her name was Berry Benjamin and she had a sixteen-year-old accomplice, Elliott Watts. But although the British police had been helpful, they'd had no real information on either of them. There was no record of the girl ever attending school and she had no next of kin. The boy's father had shown no interest in tracking his son down and had actually seemed quite pleased that he was gone. And despite the police putting a watch on all bus and rail stations, both of them had disappeared and the trail had gone cold. Although it seemed unlikely that the pair were a direct threat to US security, it was important that they got to them before these other people did. Horton was now convinced that the girl had the missing item and the group at the hotel were obviously prepared to use extreme violence to get their hands on it. But all Horton had to go on was a few vague sightings of three men acting suspiciously and a description of a middle-aged blond man leaving the hotel in a hurry. A description that would probably fit a couple of hundred thousand Americans.

It wasn't looking good.

'There you go,' said the man, dropping a thick lever arch file on to the counter. These are all the orders we've had since January of this year.'

'Mind if I take a look?'

'Be my guest.' The man pushed the file across the counter towards him. 'Take as long as you want.'

Horton spent the next twenty minutes flipping through the sheets, just as he had done in each of the other places. He was getting used to the layout now, his eyes flicking quickly from the content of the order to the date and the customer's name. The man was right about the spring — there was a lot of fertilizer purchased in February and early March, then the orders seemed to drop off in April. They were all fairly large quantities and all of them seemed to be ordered through bona-fide companies. Horton sighed as he reached the end of April and the orders for fertilizer became fewer and farther between.

Once again, there seemed to be nothing.

But just as it was occurring to him that he might have to rethink his approach, he came across an order for 5 x 20 kg sacks of ammonium nitrate. The order was dated 20 April.

Although he knew it could be just coincidence, Horton felt his pulse quicken.

4/20. *The number on Sampson's email.*

Hitler's birthday.

'Excuse me,' he said to the man who was piling up bags of cattle feed in the corner. 'Is this a usual amount of fertilizer for you to sell?'

The man wiped his hands on the front of his shirt and walked over to the counter.

'Let's see. A hundred kilos. Well, it's not unheard of, but it wouldn't be an industrial order. You'd probably be looking at home use.'

'Home use?' Horton raised an eyebrow quizzically. 'Isn't a hundred kilos rather a lot for one garden?'

The man shrugged. 'Guess that depends on the size of your garden.'

'Any credit-card record of the sale?'

The man shook his head. "'Fraid not. Looks like it was a cash transaction. Hang on though. He should have signed for receipt of the goods.' He flipped over the page to a green back sheet. 'Yeah, here you go. It was a Mr Jones. Matter of fact, I remember him now. He was a middle-aged guy. About fifty, maybe? Yeah, that's it. And he had this kind of wispy blond hair.'

As he floored the accelerator and left the bemused store owner staring after him in a cloud of dust, Horton knew that his luck might finally have changed. In his pocket was the piece of paper he hoped would reveal the identity of the man who had killed Andy Sampson. The man who he now believed was the biggest threat to national security that the United States had ever seen.

44
KRUGER AND MITCHELL

THE TIME FROM THE IDENTIFICATION of the finger-print on the receipt to the moment a heavily armed SWAT team kicked down the door of William Kruger's apartment was a few seconds short of forty-five minutes. It seemed to Horton that the powers-that-be had finally woken up to the fact that he might just be on to something. Suddenly, he had all the support he needed.

He just hoped it wasn't too late.

The moment Horton saw the red flag with the black swastika on the wall and the framed black-and-white photographs of soldiers in Nazi uniform, he knew they had come to the right place. But he also knew, from the junk mail scattered across the mat, that Kruger had not been back here in the last forty-eight hours and, now they had kicked his front door in, he wouldn't be coming back at all.

'Damn it!' he hissed. Turning to the local police chief he asked, 'Can we get a description circulated?'

'Already done,' said the chief. 'We're stepping up state-border patrols too.'

'Good,' said Horton. He saw Layton making his way through the splintered doorway and grimaced.

'We missed him,' he said. 'He must have guessed we were coming.'

At the other end of the street Kruger watched, white-faced with anger, as the black-clad figures smashed his apartment door into matchwood and knew that his instincts had saved him. Aware that he might have been seen at the hotel, he had picked up a fresh hire car and made it to the outskirts of Albuquerque in two days. Driving slowly past the end of the block to check out the situation, he had immediately spotted the dark-blue Buick parked halfway down on the right.

Two guys, watching his house. Pretending to read the paper. It had been so obvious it was almost laugh-able. But now anger boiled inside of him as he thought of the heavy police boots stamping through his apart-ment, desecrating his sanctuary.

His rage, however, was tempered by the news he had recently received from Snyder.

Apparently the Oakland Angels had caught up with the girl in a bar near the border, tried to detain her and failed. But Snyder's gang had subsequently taken over at the border, trailing the pair at a discreet distance. There had been some sort of accident and they had followed the ambulance to the Memorial Hospital. As far as they knew, the boy was still there, but the girl had gone.

Snyder had been very apologetic about that one. Said he couldn't understand how they would let her out after a crash like that.

But Kruger wasn't worried at all.

Quite the opposite, in fact.

Because he knew now that his hunch had been right. Mitchell had told the girl the location just before he died. And now the little fool was trying to return the bracelet for him.

As he watched more police cars pull up outside his apartment, Kruger realized that his mistake had been in making all the running. What he should have done was simply let the girl do exactly what she was doing. To let her bring the bracelet back.

But he knew she might need a little persuasion to see things his way.

Punching a number into his mobile, he waited for a woman's voice to answer and then told her exactly what he wanted. He knew she was good; she wouldn't let him down.

'Keep me informed,' he said. 'I'll be waiting.'

All he needed now was patience. Just a little longer and the bracelet would be his, just as his father had wished all those years ago. He smiled bitterly.

Soon the whole world would know the name of William Kruger.

Layton stared at the swastika on the wall and whistled. 'Guess you were right about the whole Nazi thing. So what do we know about this guy Kruger?'

'We got lucky, Jack. Seems he committed a traffic offence about twelve years ago and assaulted the arresting officer. He only got thirty days, but it meant we were able to identify him from the fingerprint on the receipt. And that's not all.'

'Go on,' said Layton.

'The name Kruger threw up a classified file on the CIA database dating back to the 1940s. Given the current threat to US security, we've been given access to it for the first time.'

'The 1940s? But Kruger wasn't alive then.'

'No,' agreed Horton. 'At least, *William* Kruger wasn't. But Franz Kruger was.'

'Franz Kruger?'

'His father. He was one of the German scientists flown over to the White Sands Missile Base in New Mexico after the war.'

'Project Paperclip?'

'That's the one. Each German scientist was assigned to work with a scientist from the US, remember? Franz Kruger was assigned to work with one Joseph Mitchell.'

'Wait. The same Joseph Mitchell who went missing after the Roswell Incident? The old guy on the CCTV tape?'

'That's right.'

Layton looked puzzled.

'So where do the Krugers fit into all of this?'

'According to the CIA report, Franz Kruger and Joseph Mitchell were part of a specialist Crash Investigation Team sent to sift through the wreckage south of Roswell.'

'The UFO crash?'

'Well, the report doesn't specify the type of aircraft involved. But, two days later, Mitchell went missing, taking item X3472 with him. And whatever that item was, the CIA was desperate to get it back. They thought Kruger was involved in some way and kept a watch on him. In the course of their investigations they discovered that he had formed a secret group dedicated to keeping Nazi ideals alive, and as a result he lost his job at the airbase. He spent the rest of his life living in low-cost housing on the outskirts of Albuquerque until his death in 1972.'

'So how come the CIA kept the file going?'

'Partly because he was a known Nazi sympathizer. But mainly, I guess, because of the importance of the missing item. Same reason they spent so long trying to locate Mitchell. Maybe they were afraid that, because Kruger was one of the few people who knew of its existence, he would try and find a way of getting his hands on it. They closed the file on him after his death. But I guess they hadn't counted on his son William keeping the Nazi flame burning.'

'So you think William Kruger is close to finding this item, whatever it is?'

'I'm sure of it. That's why he was at the hotel in San Francisco. He thinks the girl has got it.'

'And what about you? What do you think?'

'I think she's got it too.'

Horton's phone rang. He pulled it from his pocket and flipped open the cover. 'OK,' he said. 'I'll be right over.'

'Problem?' Layton asked as Horton snapped the phone shut.

Horton shook his head and, when he looked up, Layton saw the beginnings of a smile.

'That was the Traffic Unit,' he said. 'They think they may have found them.'

45
A Late-night Visitor

Berry awoke with a start and felt at once that something was wrong. Strange warnings began to tremble through her body and she felt certain that Ell was in some kind of danger. What if he had woken to find himself alone in a strange place? Would he think that she had abandoned him, just as everyone else in his life had done?

Tumbling out of bed, Berry pulled on her clothes and decided to wake Polly. She already trusted her implicitly and knew that she would listen to her fears. If they hurried, they could be at the hospital in less than an hour. But as Berry was about to turn the door handle, she heard the low murmur of voices downstairs.

Opening the door slowly she tiptoed out into the hallway, wincing every time the floorboards creaked. As she approached the edge of the landing she dropped down on to her hands and knees, crawling across the carpet until she was close enough to see through the banister rail.

A man stood outside the front door, illuminated in the glare of a security light. He wore a sand-coloured trench coat and Berry noticed that his black shoes had lost their shine beneath a layer of dust. Perhaps self-conscious of the fact, he casually rubbed the toes on the back of his trousers as he spoke.

'Could I see some ID?' Polly was saying. She clutched the front of a pale-blue candlewick dressing-gown to her chest and Berry guessed that she must have been asleep when the doorbell rang.

The man flashed his ID card at the same time as he stepped through the door into the hallway. 'Special Agent Horton. I'm with the FBI.'

Berry felt her stomach flip. She guessed the FBI didn't come round in the middle of the night just to talk about parking offences.

'It's very late,' Polly said and Berry heard a quiver in her voice. 'Is there something I can help you with, Agent Horton?'

'Yes, ma'am,' replied Horton. 'I believe there is. Are you Ms Polly Washington?'

'That's correct.'

'You're on the force? A police sergeant?'

'I am.'

'Sergeant Washington, I need you to tell me if you witnessed a traffic accident earlier today.'

'Yes, I did,' said Polly. 'I was on my way back from California.' A pause. 'But then I guess you knew that already, huh?'

Horton grunted. 'So what happened when you arrived at the scene?'

Polly shrugged. 'I called the paramedics and got the injured parties to hospital, same as anyone else would have done.'

'Injured parties?'

'Injured *party*,' Polly corrected herself. 'A young male in his mid-teens. He suffered trauma to the head and they admitted him to the Memorial Hospital. It was a motorcycle accident. No other vehicle was involved.'

'You said "injured parties",' Horton persisted. 'Tell me, Sergeant Washington. What happened to the girl?'

'Girl?' Polly repeated. 'What girl?'

'I think we both know who I'm talking about,' said Horton.

'Look Mr, uh, Horton,' said Polly. 'It's very late and I have to be up early in the morning. Couldn't we discuss this tomorrow?'

'What's going on, Ms Washington?' asked Horton, his voice suddenly sharp and accusatory. Berry saw his eyes flick across the hallway and she shrank back into the shadows.

'What do you mean, "What's going on?"?' Polly asked innocently.

'Why don't you want to tell me about the girl?'

'I don't know what you mean,' said Polly and Berry noticed a harder edge to her voice now; the shutters were coming down.

'Do you mind if I take a look around?' asked Horton, changing tack.

'Actually, I do,' said Polly. 'Like I said. It's very late and I have to be up early.'

'I thought you might say that,' replied Horton, reaching into his pocket. 'That's why I brought this along.' He took out a piece of paper and handed it to Polly. 'It's a search warrant.'

'Look, can't you come back in the morning?' asked Polly, but her tone indicated she already knew what the answer would be.

'I'm sorry,' said Horton, stepping past her. 'This won't take long.'

Polly glanced up at the banisters and when Berry saw the look in her eyes she knew that it was time to move. Crawling quickly across the carpet to her room, she looked around frantically for a place to hide. There were two options: in the closet or under the bed — both completely useless. The guy might be getting on a bit, but Berry guessed he wasn't stupid.

Her eyes fell upon the window. It was a two-storey

house and although she knew she had recently survived a much greater fall, she couldn't be certain that the bracelet would protect her again. But on the plus side, there was a garden below which would provide a softer landing if she fell.

Footsteps creaked on the landing and Berry felt the bracelet tingle on her wrist. Flinging open the window, she swung out on to the drainpipe and scrambled down it. By the time the bedroom door opened she was already out of the front gate, running past the neat suburban gardens into the hot New Mexico night.

After about a mile, Berry staggered against a street lamp and slid down into a pool of orange light. A few hours ago she had seemed so close to achieving her goal, her foot resting on the last rung of the ladder. Now here she was, slipping down snakes again. She guessed that Polly's visitor was linked to the hotel incident. If the FBI knew about the bracelet then they probably wanted to get their hands on it, same as the others. She knew there was no way she was going to let that happen; not after she had come this far.

But perhaps she was just kidding herself, trying once again to find some meaning in her life when in reality there was none. Perhaps it was all just one more lie and returning the bracelet to its proper place wouldn't make the slightest bit of difference to the world. But at that moment, sitting alone beneath the orange glow of the street light, Berry decided to carry on believing that, somehow, it would. After all, what else was there?

She turned her head at the sound of a car engine and saw a brown Ford driving slowly down the street towards her. As the car slid to a halt she got to her feet and saw that the driver was Special Agent Horton, the man from Polly's house.

'Hello,' he said as he got out. 'It's Berry Benjamin, isn't it?'

'No,' said Berry, walking away. 'I think you must have the wrong person.'

'Look, you're not in trouble,' Horton said, increasing his pace to keep up with her. 'I just want to talk to you, that's all.'

'No,' said Berry. 'Go away. Leave me alone.'

She began to walk faster, the soles of her boots scuffing up the pavement as she quickened her pace. But Horton was quickly beside her again and, despite his age, she realized she would probably not be able to outrun him.

'Just stop for a moment,' he said. 'Stop and talk to me.'

Berry felt the familiar tingling sensation in her arm then, growing stronger and stronger, spreading through every part of her body. She saw the yellow light glow beneath the bracelet's skin like winter sun-shine and before she knew it her finger was pressing down into its warm centre. Suddenly, her legs began to fizz as though they were full of sherbet and gunpow-der.

'Sorry,' she said. 'Gotta go.'

And with that, she took two steps forward and began to run.

46
ROAD RUNNING

AT FIRST, she didn't realize what was happening. The pavement slid away beneath her and Horton's words faded to nothing, like a voice heard from the window of a speeding car. Then, as she looked around, she saw that the lights of the houses had blurred into bright, continuous strings and realized that the curious *fwup–fwup–fwup* she could hear was the sound of her slipstream, whirling between street lamps as she raced past them at the rate of seven or eight a second. 'Ohh-hhhhhhhh!' she gasped, veering off into the road and accelerating at a speed that was both frightening and exhilarating. With a flick of her heels, she overtook a lorry and a sports car, then – feeling the power surge in her feet – she ran harder and the lights of the town disappeared into darkness behind her. It was easy, scary – beautiful – and she flew down the open road like a rocket with the stars bright above her and the warm wind whipping through her hair.

Her legs powered her so smoothly across the desert landscape that she found it hard to judge exactly how fast she was going, but as a series of telegraph poles flashed past her she experienced the same sensation of speed she had felt in the aeroplane as it accelerated down the runway. Although at first she found it hard to comprehend that she could be running this fast, it soon felt so flowing and natural that she began to relax and enjoy the sensation. Despite the fact that she was travelling at speeds far greater than she had ever travelled before, it seemed hardly to take any effort at all. She felt simply as though she was going for a gentle run and her feet bounced so lightly across the ground that it was like skipping over the surface of a trampoline. Whenever she saw headlights approaching she would veer off on to the rough scrubland, jumping boulders and ditches without even breaking sweat, kicking up a dust cloud that streamed like a vapour trail in her wake.

After a while Berry found her surroundings changing dramatically; the dry, dusty plains gave way to a strange, eerie landscape of white sand, piled here and there in huge dunes which in turn were dwarfed by the distant Sacramento mountains. It reminded her of the big winter freeze when storms had brought heavy falls of snow across the fields behind the travellers' camp. But back then it had been bitterly cold, so cold that the puddles and streams had frozen hard as iron; here a warm blanket of air hung over the milk-white dunes so that they seemed surreal and out of place, like snow in summer. *White Sands*, thought Berry. She remembered seeing the words on Polly's map and realized she must already be nearly halfway to Las Cruces.

Less than twenty minutes after she had started running, Berry found herself on the outskirts of Las Cruces with its dazzle of bright lights, billboards and motels. Deciding that running at high speed through the city centre was not the best way to stay anonymous, she slowed down to consider her next move. Seeing that her trousers were now covered in a fine layer of white dust, she bent over to brush herself down.

She was just straightening up again when she became aware of a hooting sound in the distance. She turned to see a huge chrome truck thundering down the road towards her, its smoke stack puffing clouds of white steam into the evening sky. As she watched it approach, an idea occurred to her and, when the truck swept past in a rush of wind and noise, she immediately began running again. Within a few seconds she had caught up with it, keeping pace alongside for a few seconds before grabbing the door handle and pulling herself up on to the footplate. As the truck rumbled on through the city streets, she watched the bright shop windows slide past and tried to remember where the hospital was.

Then, with a hiss of air brakes, the truck stopped at a set of traffic lights. Berry watched an ambulance shoot over the crossroads with its siren blaring and, making the connection, she jumped down from the footplate and was off running again. Abandoning all thoughts of remaining anonymous, she sprinted after the ambulance like a whippet, catching the occasional glimpse of a surprised onlooker from the corner of her eye. She raced down the street at high speed, skidding round corners with yellow sparks shooting from her heels. As the ambulance approached the hospital gates, she slowed to a walking pace and felt a burning sensation, as though she was walking over hot sand. Glancing down at her boots, she saw smoke billowing from the soles and took a rapid detour across the hospital lawn to dip them into a small fountain where they hissed and spat like bacon in a pan.

'What was the patient's name again?' asked the lady on reception, squinting at her computer screen.

'Ell. I mean, Elliott. Elliott Watts.'

The woman tapped a few keys and shook her head. 'Elliott Watts. I don't think we've got anyone here by that name.'

Berry thought for a few moments.

'Maybe they didn't get his name. He was in an accident, you see. He was unconscious when they brought him in.'

The woman looked up from her computer and Berry saw that, although her expression was not unpleasant, she wasn't about to let just anyone walk into her hospital.

'Are you related to the patient?' she asked.

'No,' said Berry. 'He's a friend.'

She noticed the woman steal a puzzled glance at her boots and realized that they were still smoking.

'I was in a hurry,' she said, by way of explanation.

Raising an eyebrow, the woman turned back to look at her computer. 'How old is your friend?'

'Sixteen,' said Berry. 'It was a motorbike accident.'

'I see,' said the woman. 'Let me check emergency admissions for you. They don't always show up on the main system right away.'

'OK,' said Berry. 'Thank you.'

She watched an old man shuffle through the sliding doors with a bandage around his hand and thought about the way the bracelet had protected her, stopped her from being hurt. She wondered what the world would be like if no one ever felt any pain. Would it be a good thing? Or was life somehow more complicated than that?

'Oh here he is,' said the woman. 'I've found him. He's in Intensive Care on the sixth floor. But I need to check a few details first. What did you say your name was again?'

Berry turned and saw that the woman was looking at her suspiciously.

'I didn't,' Berry replied.

'Ah,' said the woman, suddenly understanding. 'Weren't you involved in the accident? The girl who came in with him?'

Berry saw then that the penny had dropped; that the police must have told this woman to keep her eyes open and now she had finally figured it out.

'I have to go now,' she said, walking towards the lift. She saw the woman pick up the telephone and broke into a run.

'Wait!' shouted the woman. 'Come back!'

47
ABOVE THE CLOUDS

BERRY WATCHED button number 6 illuminate and as the doors slid open she stepped out into the corridor, finding herself behind a cleaner who was pushing a trolley towards the nurses' station. She followed a few paces behind and, as they approached the brightly lit office at the end of the corridor, she noticed a uniformed police officer sitting outside one of the rooms.

So they weren't taking any chances. They knew that Ell had been with her at the hotel. And, judging by the recent visit from the FBI, they were working pretty hard to find the bracelet.

Berry knew it didn't belong to them. Or to her. Or to anyone else.

But for now, all of that could wait.

She just wanted to see Ell and make sure he was all right.

The chair where the police officer sat was only a few more steps up the corridor. Berry wasn't at all sure what she was going to do when she got there. If she owned up to who she was, then at least they might let her see Ell for a few minutes.

But then what?

They would almost certainly take the bracelet away and send her back to England. If that happened, then everything that they had done, everything they had been through would have been for nothing.

There *had* to be another way.

As she passed, Berry stole a quick sideways glance at the police officer, trying not to be too obvious about it. She saw that his chin was resting on his chest and this gave her the confidence to slow down and take another quick look. This time she saw quite clearly why he hadn't glanced up at her: the man was fast asleep.

Unable to believe her luck, Berry waited until the distance between herself and the cleaner had opened up a little, then walked a few paces back until she was level with the police officer again. She peered down at him and saw that his eyes were definitely closed.

It was now or never.

Pushing the door handle down slowly, she was relieved to find the door opening without a sound. With a final glance at the policeman, she slipped quietly into the room and pulled the door shut behind her.

She found herself in a small, dimly lit private ward. Drips hung on metal stands and machines beeped softly, tracing little green lines across their screens. But as Berry walked towards the bed in the middle of the room she was shocked to see that it was empty; its sheets had been ripped off and now hung untidily over one edge, soaking up water from a glass that had fallen and shattered on the floor. Sensing a movement to her left, Berry turned and saw that she was not alone.

A nurse in freshly laundered blue scrubs was watching her from the corner of the room and Berry noticed that she was holding a syringe in her hand. Although she was wearing a blue face mask, there was something about the eyes and the wisp of dark hair, escaping from beneath the sterile cap, that made Berry uneasy.

'Oh,' she gasped in surprise. 'I'm sorry. I didn't see you there.'

'Please,' said the nurse. 'No need to apologize.'

Then, as she removed the face mask, Berry saw to her utter horror that it was the woman from the hotel.

'What are you doing here?' she whispered, hearing how small and shaky her voice had suddenly become. 'What have you done with Ell?'

'My, my,' replied the woman, 'such an inquisitive little thing.' She sighed and squirted a small amount of liquid from the syringe. 'You know, all this unpleasantness could have been avoided if you and your friend hadn't made life so difficult for us.'

'Who *are* you?' Berry asked, squeezing her hands together to stop them from shaking.

'Who *are* we?' hissed the woman, her face changing suddenly, contorting with bitter rage. 'I'll tell you who we are! We are the people who should have been running this world for the last sixty years! But they destroyed our Fatherland and turned the world into a garbage dump run by scum!'

'But Ell's got nothing to do with it!' Berry protested. 'Why would you take him?'

At this, the woman seemed to regain some self-control. She even managed to produce a thin, tight-lipped smile.

'Because, my dear, Mr Kruger knows how much you care about him. And so he just wants to make sure he is looked after — how shall I put it? — *properly.*'

'Look,' said Berry in desperation, seeing the madness in the woman's eyes and realizing that Ell must be in terrible danger. 'There's a policeman outside this room. Unless you tell me what you've done with Ell, I'll call him.'

'Oh, please,' spat the woman. 'Do you take me for a fool?'

Then, suddenly, it dawned on Berry how naive she had been. The reason that the policeman had failed to look up when she sneaked past had nothing to do with him being asleep. She guessed that, from now on, he wouldn't be answering anyone's calls.

'Please,' said Berry as the woman's thumb caressed the top of the syringe. 'Just tell me where he is.'

'But of course,' replied the woman, moving forward a little. 'Your friend is with Mr Kruger. And Mr Kruger wants you to know that he would very much like for you to be there too.'

Berry took a step backwards, maintaining the distance between herself and the woman.

'Get away from me,' she said.

'There's really no need to be nervous,' replied the woman softly, taking another step forward. 'I'm here to help.'

As Berry moved away again, she heard the sound of a phone ringing. The woman reached into her pocket, took out a mobile and flipped open the cover. Then she smiled.

'Yes, she's here. Would you like to speak to her?'

She held out the phone.

'It's for you.'

'*What?*'

'Go ahead. Take it.'

'Put it down on the bed,' ordered Berry, her voice trembling. 'Put it down and move back.'

The woman shrugged.

'As you wish.'

Berry waited until the woman had moved away from the bed, then picked up the phone and retreated back against the wall.

'Who is it?' she said.

'Guess,' said the voice on the other end, a voice she recognized immediately as belonging to the man from the hotel.

Kruger.

'Please,' Berry pleaded. 'Don't hurt him!'

'I am touched by your concern,' replied Kruger, 'but I really don't think you are in any position to tell me what to do.'

'Please,' said Berry again. 'I'm begging you . . .'

'Begging?' asked Kruger, his voice tinged with amusement. 'That doesn't sound like begging at all. Let me show you what begging sounds like . . .'

There was a short pause, followed by a loud scream. 'No, I swear! I swear I don't know where she is! Don't hurt . . . don't . . . no, no, no!' More screaming. The sound of a door banging.

Then silence.

'Oh dear,' said Kruger. 'I'm afraid your friend seems to be having rather a difficult time just now. I think he really needs you to be here with him. What do you say?'

Berry was crying now, the tears running down her

face. 'Why are you doing this?' she sobbed. 'Why?'

'But, my dear,' replied Kruger, 'I'm not the one who's doing it. Don't you see? It's all down to you. You took something that didn't belong to you, and these are the consequences. You may not like it, but that is the way the world works. And if your friend dies, well, then I am afraid it will be all because of you.'

'What can I do?' sobbed Berry. 'How can I save him?'

'Well, that's really very simple,' said Kruger. 'You can give me back what is mine.'

'I will,' said Berry frantically, 'I'll give it to you. But please. Don't hurt him any more. Just tell me what I have to do.'

'There,' said Kruger. 'You see? That's much better. Now. You are with one of my associates at this moment, yes?'

Berry wiped her eyes and saw the woman smiling back at her.

'Yes,' she said.

'As I thought. Then you must remove the bracelet and accompany her immediately to the Sacred Place. I will be waiting for you there with your friend. If everything is as we have agreed, then you will both be released unharmed. But I warn you now, Miss Benjamin, don't try anything foolish. If I do not have the bracelet in my possession by 2 a.m. at the latest, I shall assume that you are still playing games with me. In which case, your friend will die knowing that you chose to abandon him. Do you understand?'

'Yes,' said Berry. 'I understand perfectly. But . . .'

There was a click on the line, followed by the dial tone. Berry glanced up at the clock on the wall and saw to her horror that it was five past midnight.

Less than two hours to go.

'So,' said the woman. 'Are you going to let me help you now?'

Berry nodded weakly.

'Yes,' she replied, unable to see a way out. 'I suppose so.'

The woman smiled coldly and held out her hand. 'Good girl,' she said in a soothing voice. 'In that case, take off the bracelet and place it on the bed. Then I can give you a little something to help you relax. Before you know it, this whole thing will all be over . . .'

'Yes,' said Berry helplessly. 'I understand.'

Shaking, she began to slide the bracelet down her wrist. But the moment she touched it, an image flashed through her mind of men with guns, running down a hospital corridor. Heat sparked through her veins like wildfire and suddenly she saw that this was not the answer; that everything was too close and too dangerous.

'They're coming,' she said nervously. 'They're coming right now. What shall we do?'

The woman froze.

'Who's coming?'

'I don't know – police, people with guns . . .'

The woman's expression changed to one of disgust.

'Your lies won't work on me this time,' she said. Then, quick and vicious as a snake, she sprang across the room with the syringe raised, ready to strike. But Berry's fingers were already dancing down her arm and into the green light. With a loud bang, the world slowed; as the woman froze into a statue of herself, Berry looked past her to the open door and saw a police officer holding a gun. She watched, horrified, as a shiny brass bullet emerged from the end of the barrel and flew slowly across the room before disappearing into the woman's chest. In an obscene, slow-motion ballet, the woman dropped the syringe and twisted sideways before both her feet left the floor and she crashed back against a trolley of surgical instruments, sending scalpels and kidney dishes spinning like sycamore seeds to the floor.

'No!' shrieked Berry as the woman rolled over and lay still. 'I need to find him!' Leaping up on to the windowsill, she gazed out at the lights of the city and pressed her forehead against the cool glass. 'Help me,' she whispered. 'Help me, please . . .'

Then time and the world whooshed back into its

well-worn groove and three more police officers burst into the room with their guns drawn.

Berry looked up at the bright moon, just visible above the clouds that gathered above the warm streets, and suddenly the frantic scene unfolding behind her seemed of no more significance than a television playing somewhere in another room.

And when a police officer shouted for her to come down and that no one would get hurt, she knew she no longer wanted to be part of all the violence and the madness. With a last look back at the shouting men, and the guns, and the red stain spreading across the dead woman's uniform, she swung her leg back, kicked out the window and stepped out through a glitter of glass.

There was no fear, no sudden drop downward or dark streets rushing up to meet her. Just a gentle drift upwards, breaking the bonds of earth as the bright hospital room faded to a tiny square of light behind her, soon to be lost among a thousand others as she rose into the night sky, light with the knowledge of who she had been and what she might become.

Walking on a bed of white clouds she watched her shadow dance beside her in the moonlight, like a child skipping across fields of freshly fallen snow. At length she came to a place where the clouds were so deep that she sank down into folds of cool, damp mist. As white moonbeams punctured the clouds all around her she saw the bright stars shining above her and suddenly everything was simple and true and she cried out, for it was too much to bear.

'No!' she screamed. 'This is not where the road ends!'

Then, her eyes bright with anger, she stepped through the clouds, down towards the earth once more.

48

A Long Way from Home

Berry crouched among the fruit bushes at the end of Polly's garden, looking back towards the brightly lit kitchen. As the cicadas chirped and whirred, she saw Polly standing at the window, staring into the darkness. A woman police officer appeared next to her, at which point they both walked towards the hallway.

Berry ran around to the back of the house and tried the back door, but it was locked. Running to the side of the house again, she peered through the kitchen window and saw that Polly had followed the police officer to the front door. The pair of them now appeared to be engaged in conversation.

'Come on, Polly, *please*,' she said in frustration and leaned against the brick wall. Immediately she felt the familiar tingle in her wrist and without warning the wall went soft, like melting chocolate. Suddenly she was looking at wires and cobwebs and the next moment she was blinking up at the bright lights of the kitchen. With a start, she realized that her head and shoulders had sunk through the brickwork and were now sticking out of the wall on the inside of the house.

As she let out a small cry of surprise she noticed Polly look over her shoulder with an expression of disbelief. But the years of police training had paid off and instead of exclaiming loudly at the sight of Berry's head poking through her kitchen wall, she merely turned to the police officer and said, 'Of course. I'll let you know the moment I hear anything.'

As soon as she had shut the door, Polly hurried down the hallway into the kitchen and stopped in the doorway, her mouth hanging open as if her jaw had come unhinged.

'Oh, my sweet Lord!' she exclaimed. 'What in heaven's name are you doing stuck in my wall like that?'

Berry shifted her weight so that the rest of her body passed through the brickwork and into the kitchen. She felt a slight resistance as she moved, as if she was walking through treacle.

'Sorry,' she said. 'Didn't mean to frighten you. I've never actually done that before.' Although Berry's new-found ability to pass through a solid brick wall was something of a shock to her, she had already experienced enough of the bracelet's powers not to be entirely surprised. But she could see that, for Polly, it was going to take some getting used to.

'But how—how—how on earth did you do that thing that you did just then just now?' Polly gabbled in a squeaky, high-pitched voice.

'It's the bracelet,' Berry explained breathlessly. 'Polly, listen, you've got to help me. They've got Ell. They took him from the hospital!'

'What?' This information sent Polly's eyebrows back up where they'd been a few moments before. 'Who took him?'

'The people I told you about. Someone called Kruger. He says he'll kill him if I don't give him the bracelet by two o'clock.'

'Two o'clock *this morning?*'

'Yes!'

'But it's twelve thirty now!'

'I know!'

'Oh, my *Lord!*'

Polly tapped the kitchen worktop. 'OK, let's . . . let's just calm ourselves down here for a moment and think. Where did he tell you to bring it?'

'That's just it – I don't know. This woman – one of his gang – was going to take me there, but then she got shot. He said something about a Sacred Place, but it could be anywhere.'

'It could,' said Polly. 'Or it could be the same place that Mitchell wanted you to take it.'

Berry nodded and her eyes grew wider. 'Polly,' she said, 'you're a genius.'

'Not yet I'm not,' said Polly. 'We still haven't worked out where it is, remember?'

As they laid the map out on the dining-room table, Berry stared at the three towns circled in pen — Eunice, Vaughn, Anthony — and began to feel increasingly desperate.

'What do you think?' asked Polly. 'Check the computer again?'

Berry glanced at the clock and shook her head. 'There isn't time,' she said. 'Oh, Polly, what are we going to do?'

'Maybe we've done all we can,' said Polly. 'This is serious stuff, honey. Maybe it's time we got the authorities involved.'

'Then Ell will die,' said Berry, 'and it will be all my fault.' She thought of Ell sitting next to her on the plane like a small child, clutching his bag of sweets, and she started to cry.

But then, as Polly put an arm around her and said, 'Shhh, it'll be all right, sweetheart, just let me make a few phone calls', she remembered something else. Something that Ell had said.

The more you focus on something, the more you see it.

'All right, wait a second, Polly,' she said, wiping her eyes and turning back to the table. 'All we've got to do is focus. Think hard. We can do this, Polly, I know we can. Three towns. Eunice, Vaughn, Anthony. Centre. Think of anything at all. Anything that comes into your mind, just, just say it. OK?'

'But I don't think –'

'Please!'

'Well . . . OK,' said Polly uncertainly. 'Three towns, three names, letters, E, V, A, spells Eva, girl's name maybe . . .'

'Girl's name, three letters . . .' said Berry, spinning her hand around in an effort to keep the thoughts coming. 'Anagram, Ave, Vea, no, not working, OK, three towns, triple towns, come on help me out here, Polly, help me out . . .'

'Three towns, Centre, the middle, town centre, Eunice centre, Vaughn centre, what did we have before? Railways, community centre . . .'

Polly looked up at the clock, saw it was 12.45 a.m. and held her hands to her head.

'Oh, I'm sorry, honey, but my mind's gone a blank here. We just seem to be going round in circles.'

'Circles,' repeated Berry. She stared at the three blue circles around the towns on the map. 'Circles, squares, triangles, quadrilaterals.' She picked up a pen and drew a big square around the whole area.

'Squares.'

She moved back a little way, folded her arms and stared at what she had done.

'Squares, circles . . .'

Picking up a magazine, she laid it carefully on the map so that its edge was touching two of the blue circles. Then she took the pen and drew a straight line between them.

'You on to something girl?' asked Polly.

'The centre, remember? Eunice, Vaughn, Anthony, *Centre*.' Berry drew two more lines and when she had finished joining all three circles, there was a large blue triangle on the map.

'Oh, OK,' said Polly. '*Now* I see what you're doing.'

'Haven't finished yet,' said Berry. Taking the edge of the magazine, she lined it up with each point of the triangle and drew a line down to the middle of the opposite line. When she had finished, the three lines crossed over a point at the very centre of the triangle.

'There,' she said, drawing a final circle around the middle point. 'Eunice, Vaughn, Anthony . . . centre. What do you reckon?'

She stepped back from the table again and Polly leaned forward to take a closer look. Berry watched Polly stare at the circle for a long, long time. It was at the exact centre of the triangle formed between Eunice, Vaughn and Anthony, precisely at the point where the border between Eddy County and Chaves County was intersected by a narrow, secondary road which ran from the small town of Dexter in the north to Route 82 in the south.

'That's not possible,' whispered Polly, putting a trembling hand up to the side of her face. 'That's just not possible.'

'What do you mean?' asked Berry, her voice anxious and concerned. 'What's not possible?'

'That place you've marked on the map,' replied Polly. 'It's the exact same place I saw the UFO.'

As Polly took the standard issue 9 mm Beretta pistol from the desk drawer and slotted it into the holster beneath her jacket, there was a knock at the door.

Berry glanced down the hallway and saw a woman's face peering through the opaque glass panel.

'It's that woman again,' she whispered, stepping quickly back into the kitchen. 'Do you think you can get rid of her?'

'I'll do my best,' replied Polly, 'but my guess is she's been sent back to keep an eye on me.' She looked up at the clock again and saw that it was five past one. 'Dammit! Look, just stay hidden, OK?'

Berry hid behind the kitchen door and, as the police officer came back up the hallway, she heard her say, 'I'm sorry, Ms Washington, but those are my orders. I got to stay here until such time as I'm told otherwise. So maybe we should just make the best of it, you know, sit down and have ourselves a nice cup of coffee until someone tells us different. What do you say?'

As they entered the kitchen, Berry knew that if they wasted any more time, Ell would die. Her mind whirled back to Ricky's Bar & Grill and the emergency room and then she remembered exactly how to do it. Touching the bracelet, she watched the woman's movements freeze to a virtual standstill before walking calmly across the room, taking her radio from her top pocket and removing her gun from its holster. She opened the chamber, removed the bullets and threw them into the bin. Then, deciding she ought to try and keep Polly out of trouble, she walked over to her, held the gun to Polly's temple and, as she touched the bracelet again, time zipped back to its normal rhythm.

'I'm very sorry,' she said as the woman's hand flew to her empty holster and her expression turned to one of horrified confusion, 'but I'm afraid the coffee will have to wait. And let's be clear about this: unless you do exactly as I say, I'm going to blow this nice lady's head off. Do you understand?'

Her face draining of all colour, the woman could only nod dumbly. And as Polly pleaded, 'No, no, please, don't kill me!' Berry pushed her out of the front door and hoped that she wouldn't overdo it.

'OK,' said Berry as she looked at the two of them standing together in the garage. She waved the gun at Polly. 'You. What's your name?'

'Polly,' said Polly.

'All right then, Polly. I want you to come out here with me.'

'What for?' asked Polly, still pretending to be nervous.

'Just do it,' said Berry sharply, aware that the hospital incident would probably have stirred up the New Mexico Police Department's finest by now. They were going to have to move fast if they were to reach Ell before the police caught up with them. Berry noticed that the police officer looked genuinely worried for Polly's safety and, for a moment, she felt ashamed of her actions. The woman was only doing her job, after all. But then she thought of Ell, alone and terrified, and she knew that she had no choice.

'Close the door,' she ordered Polly.

'Hey!' shouted the woman as the door rattled shut.

Polly locked the garage and put her thumbs up. 'Nice going,' she whispered. As Polly unlocked the car and started the engine, Berry threw the empty gun into the porch and jumped into the back seat. 'All right,' she said. 'Let's go!'

A few minutes later, Polly's foot was pressed firmly to the floor and they were accelerating fast down Route 82 towards the Eddy/Chaves border. As Berry watched the street lights fade she felt strangely fragile, as though something inside her might fall and shatter. And as the car sped her closer to a man who knew neither love nor mercy, she thought of Ell, and her mother, and the painting of the blue house and the cherry tree, and she felt further away from home than she had ever felt before.

49

WAITING FOR GLORY

TURNING OFF THE MAIN FREEWAY on to an unlit side road, Kruger headed north for a few hundred yards until he reached the first bend. Here, instead of following the road around to the north-east, he pulled over and reversed back over the rough ground. Cutting the engine, he checked the map again, more for reassurance than for information. After all, he had been here many times before. And when he had heard Mitchell's last desperate plea, it had made him smile. It seemed that, at the end of his life, Mitchell had finally found his conscience. Perhaps the son of a Southern, God-fearing Baptist had finally remembered the eighth Commandment: *Thou shalt not steal*. But whatever Mitchell's motives, Kruger knew Eddy Chaves was the place where his own father had taken him all those years ago.

'This is where it all happened,' his father had told him. 'Right here on the border.' He had pointed to the dust beneath a single tree, its twisted branches blown into jagged fingers by the westerly winds that swept across the plains.

'This is the Sacred Place. This is the place where the secrets of the stars fell to earth.'

Kruger knew that if one was to gain ultimate power, one could not be sentimental about the lives of individuals. But, he told himself, that did not stop him appreciating order and symmetry. His father had died at two o'clock in the morning, a bitter and broken man. Now, years later, there was something wonderfully symmetrical about gaining the power that had eluded his father at exactly the same moment. Gaining power and taking revenge on those who had stood in his way.

It was more than just symmetrical, in fact.

It was beautiful.

Kruger was finally done with keeping control of his emotions. At last he allowed the years of anger and frustration to wash over him like a cold drink on a hot day. People always said that anger was a bad thing, that it should be avoided, as if it were a mad dog or a tornado. But Kruger knew that this was the reason the other members of his group had failed him: they weren't angry *enough*. Now that he had given in to it, he understood why his whole life up until now had been so hard, so frustrating, so *unrewarding*. He saw it all clearly now. It was a test. No, more than that. It was a gift. The years of disappointment had been part of it — they had been *necessary*, allowing him to build up enough anger to succeed. Everything in his life until this point had been preparation, that was all. And now the time was right. At last, everything was coming together. Like a fighter at the peak of his training, Kruger was poised and ready to unleash his anger and hatred on the final obstacle that stood between him and glory.

Unlocking the trunk of his car, he shone his torch on the pathetic, snivelling figure of the boy and smiled.

His destiny was written in the stars.

All he had to do now was wait.

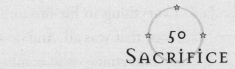

☆ 50 ☆
SACRIFICE

'THIS IS IT,' SAID POLLY as her headlights picked out a sign showing the road number 1 3 and an arrow pointing left. The car swung off the highway on to the narrow link road and as Berry listened to the tyres bump and rumble across the rough surface, she felt hollow and scared, as if all of her fears and dreams had suddenly been scooped out and held up to the light. All along she had wanted to believe that there was some reason for this, that somewhere out here was an answer that would make sense of her journey at last. But it seemed that nothing good awaited her at the end of the road; no blue skies or fields of gold. Just Kruger and his bitter crop of violence.

Polly spun the steering wheel hard to the left, the car slewing sideways in a cloud of dust before skidding off the road and accelerating over stony ground.

'How far now?' asked Berry anxiously, glancing at

the clock on the dash. The clock read 1.53 a.m. Seven minutes to go.

'Not far,' said Polly, zigzagging between the bushes that seemed to rise out of nowhere. 'But I'm worried about how this Kruger guy's going to react when he sees you with me instead of the woman from the hospital.'

'Then maybe,' said Berry, staring out into the darkness, 'he shouldn't see me at all.'

Kruger watched the two pinpricks of light approaching across the plain before turning to the boy and stroking the gun barrel against his cheek. 'I don't think your little friend is going to make it in time,' he said.

'Please,' the boy whimpered. 'Don't shoot me.'

'Please,' Kruger repeated, a cruel, high-pitched imitation. 'Don't shoot me.' Then he pressed the gun barrel against the boy's temple and tightened his finger on the trigger.

'This is the place,' said Polly in a whisper, lifting her foot from the accelerator so that the car slowed to a crawl. 'Definitely.' In the distance, Berry saw the dark silhouette of a thorn tree clawing at the sky. 'And look. There they are.'

It was then that Berry saw Ell. He was still dressed in the thin hospital robe and his wrists were tied to the branches of the tree. He stood with his arms outstretched, white-faced and terrified, frozen in the glare of the headlights. Next to him stood Kruger, staring into the light and holding a pistol against Ell's head.

'Oh, my dear sweet Lord!' exclaimed Polly in horror, slamming on the brakes and twisting around to look at Berry. 'That poor boy! What do we do now?'

But when she turned around, the car was empty and Berry had disappeared.

As she hit the dirt, Berry caught the sweet perfume of gorse flowers and sensed the warmth rising from the earth all around her. Looking up at the glittering stars, she felt as though she had waited all of her life for this moment. She felt the weight of the sky pressing down into the dust, crushing all the world's complications beneath it. For a brief moment, she saw how simple everything was and felt sad for those who would never know. And as music sang through her blood and the bracelet spun sweet light inside of her she knew that the end of the road was near. A few more steps, a few more paces towards the tree, the light and then, and then . . .

'Where is she?' Kruger shouted angrily, grabbing a fistful of Ell's hair and pushing the gun harder against his head so that he cried out in fear and pain. 'Where is the girl?'

Polly stepped cautiously in front of the headlights

and held up her hands to show that she was not carrying a weapon. 'That's what I came to tell you,' she explained. 'Your friend was involved in a crash but Berry was protected by the bracelet. She phoned me straight away and asked me to tell you that she was on her way. She'll be here any minute.'

Instead of calming Kruger, Polly's words seemed to have the opposite effect. His eyes darted frantically from side to side and then, without warning, he suddenly pulled the gun away from Ell's head and pointed it straight at Polly. 'You're lying!' he screamed. 'She's here! I know she is!'

'I swear, I'm n—' Polly began but, before she could finish, Kruger pulled the trigger and then she was lying face down on the ground, clutching her shoulder and watching blood leak out into the dirt.

'I know you're here!' Kruger screamed into the darkness, returning the barrel of the gun to Ell's temple. 'Show yourself, or I'll kill him!'

He was less than ten paces from her now. A few more seconds and she would have made it. But when Berry saw Polly fall, saw how all the hate and madness in Kruger was about to explode, she knew that a couple more seconds was something she did not have.

'Stop!' she cried, touching the bracelet. 'Stop! I'm here!'

As Berry appeared, Kruger gave a shout of triumph and then smiled nastily. 'You tried to trick me,' he said. 'See what happens when you try to trick me!'

He fired at Polly again, the bullet throwing her sideways and making her cry out in agony. As Berry looked into his eyes, she saw the cruel pleasure he got from her pain and was suddenly very, very afraid.

'Don't hurt them any more,' she pleaded. 'Please. It's me you want. Not them.'

Kruger glared at her, and pointed the gun back at Ell's head.

'Do you think I don't know?' he hissed.

'Know what?' asked Berry.

'I saw how you hid yourself from me just now. I saw what you did at the hotel. I *know* what it can do.'

He moved closer to Ell, keeping his eyes firmly on Berry all the while.

'But think about this, little girl. However fast you can move, however quickly you can cover the ground between us, there's one question you have to ask yourself.'

Kruger's eyes shone with vicious excitement as he pressed the gun barrel harder against Ell's temple.

'Can you move faster than the split second it takes me to pull the trigger?'

Berry blinked and, seeing her hesitation, Kruger nodded as if his question had been answered.

'Then give it to me. If you want him to live, give me back what is mine.'

At this, Berry felt powerful waves of desire sweep through her body, each one stronger than the last and each one binding the bracelet closer and closer to her heart until she felt that she never, ever wanted to let it go. But then, somewhere deep inside her, something resisted. And with a low moan of pain, she moved her hand towards the bracelet.

'No!' screamed Ell suddenly. 'Don't do it! Don't give it to him!'

Berry shook her head.

'I have to,' she said quietly. 'I couldn't stand to lose you again.'

As her fingers touched the bracelet and began to push it down her arm, she felt an excruciating pain, as if a thousand knives were dragging through her veins and ripping her insides out.

'If you give it to him he'll kill you!' shouted Ell.

'But if I don't, he'll kill *you*,' cried Berry, her face contorted with agony as she continued to push the bracelet down towards her wrist.

'Remember the poem,' gasped Ell. 'Remember I said I didn't know who it was for?'

'Shut UP!' shouted Kruger.

'Well, now I do,' cried Ell. 'It's for you, Berry. It's for you!'

Berry remembered the words then, spoken far away, in a field on the other side of the world.

> If you ask me I will die for you
> I'll walk into the sky for you . . .

'Give it to me!' screamed Kruger.

Berry looked at Ell and Polly — her only friends in all the world — and realized that she no longer knew what the right thing was any more. But she knew that she had loved and been loved; from now on she would just have to take her chances.

But as she pulled the bracelet from her wrist, a clatter of rotor blades filled the night air and a bright light shone down with such intensity that Berry was momentarily blinded. As the sound became deafening she heard Kruger shout and when she opened her eyes again she saw a helicopter hovering above them, the powerful beam of its searchlight illuminating the scene. But when Berry saw the flashing lights of approaching police cars, the circle of soldiers rising from their hiding places and heard the crackle of loudspeakers above her, she knew that this was not the ending she had hoped for.

'Put down the bracelet,' instructed a loud, amplified voice from the police helicopter. 'Place it on the ground in front of you and move away.'

'No!' screamed Kruger, stepping forward and stretching out his hand towards the bracelet. 'Give it to me! It's mine, it's mine!'

But as Berry clamped her hands over her ears in a desperate attempt to shut out the noise and confusion, she noticed the red dot on Kruger's chest and turned to see a police marksman crouching in the door of the helicopter, squinting through the laser sight of his rifle. She sensed something else then, something beyond all fear which filled her with a fierce and terrible certainty of what she must do. Her fingers fluttered into the blood-red light glowing at the centre of the bracelet. And suddenly she knew in her heart that, whatever Kruger might have done, she didn't want to be the cause of any more death or sadness in the world.

Which is why, without stopping to think, she dropped the bracelet, ran forward and pushed Kruger to the ground at the same moment that the rifle cracked and her world exploded into blood and pain.

Lying half conscious in the choking dust, Berry saw Kruger being dragged, handcuffed, across to a police car. Through a crimson mist, she saw the tree, and the sky, and the outline of Ell's face.

'Did I save them?' she whispered. 'Did I save them all?'

'Yes,' said Ell and Berry noticed the rope burns on his wrists and saw that he was crying. 'Everyone but yourself.'

She caught sight of Horton then, standing in a pool

of light beneath the circling helicopter.

'Where's Polly?' she asked breathlessly. 'Is she all right? I have to speak to Polly.'

'I'm right here,' said Polly, clutching her injured shoulder as she crouched down next to Berry. 'And don't you worry about me. They're flesh wounds, that's all.' She squeezed Berry's hand. 'The ambulance is on its way, sweetheart. You just hang on in there.'

'Polly,' whispered Berry. 'I think they've come for the bracelet. They've come to take it back.'

'I know, my love,' said Polly, stroking Berry's forehead. 'But you did everything you could to stop them. No one could have done any more. And now that you've told me about it, I'll do everything I can to stop them using it for bad things.'

'No,' said Berry. 'Not them. *Them*.'

Polly and Ell turned to stare in amazement at the strange, blood-red light that pulsed like a heartbeat in the sky above them. Berry looked at the bracelet lying in the dirt and whispered, 'We did it, Ell. You and me. We did what we set out to do. And that's what matters, isn't it? That's all that matters in the end.'

As she spoke, a powerful draught of wind swept down upon them, creating a sudden dust storm so fierce and intense that the force of it knocked Polly to the ground. There was a loud whirring of rotor blades followed by a crunch of metal as the helicopter crash-landed somewhere near by. The wind swirled around her in a thick, impenetrable cloud and Polly felt the dust stinging her eyes and clogging her throat.

'Berry!' she cried. 'Berry, where are you?'

But her voice was lost in a whirlwind of dust and noise. Crawling on her hands and knees in search of the others, she saw coloured lights — blue, yellow, green, violet and red — twinkling briefly in the darkness. Then they were gone and, as the dust settled, she saw Special Agent Horton stagger towards the crumpled helicopter.

'What happened?' he shouted as the pilot clambered from the wreckage. 'Something wrong with the motor?'

'No, sir,' replied the pilot shakily. 'Whatever that was had nothing to do with the helicopter. To tell you the truth, I ain't never seen anything like it.'

Horton turned to look at Polly and she saw that his face and clothes were covered in a thin layer of orange dust.

'Hey, Sergeant Washington!' he barked. 'What the hell have you done with them?'

Polly shook her head. 'Who?' she called back. 'Who are you talking about?'

'Who do you think I'm talking about?' Horton shouted. 'The two kids of course.'

Her heart in her mouth, Polly spun around. She saw

the impression in the ground beside the thorn tree, the scorched circle of blackened earth and the empty space where Ell and Berry had been huddled together only moments before and knew at once that they were gone.

And as Horton ordered his men to spread out and search the area, Polly watched the wind blow dust across the place where they had been. Then she began to cry, knowing that once more the truth would be buried beneath lies and that the things she had loved would be lost for ever, just as they had always been.

51
MORE THAN THIS

'YOU KNEW, DIDN'T YOU?' said Horton. 'You knew all along. That's why the soldiers were already there.'

Layton poured two generous measures of malt whiskey into a couple of crystal tumblers and slid one across the desk towards Horton.

'It's not like you think, Bill,' he said. 'If I could have told you, I would have done. Hell, I gave you the forensics information on the fertilizer bomb, didn't I?'

Horton stared back at him across the desk. 'You knew I'd have found that out anyway. And my guess is, the CIA was already on to Kruger by then.' He looked at Layton's face and knew that he was right. 'They were hoping he'd lead them to the bracelet, weren't they?'

'Look,' said Layton, 'you've got to understand that none of this was my decision. This stuff came all the way from the top.'

Horton took a slug of his whiskey and felt it burn the back of his throat as it went down.

'So you're saying that makes it all right?'

'No, I'm saying that some things are classified information and some aren't. This one was classified. You know as well as I do that however much I might want to, I can't go around choosing who I share that kind of information with. We might not like it very much, but hell – that's the business we're in, Bill. Classified is classified. End of story.'

'Is that what you told Andy's wife?'

'What?'

'Is that what you told Andy's wife? You know, when they buried what was left of him?'

'That's not fair, Bill. Andy knew how dangerous this whole thing was.'

'Yeah, and he tried to tell you about it, didn't he? But I guess you told him the same as you told me. What was it again? Oh that's it: "You've got a good reputation. Don't throw it away over this."'

'You're missing the point,' said Layton.

'Am I?' asked Horton. 'Tell me then, Jack. What is the point exactly?'

'The point is,' Layton went on, 'that you have to look at the wider picture. People can't cope with too much reality. Look at what happened in the forties after Roswell. And again with all the UFO sightings over Capitol Hill in '52. The idea that there might be more to this life than what people already knew damn near caused a riot. It threatened to turn society's values every which way and once that starts happening, the whole economy goes to hell in a handcart. So the government decided then and there that any such information was never to be shared with the public again. It was just too risky. That's how Operation Starlight came into being in the first place.'

'Operation Starlight? What the hell is that?'

'It's a whole bunch of ways in which the government makes sure none of this stuff gets out.'

'Like what?'

Layton shrugged. 'Like sending aircrews for psychological assessment if they report a UFO sighting. Like ensuring that all aircrew sightings remain classified, blaming the Roswell crash on Skyhook balloons and finding A-grade nutters who will go on TV to talk about being abducted by aliens. All of which helps convince Joe Public that the world is exactly the way he always thought it was.'

'So how much information does the government actually have on all this?'

'Who knows? Personally I've only been briefed on Mitchell and the Roswell crash. But you saw yourself how quickly those things appear. They come and go in the blink of an eye. My understanding is that any information the government has got is still pretty sketchy, which is why they were so desperate to get their hands on the bracelet. But one thing is certain: they know enough to want to keep it to themselves.'

Horton swilled his whiskey around the glass and tried to remember himself as the young man he had once been, in the days when he still believed that his job could make a difference. But he wasn't that person any more, and he knew it.

'Knowledge is power,' Layton went on. 'There was more knowledge in that small circle of gold than in all the science books in the world. Think what that knowledge would have done for us as a nation.'

'Mitchell did think about it,' said Horton. 'That's why he took it.'

'Is that what you think?' asked Layton. 'That Mitchell stole the bracelet out of the goodness of his heart?'

'Yes,' said Horton. 'Actually, I do. I've seen his file and I know Mitchell was no thief. An idealist, maybe, but not a thief. The only reason he became a scientist in the first place was because he believed he could change the world for the better. That's why he took the bracelet.'

'So theft of government property is a good thing? Is that what you're saying?'

'No,' replied Horton, fighting to keep his voice

calm. 'I'm saying that Mitchell was afraid of the consequences if one nation gained that kind of power above all others. He'd seen what happened with the atomic bomb and he didn't want to be another Oppenheimer. That's why he was desperate for it to go back where it came from. He realized it didn't belong in this world and that he could no longer keep it out of harm's way.'

'So that's why he sacrificed the life of a fourteen-year-old girl,' said Layton. 'In order to save the world. Well, I guess he was all heart, wasn't he?'

'I don't believe that was ever his intention,' said Horton, feeling the anger rise within him.

'Same as it was never the government's intention to sacrifice Andy Sampson,' replied Layton. 'But sometimes, unfortunately, these things happen. In the end, it's all about the greatest good of the greatest number.'

Horton looked at his boss then, saw how he was trying to find some kind of validation for all the lies that had been told and suddenly he didn't want to be a part of it any more.

'No, it isn't about that,' he said angrily, standing up and leaning forward on the desk. 'You know what it's about? It's about treating people decently and having enough faith to keep on following those things you believe to be true. And that's something that you and all the others like you will never understand. Because behind all the numbers and figures, there are ordinary people like Andy Sampson, and Mitchell, and the girl and her friend, just trying to do the right thing in this life.'

'Yeah,' said Layton, 'and look where it got them. Can you honestly tell me that anything in the world is worth that?'

But as he walked through the quiet streets across town towards his apartment block, Horton wasn't thinking too much about the world any more. Instead he was walking past the deserted factories and burned-out cars, the abandoned tenements with their broken windows and graffiti, breathing in the night air and filling his lungs deep in an effort to cleanse all the years of dirt and grime that had accumulated inside him, turning his face up to the stars, searching for something that would tell him, please God, that life was not just these endless days of anger and greed and disappointment and lies. That somewhere, somehow, there was something else, something more than this, more than this, more than this . . .

EPILOGUE

WHETHER IT WAS BECAUSE she had put in over forty years of good service or whether it was because they had wanted her to go without making a fuss, Polly wasn't sure. She suspected it was probably the latter. But at any rate, they had treated her well enough – giving her an incredibly generous package that would ensure she could live out the rest of her days in comfort, here in California. She had been surprised at first, expecting there to be trouble over the way she had hidden Berry from the police.

But it had soon become obvious that the US government was not interested in punishing her. It seemed they had learned their lesson, remembering only too well how the supposed UFO crash at Roswell in 1947 had been splashed all over the newspapers and the 1952 sightings of strange lights in the sky over the

White House had practically led to mass hysteria. Back then they had managed to gloss over both incidents by blaming weather balloons, aircraft, or people with over-active imaginations, but it had been a close-run thing.

Now they knew that Polly had seen the truth. And what they wanted was not justice, but silence. They wanted to make absolutely sure that the public continued to live in quiet ignorance, without fuss, forever unaware of the extraordinary forces that were at work all around them.

And, in the end, Polly had decided to go along with it. She knew, after all, what had happened the last time she spoke of such things.

So she took their generous offer and retired quietly to her house in California, where she could spend her twilight years listening to the sea and trying not to think about what had been lost.

It was a clear, bright morning and, although it was still early, Polly could feel the heat settling across the stone terrace. Her shoulder was healing nicely now; the doctor told her that she had been lucky. The bullets had passed clean through her without damaging any bones and already the pain had settled down into little more than a dull ache.

Placing her glass of freshly squeezed orange juice on

top of the low wall, Polly watched a seagull ride the warm air currents above the waves and, as the sun sparkled across the ocean from a sky of glorious blue, she wondered if she might learn to be happy in the time she had left.

It was certainly beautiful up here on the cliffs. Behind the house were fields that stretched for miles while in front were those wonderful sea views. The climate was always warm, even in winter. And although, up until now, she had always woken with a feeling of heaviness, this morning felt different somehow. It had a strange, almost luminous quality to it and she felt curiously light and excited, like a schoolgirl waking up on the first morning of the holidays.

Quite what it was that made her want to go quickly across the terrace and around to the front of the house, she couldn't say, but as she walked up the path towards the garden gate and looked out across the golden fields of corn, she stopped suddenly and her heart fluttered like a butterfly at a window.

'Oh,' she said faintly, leaning unsteadily against the white picket fence and putting her hand to her mouth. 'Oh my . . .'

At first, Berry thought she must still be dreaming. But for so long her dreams had been of starlight and silver that she knew at once this was different. She smelled the rich, warm earth and felt the gentle heat of sunshine on her back. Opening her eyes, she saw that she was surrounded by stalks of yellow corn. Blinking in the bright sunlight, she noticed that Ell was curled up next to her, sleeping peacefully. As she knelt up, Berry was puzzled to see a small, tattered card pressed into the corn beneath where she had been lying. She picked it up and stared at the picture on the front for a few seconds, trying to remember.

Still leaning against the fence, Polly gazed in awe and wonder at the incredible patterns that had been woven into the field during the night. A dozen or more circles had been flattened into the corn, all linked together by straight lines to form a complex, symmetrical pattern that was both strange and beautiful. But it was the smallest circle, the one closest to her, that most held Polly's attention. For in the very centre of it stood a figure, and as Polly watched, she saw that the figure was moving.

Berry stood beneath the blue sky in the middle of a perfect circle, looking out across the cornfield. Then, hearing a voice somewhere in the distance behind her, she turned around.

'My child,' said Polly as her fingers shook and fumbled on the gate latch. 'My darling child . . .'

For a few seconds, Berry stood at the edge of the circle and stared, unable to move. 'Ell,' she whispered. 'Oh, Ell, look . . .'

Then, with a little cry, she began to run, slowly at first, then faster and faster, running through the field of corn and suddenly her heart was full and she knew that everything mattered; her mother, the hospital, Ell and the old man, the bracelet and the poetry and all the fear and laughter and sadness and loss – all of them were here in this moment, breaking inside her like a wave as she ran barefoot through the golden corn and out at last on to the road; the road that led to the blue house and the cherry tree, and the garden where Polly had unlatched the gate and was now on her knees with her arms wide open, waiting to greet her.